YOU
EVERY
MOVE

Also by Sam Blake

Little Bones

In Deep Water

No Turning Back

Keep Your Eyes on Me

The Dark Room

High Pressure

Remember My Name

The Mystery of Four

Three Little Birds

The Killing Sense

For young adults:
Something Terrible Happened Last Night
Something's About to Blow Up

YOUR EVERY MOVE

SAM BLAKE

First published in trade paperback in Great Britain in 2026 by Corvus,
an imprint of Atlantic Books Ltd

Copyright © Sam Blake, 2026

The moral right of Sam Blake to be identified as the author of this work has been asserted by her in accordance with the Copyright, Designs and Patents Act of 1988.

All rights reserved. No part of this publication may be reproduced, stored in a retrieval system, or transmitted in any form or by any means, electronic, mechanical, photocopying, recording, or otherwise, without the prior permission of both the copyright owner and the above publisher of this book.

No part of this book may be used in any manner in the learning, training or development of generative artificial intelligence technologies (including but not limited to machine learning models and large language models (LLMs)), whether by data scraping, data mining or use in any way to create or form a part of data sets or in any other way.

This novel is a work of fiction. Apart from the well-known actual people, events and locales that figure into the narrative, all names, characters, places and incidents are the products of the author's imagination or are used fictitiously.

10 9 8 7 6 5 4 3 2 1

A CIP catalogue record for this book is available from the British Library.

Trade Paperback ISBN: 978 1 80546 538 6
E-book ISBN: 978 1 80546 539 3

Printed and bound by CPI (UK) Ltd, Croydon CR0 4YY

Corvus

An imprint of Atlantic Books Ltd
Ormond House
26–27 Boswell Street
London
WC1N 3JZ

www.atlantic-books.co.uk

Product safety EU representative: Authorised Rep Compliance Ltd., Ground Floor, 71 Lower Baggot Street, Dublin, D02 P593, Ireland. www.arccompliance.com

*For all the missing women – and
for Suzy Lamplugh.
Forty years on.
Gone but not forgotten.*

But O, how a bitter thing it is to look into happiness through another man's eyes.
William Shakespeare, *As You Like It*, Act V, Scene 2

Prologue

SHE DIDN'T FEEL the shove from behind; she was too busy focusing on the howl of the wind, the pain in her ears, and the icy whip of rain against her cheeks as she ran along the narrow cliff path.

Jago was here somewhere, and she *had* to find him.

Above her, the foghorn reached out from the lighthouse with an eerie high-pitched wail. Earlier she'd been thinking about how different it sounded from the one at home; the sound she'd heard every winter growing up had been a much deeper, more comforting tone. Randomly she'd found herself wondering if foghorns were all different, if somehow sailors knew where they were by the pitch of the alert, like the flashes from lighthouses. She pushed the thought away now; there was no space in her head for anything except finding Jago.

But she should have listened to the warning signals.

Now she knew what had been going on, there had been so many signs. How could she have been so stupid?

Below her, she could hear angry waves breaking over the jagged black rocks, the spray spitting up into her face. There was no barrier along the cliff edge, just a carpet of long stalky grass flattened by the wind, something that had surprised her when she'd walked here yesterday. Then the mist had been swirling like spectres gathering. Now the spectres had joined together to form an army, fog so dense in patches that she could only see a few metres ahead.

A wave crashed below, and she felt its freezing fingers reaching for her.

He had to be here somewhere; it was only a short walk to the lighthouse. Had he climbed down to the caves? The thought suddenly occurred to her as another wave broke, the sound explosive. It seemed mad in this weather, but these cliffs had been his playground, growing up. Had he seen someone acting suspiciously and followed them down?

The fog was comforting at least. If Rosie couldn't see anything then she must be almost invisible too. And she needed to be invisible. In the city she always felt as if someone was looking; there were so many people, anyone could hide among them, watching her. Out here there was nobody, and the wind was stinging her ears, but the salt smell of the storm was as familiar as it was dangerous.

If Rosie Kinsella had realised *how* dangerous, perhaps she wouldn't have run from the house so fast. If she'd realised how hard it was going to be to find Jago, maybe she'd have …

And then she felt a push and she was falling.

And she couldn't see anything at all.

How it started ...

TO: Rosie Kinsella

DATE: 14 February 2025

SUBJECT: Lilies

FROM: Outlander

Hey Rosie,

Congratulations on the new job! I know lilies are your favourite. I thought I'd wait to let you settle in before sending them. Lilies represent purity and renewal, isn't that perfect? I love their scent too, it reminds me of summer, like your perfume. Dioriveria is so perfectly you. I close my eyes and breathe it in whenever you pass me, the French Riviera meets Paris. I can see us sitting in a pavement cafe looking out at the sea in Antibes, or you showing me your favourite cafe in Paris. London must be a big change – this weather! I got caught in the rain as well the other day! I called out to you to share my umbrella but I don't think you could hear me, and your bus arrived right then so hopefully you were able to get warm.

Michael

TO: Rosie Kinsella

DATE: 16 February 2025

SUBJECT: What a coincidence/work party

FROM: Outlander

Hey Rosie,

Great to see you last night, who knew you loved dim sum too? Your work crew are great fun – that Nick, though? He's a bit of a privileged prick, isn't he? You looked fabulous, he couldn't keep his eyes off you. Did you notice? Grace seems very nice, caring. She thinks he's a bit of a prick too, I could see from the way she was talking to him. Hope you managed to get a cab OK, you could have shared mine. Maybe next time.

Michael

Private number

Hey Rosie, I know you haven't been to the theatre since you came to London – Hamilton is such a fabulous show, I know you'll love it. I've booked for 26th March, it's a good few weeks away so you should be able to clear your diary if there's a clash. Our tickets are at the box office under your name, it's the Victoria Palace Theatre, right next to the station. We can have a drink afterwards. Can't wait!
Love Mike x

13:05

Add your message here:

Hey Rosie, I thought you could use this cute umbrella. Open it up and see the inside, it's printed with a stunning painting of the cosmos. So many shining stars, just like you. It's a tiny one so it should fit in your bag. I'd hate you to get so wet again!
Love Mike x

Thank you for shopping at London Undercover

How it's going ...

Chapter 1

'FECK'S SAKE.' It came out more aggressively than Rosie had intended. Sitting down hard on her chair, she looked again at the image she'd just opened on her phone.

On the other side of the table, Grace pushed a blonde Ghd ringlet over her shoulder and looked around her open laptop lid at Rosie. Even with the harsh light from the floor-to-ceiling windows throwing her face into shadow, Rosie could see Grace's blue eyes widening as she registered the look on Rosie's face.

'What? What's happened?'

Unable to form any words that passed as polite, Rosie's eyes met Grace's. Rosie could feel her mouth set in an angry line. Her heart pounding, she fought with the need to throw her phone across the room and scream.

She glanced down at the email that had just arrived, anger swirling like molten glass, red-hot and liquid now, but as soon as it cooled, she knew she'd feel dark and brittle. And liable to crack.

She was going to have to tell them now.

The part of her that wasn't fuming, cringed. Rosie had been praying that this was someone from home arsing about – that it was some sort of joke – but as each email and text message had arrived, she'd felt more tense, more intruded on, more pissed off and, if she was honest with herself, more afraid.

Why was this happening? It had taken her so long to find the right job, and then find a flat in London, and now this. When the flowers had arrived a few weeks ago, 'coincidentally' on Valentine's Day, she'd laughed it off, not mentioning the weird email, pretending Michael must be a friend whom she hadn't heard from in ages.

Then *that* email had arrived the day after their night out.

She hadn't noticed anyone creepy in the restaurant, but then she'd been celebrating, thrilled to get her first sale. She'd only been a fortnight into the job, and she'd closed on a stunning prime property that had been on the books of Sterling & Co for a lot longer than the vendor was happy about. It had been a breakthrough moment: any rumours that she'd been hired because of her Instagram account had been firmly quashed with a multi-million pound sale. Sitting in that Chinese restaurant in Mayfair, sipping her champagne, she'd felt as if everything was actually coming together. The drama of Paris was firmly behind her. It had been her moment. Finally.

She'd loved Paris. She had found her feet in high-end residential sales, starting her @RosiesParisLife IG account, loving the feeling that came with being seen – with being an influencer. Who had expected *that* when she'd left school in Cork with a crappy Leaving Cert and a summer's work experience at a luxury boutique? Or that she'd take to French as if she'd been born to it? She'd always been good at Irish, had picked up bits of Spanish on holiday, but becoming fluent in French had turned out to be a lot easier than she'd expected. When she'd met Xavier Verdier, she'd thought she'd found everything she'd ever dreamed of in the City of Love. With his liquid brown eyes, his money and family connections, he'd swept her off her feet, and helped her build professionally, introducing her to clients, becoming an intrinsic part of her life. It had all been perfect … until the wife Rosie didn't know Xavier had, had turned up at the office one day.

London would be the new start she needed.

Should have been …

Had been, until this Michael character had landed in her inbox.

Rosie looked back at the photo attached to the email.

It had been taken this morning.

She knew it was this morning, because she could see the package beside the doorstep from the Swedish coffee company that David Two got regular deliveries from. In the photo, it was half hidden in the foliage near the front door, but she'd spotted it as she'd come out, and picking it up, had popped it onto the hall table. She'd been about to text David Two to let him know it had arrived when her phone had rung. Pulling the milkshake-pink door behind her, she'd yanked up her coat collar against the freezing rain and forgotten all about the package, concentrating on her little brother's voice asking if he could move his drum kit into her old bedroom at home.

Hurrying down the path, she'd run for the bus, telling Conor she'd call him later, and not to dare moving anything out of *or* into her room.

The photo looked as if it had been taken right before she came out of the door. *Michael must have been watching for her to leave.* She felt a shiver run up her back at the thought. Why was she using his name, even in her head? It made him more real.

More importantly, how did he even know where she lived?

The answer to that made her feel actually sick: *he must have followed her home.* But when?

No matter how Rosie had felt during the weeks of weird emails, texts and WhatsApp messages, this had suddenly got a whole lot creepier.

This Michael character had sent photos before: a view of the Thames he thought she'd like, or a cat in a window, or something funny he'd seen on Instagram. Then a few days ago it had been his seat in the theatre; of the stage before *Hamilton* began; of the champagne he'd thought he would be sharing with her after the performance. *Who did that?*

When the flowers had turned up, right at the start, she hadn't really taken it seriously. But then the email about their work dinner had arrived, and then the texts had started.

And *then* the first gift box had been delivered, the note signed with a kiss.

Ick. Jaysus. Her skin crawled at the thought.

Back at the start, she'd called both her older brothers to see who this Michael joker was – thinking he had to be one of their friends taking the proverbial. Fiacra and Eoin had both lived in London; both had played rugby for London Irish. They both knew loads of Michaels, Mikes, even a Mikey, but none of them seemed to be *this* Michael.

From the other end of the huge table forming the main workstation in the open-plan office, Nick finished his call. Her mind still swirling, Rosie could feel him looking at her.

'What's up, Rosie? You look like you're going to belt someone.'

She glanced over at him, only half concentrating.

'Shut up, Nick. Did you leave your common sense at home with your comb?' From her seat opposite Rosie, Grace scowled down the table at their colleague and stood up, her stiletto heels tapping on the wooden floor as she came around to Rosie's side to look at the image.

Rosie held the phone up so she could see.

'It's my front door. It's that guy who sent those flowers. He's emailed me a picture of my front door. But, *seriously*, I *really* don't know anyone called Michael.'

Chapter 2

'ARE YOU SURE you don't know him? There was that fancy box with the umbrella – that shop's *really* expensive.' Rosie felt frustration rising as Grace continued. 'Could you have met him in a bar and got chatting? Maybe you met him at the group you mentioned, that drinking club for blow-ins?'

'What the hell's a blow-in?' From the other end of the table, Nick looked at them as if they were talking a foreign language. They probably were some of the time. Between Grace's soft midlands Irish accent and Rosie's Cork lilt, she knew when they got chatting, nobody could keep up. Grace looked at Nick, rolling her eyes at his lack of understanding. 'Someone from out of town, like, not born here. Obviously.'

Ignoring Nick, Rosie shook her head in reply to Grace. 'I definitely haven't met anyone called Michael since I got here, I'd have remembered.' She put the phone down on the table and, taking a deep breath, hooked her dark blonde hair behind her ears, trying to centre herself, to calm the maelstrom of emotion threatening to overwhelm her. She couldn't lose it in the office. She hadn't been here long enough, for one thing. Professionalism was vital in this job; the clients were allowed to get hysterical – they could afford it – but not the sales team.

Rosie let out the breath she'd been holding, deliberately keeping her voice level. 'This is actually starting to freak me out.'

Rosie felt Grace's hand on her shoulder, giving her a reassuring squeeze, and for a moment was incredibly grateful that there was someone here in the office who really understood her. Their co-worker Hallie was *so* nice, but at least ten years older than them both, and every time she got caught in the rain, threatened to go home to Australia. And their boss, Yaraslava, was a bit inaccessible, to say the least. She came into the office every morning looking as if she was about to do a cover shoot for *Forbes. Not daunting at all.* Rosie had been super-impressed by her when they'd first met, with her dusky looks, heavy Belarusian accent and even heavier gold jewellery. She was so poised, so polished, she was exactly what Rosie aspired to be. Sebastian Sterling, the Sterling of Sterling & Co, was the ultimate boss – he'd sat in on Rosie's interview and came to their team meetings – but Yaraslava was definitely running the show.

At the other end of the table, Nick leaned back and linked his hands together behind his head. His jacket was slung around the back of the chair, his tie loose at the open neck of his pale blue shirt. With his long, heavily highlighted hair, he looked more like a male model than an estate agent, and he knew it.

'But why would this dude do that – take a picture of your house? That's so random.'

Rosie and Grace both looked at him and then at each other in a moment of shared understanding. Grace answered for them. 'Because he wants to show her that he knows where she lives, that he's followed her without her realising.'

Nick's brow furrowed. 'I don't get it. What's the point of that?'

Grace threw him a withering look. 'It's usually about power, Nick. Control.'

Rosie glanced down the table at him. 'God knows what it's about. He's delusional. It's like he's got it into his head that he knows me, that we're friends. That's the weirdest bit. He keeps texting random stuff, like you would your best friend.'

Nick sat forward in his chair. 'Like texting a lot?'

Rosie hesitated, not sure she could admit to the full truth. 'Three or four times a day, sometimes more.'

His eyes widened slowly. 'What sort of stuff? Personal?'

'Not super-personal.' Rosie felt her voice catch. She put her elbow on the table and rubbed her eyes before answering. 'Things like he was worried I might miss my bus, or he almost missed his. Or work was tough and his boss is a nightmare. He doesn't like his job much, and there's someone in his office he really hates. He's pretty nasty about them.' Rosie sighed. 'God only knows why he needs to tell me that, or what he thinks I can do about any of it. It's way too much information. I mean, even if I did know him, it would be like you texting me and giving out about Hallie and Yaraslava all the time. Except he only uses horrible nicknames, and I don't have an earthly idea who any of the people are he's talking about.'

Nick frowned. 'That's weird shit, all right. Has he given you any clues about where he works?'

Rosie shook her head. 'I was so confused at the start, I thought maybe I *had* met him somewhere and I didn't want to be rude. I answered the first one, saying he'd have to remind me who he was, that I had a terrible memory. He thought I was joking, I think. Then the messages just kept coming.' She sighed. 'He must work in London because he knows which buses I get, the actual numbers, and obviously he knows where I live.' She could feel tears pricking at her eyes. 'He knows I lived in Paris. I just …'

Rosie's phone pinged and a notification appeared at the bottom of the screen. Another email had arrived. Fear clutched at her stomach. She glanced up at Grace.

'You'd better open it. See what he's got to say about why on earth he's sent that photo.' Rosie could see Grace was trying to appear calm, but her eyes were wide.

Rosie looked at the screen. At least it wasn't a voice message. Hearing his super-smooth voice made her feel like heaving. And an email didn't feel as personal as a text, somehow.

Clicking to her inbox, Rosie glanced up at Grace again for reassurance.

'Go on, we're all here, you're safe. Let's see what he's got to say.'

'Can you read it out?' Nick's face was a picture of curiosity. Rosie's eyes flicked to him. *Honestly, men just didn't have these problems.* It never occurred to them they might be attacked on the way home after a night out, or crossing a dark car park; they didn't have to think constantly to avoid becoming prey.

She opened the email. The sender's name was the same as the previous ones: Outlander. What was that supposed to mean?

TO: Rosie Kinsella

DATE: 28 March 2025

SUBJECT: Hamilton

FROM: Outlander

Hey Rosie,

I waited for you for ages the other night, you must have got caught at work, did you? Hamilton is so good, mesmerising – I know you'll love it. I felt bad you were probably stuck at the office, but sad we couldn't catch up.

There's a cosy cafe right near your flat that does the most perfect croissants, they crumble in your mouth and their coffee is so French. Why don't we meet there and you can tell me all about that house in Kensington, wow, that swimming pool is amazing. And the secret room off the bedroom? What do you think that could be for?

Mike xx

Rosie closed her eyes, her stomach churning.

Chapter 3

SITTING IN THE rear of a black cab, her hand resting on the top of her handbag, Yaraslava Kavalenko felt her phone vibrating inside it. Glancing out of the rain-splattered window to see where they were, she pulled the bag onto her knee and rooted for her mobile. It was probably her brother. It was always her brother.

Finding the phone, she looked at the screen, seeing the missed call and multiple WhatsApp messages. She felt a red-hot stab of irritation and deliberately closed her eyes, stilling her temper. She knew he was tense because things weren't going the way he wanted – but there wasn't much more she could do. She could feel her jaw clenching.

He picked up the moment she returned his call.

'Dimitri, good morning.' She kept her voice deliberately calm, always more comfortable in her native language.

'There's nothing good about this morning. I thought you had the Hampstead house sold?'

Yaraslava bit back her response. Their conversations over the last few days had revolved about this one thing, and it was *really* starting to get on her nerves. She was hardly going to forget they needed to sell it. She knew he needed to urgently liquidate the asset and get the money moving, but she couldn't work miracles.

'The buyers we have are very interested, I keep telling you. I can't hurry them too much or they'll get suspicious. None of us can afford that.'

'I thought you said they were old? Why would they worry about who the previous owner was?' At the other end he snorted, sending Yaraslava's hackles up even more.

Why did he involve her at all if he didn't trust her?

She already knew the answer to that; they both did. Was this a good time to remind him that these deals wouldn't go through at all if she wasn't orchestrating them? Any other property agency would be running background checks when a foreign registered company approached them for the quick sale of a property of the value of Park House – of any prime property, in fact. Dimitri was well aware that the Suspicious Activity Report had been created by the UK Financial Intelligence

Unit for a reason, and the obligation was on the property agents or solicitors involved to file the report. He knew damn well that they could be prosecuted for not filing, regardless of whether an offence of money laundering was ever substantiated. Yaraslava couldn't afford for that to happen at Sterling & Co.

Dimitri's business prospered because of her. She'd been the one who had met the Grigori brothers first in that Mayfair bar, who had seen the opportunities. He should be thanking her.

Everyone knew there was a lot of overseas money tied up in London properties: money that went in dirty and came out squeaky clean; money that was of great interest to the National Crime Agency. And keeping it away from the NCA required a fine balancing act – something Yaraslava was very good at.

It was a service worth paying for: the Grigoris had seen that immediately. But the properties had to sell quickly and quietly for everything to run smoothly.

'They might be old, but Major Bradford is very sharp. I told you I'd call them again this morning and give them the new price. I'll see if I can get them back for a viewing. The major has taken a shine to Nick. He's a good closer. You have to trust me.'

'I'm starting to think we should move the listing to Hunt's.'

Yaraslava's anger exploded inside her, flowing like an electric charge. Physically sitting up straighter as she answered, she found herself leaning forward in her seat, as if she was about to go in for a kill. But she kept her voice very low, under control. He couldn't know how close she'd come to Hunt's discovering the truth behind their main holding company, Landmark. She'd managed to deflect a report being filed, but only just.

'You know damn well that Hunt's will ask difficult questions – it's their policy. There are laws in place that they have to abide by. Are you ready for that?' She paused, letting the silence grow as the cab slowed at a red light. 'I thought not.'

'I'm not happy dropping the price. Seven hundred thousand is a lot of money. We'll have to absorb that loss for the Grigoris.'

'We can make up the difference on the next sale. If we lose our fee for facilitating this one, it's not the end of the world.' Glancing out of the window to see how close to the office they were, she made a noise like steam escaping. She needed time to set up this appointment and to work on Nick. 'You can't have it both ways. The Grigoris want their cash. The only way to get that quickly is to make the property so attractive the buyers can't afford to let it go. We have done this multiple times in the past—'

'But this time it's different. The Grigori brothers have something going on and don't want to wait – and we don't have ten million in cash available to keep them sweet. That's what they are expecting out of this. They know the market.'

'I understand the situation perfectly, thank you. We couldn't have got Park House up for sale any faster. It's a turnkey property, and the Bradfords aren't in a chain. It's Wednesday today. Tell the Grigoris we'll have it sorted by early next week. I'll have a private word with the Bradfords and emphasise that the vendor wants a quick sale.'

'Let me know how you get on.' He hung up.

Yaraslava looked at the phone, glowering inside.

The risks she took for Dimitri and his business were just getting too big. She'd needed the Grigori brothers when she'd first come to London, her money running out much faster than she'd expected. They had a reputation and influence, and the first sales had been easy. Hearing that his sister had fallen on her feet, Dimitri had quickly followed her, setting up companies to get the most out of every transaction. Yaraslava had moved into the early properties that Dimitri's companies bought, to make the purchases look genuine, to give the houses life. It had been Dimitri's idea. It had saved her a fortune in rent – plus empty properties attracted unwanted attention.

Arriving in a foreign country, Yaraslava had very quickly realised that the security of having money in her bank account was the key to success. Her own money. Seeing how the Grigoris operated, living on her nerves for the first few months – what did they say here? 'Fake it till you make it' – she'd started to find her way. Dimitri might be her older brother, but it had become very clear that the only person she could rely on absolutely was herself.

Coming to London, with its bright lights and opportunities, had ended up being a good decision, despite her doubts and feelings of despair in those early months, when waitressing and cleaning toilets had seemed to be her only option. Eventually she'd found a job with a property developer who needed a Russian speaker to cultivate prime buyers. Then she'd met the Grigoris.

Yaraslava's phone pinged with a text from Dimitri.

I'll tell the Grigori brothers it'll be signed on Monday.

She felt her temper reignite. Her fingers flew over the screen as she replied:

> Do NOT tell them Monday. I do not want to be on their kill list if the Bradfords have any issues.

How could Dimitri have got them into this situation, making promises they couldn't keep? Landmark was just one of his companies that provided the perfect cover for cleansing increasingly large sums of money for foreign clients – all of whom knew it was a slow game, but it was reliable, efficient and worth the wait. Clean cash and a profit thrown in. A win for everyone.

Until now. The Grigoris needed money fast, and somehow that had become their problem. Dimitri had made it their problem.

Her phone pinged again.

> We'll both be on their kill list if this deal doesn't get done.

Chapter 4

'TWO KISSES? I mean, what's that about?' Rosie crossed her arms firmly and looked past Grace out of the open coffee shop door. It was raining again, and she could feel winter in the chill breeze despite her thick tights and knee-high boots. She shivered. There were only a few people ahead of her and Grace, but Janey Mac, they were slow.

She'd needed to get out of the office. And she needed a coffee. Now.

Behind her, Grace sighed and tightened her scarf, a rich cream against the winter white of her coat. She was taller than Rosie and always dressed carefully. 'He must have sent the photo because he was pissed off you stood him up.'

Rosie did an elaborate double take. 'I don't think I stood him up. A date sort of involves one party checking to see if the other party actually wants to go, not just buying tickets and expecting them to turn up.'

'Sorry, yeah, you're right there.' Grace reached out and gave her arm a quick squeeze. Then, realising Rosie had her back to the counter, she indicated with her head that she needed to move up. 'Your turn.'

'Latte, real milk.' Rosie turned to Grace. 'What'll you have? I'll get these.'

'Oat cappuccino, no chocolate. Will I get a table?'

Rosie looked around the tiny coffee shop. The till and coffee machines faced huge windows overlooking the street. There were a couple of stools free at the counter running along the windows, but she didn't want to sit there on full view to the world. This road was a cut through, and always busy. Lined with high-end men's boutiques and restaurants, it had an olde worlde air that Rosie had loved when she'd come along for her first interview.

Rosie tapped Grace on the arm. 'Grab that one in the corner.' Beside the passageway to the loos, two dark-suited men were standing up, just about to vacate their table. But Rosie could see that Grace was looking out of the door as if something had caught her eye. A taxi had pulled up almost outside as the two men filed out the door. 'Quick, before it's taken.'

Grace was craning her neck, apparently trying to see who was getting out of the cab. Rosie turned to the counter as Grace realised what she'd said.

'Sorry, on it now. I think that was Hallie. In the cab. Why she's getting out here and not outside the office? It's only around the corner.'

Rosie glanced outside, but the black taxi had already moved away, and Hallie had disappeared, probably down the road towards the office. 'She said she'd be in late, she was meeting a new buyer this morning.'

The girl behind the counter finished making their coffees and passed them across. Tapping her card, Rosie smiled gratefully and, picking them up, turned to follow Grace to the tiny table. She'd had the sense to sit down facing the window, so Rosie could sit with her back to it.

Rosie picked up the sugar dispenser, turning it upside down and liberally adding it to her coffee.

'That's a lot.'

'I need it.'

Grace nodded sympathetically. 'So, this buyer Hallie was meeting ... Who was it?'

Rosie shrugged. 'I don't think she gave a name. Another Australian, I expect. She's got a little black book of people she worked with when she was in the yacht business.'

Grace took a sip of her coffee. 'Well, if that was her potential new buyer in the cab with her, it's someone she knows *very* well. She gave him a proper kiss.'

Rosie's eyebrows rose slightly, but right now Hallie's love life wasn't her main priority. Her lack of enthusiasm didn't stop Grace.

'She was married, you know? When she was living in Australia. Divorced by the time she was our age, apparently. She was selling superyachts then, so she moved to Monaco, and then came here and switched to property. She had some huge clients.'

Grace seemed to know everything about everybody, not only in their office, but in the whole building. But Rosie wasn't in the mood for gossip.

'Thanks for coming out to this appointment with me. I'm going to need to talk to Yaraslava, though. She won't be keen on us doubling up every time I have to meet a new client.' Rosie picked up her spoon.

Yaraslava would not be impressed by their going to a meeting together at all. Rosie was going to have to come up with another solution if this Michael thing continued. *Maybe she could swap jobs with Grace and stay in the office.* Rosie shot down that idea before it was even fully formed. Selling was her thing, and she was damn good at it. Little Rosemary Kinsella from Ballinacurra had found her niche and nailed it spectacularly.

Deep inside, Rosie could feel the hot flame of resentment igniting again. This Michael dude was starting to seriously impact her life. Constantly looking behind her, her nerves on edge, she was sleeping so lightly that she woke every time there was a sound outside, and it was starting to drag her down. Twitchy and exhausted didn't sell property at the level she was at, and there was only so much coffee you could drink to get you through the day.

Grace took a sip of her cappuccino. 'True. Empathy isn't exactly Yaraslava's signature trait. But I'm sure there will be ways around it. And hopefully this guy will get bored and move on to someone else.'

'D'you think? It feels like he's getting closer, getting into my space, rather than the opposite. If he's following me home, he's properly stalking me.' Rosie put her mug down. 'I'm going to post about it. I wasn't sure before, but I am now.' She picked up her phone, opening the app she used to create images. 'Right now, actually.' She looked up at Grace. 'And then I'm going to report it to the police.'

 rosiesparislife

[Image: the word NEWS, in large white capital letters centred on a black background]

Hey everyone, I know this image feels a bit dramatic, but I don't have a gorgeous property shot to show you today. You all know my account here on IG started as a way to keep in touch with friends from home while I was living in Paris – but it turned out lots of people were interested in #RosiesParisLife. And interested in the beautiful homes I had the privilege of selling. So many of you have joined for the ride, and shared your own experiences, that I feel like I know you.

Now I've moved to London, I've more stunning properties to share with you, plus all the fun of a new city. But I've got something else too.

It's a Big Something and I haven't been sure whether I should talk about it here at all. It's not really what my account is about. But then I thought about it, and I realised this account isn't just about me, it's about my life and it's about you too.

To be completely genuine, which you know I am, I need to share something that's been happening to me for a while. It's something that's on my mind a lot and no matter how hard I pretend it isn't, is starting to dominate my life. I know someone else will see this too, so that's part of the reason why I didn't want to post about it before.

I also need to share it because the only posts here under #stalker are memes and a film from 1979. But you don't have to talk to too many women to find out there's been a moment in their lives when they've felt uncomfortable, or had unwelcome attention. Or they've been downright freaked out.

That's what's happening to me.

The Met Police say on their website to call 101 if you need to talk to someone about a non-emergency situation.

But this is starting to feel like an emergency.

#stalker #metoo #womensaid #nomore

Chapter 5

HALLIE JUMPED AS Yaraslava arrived through the main door of the office *almost* right behind her. She'd only just sat down and opened her laptop. Now she turned it on discreetly in an effort to look as if she'd been there all morning. She needed to be more careful. *What if her arrival at the office had coincided with Yaraslava's?* The thought made her mouth dry. *When the screaming was over, she'd be lucky to keep her job.*

Yaraslava stopped dramatically in the doorway, her full-length black fur coat swirling around her. She had her phone in her hand, as if she'd just finished a call. 'Where is everybody?'

As Hallie turned towards the door, she glanced at Nick beside her, sending him a telepathic message not to say anything about her only just getting here. She'd mentioned she'd be late this morning, but not this late.

Catching the look, he swivelled his chair to face the door and gave Yaraslava a full-on charm blast. 'Grace went with Rosie to meet her new client at the apartment in St John's Wood. The client's a guy she hasn't met before, and she was a bit worried about going on her own.' His tone became much more serious. 'It turns out that guy Michael – the dude who sent Rosie the flowers and stuff when she started – is actually some sort of stalker creep. He's been emailing her and taking photos of her house. Rosie's totally freaked out. She's no idea who he is.' He paused significantly, and then, obviously trying to move the conversation on and distract Yaraslava, continued. 'They'll be back before lunch. You know, that coat's *magnificent*.'

Yaraslava took the compliment with an upturn of her Chanel red lips as his explanation for Rosie and Grace's absence fully registered with Hallie.

'Nick, are you *serious*?' She looked at him in horror. He'd said something about Rosie getting a weird email when she'd come in, but she'd been distracted – hadn't had the time, or the focus, to ask more. Now she felt terrible. She liked Rosie a lot and this sounded scary. Hallie had wondered why Rosie had been so offhand about the gorgeous bouquet of flowers that had arrived on Valentine's Day. She reached for her phone to text Rosie as Nick swung around to face her.

'She's really spooked.'

Yaraslava frowned. 'How come they *both* needed to go?' She put her head on one side, the overhead spots glinting off her glossy black curls. 'I need Grace to keep with the relocations. Faizah Noor has called, wondering about schools again, and she needs a second nanny who can drive.' Yaraslava paused. 'We charge a lot of money for Grace to manage problems. It makes us the best. She must be brilliant. And *here* when people need her.'

Hallie glanced from Nick to Yaraslava. They all knew their boss was steel-edged, but her total lack of empathy with this situation was a bit much. A lot of their job involved meeting clients in empty properties. They had safety protocols in place, to make sure the office knew who they were meeting and when, but if Rosie had picked up a stalker …

Hallie cleared her throat, masking her thoughts with an innocent tone. 'I'm sure they won't be long. I was just thinking of getting a proper coffee. Can I get you one?' She could text Rosie and check she was OK more easily from the coffee shop.

Yaraslava could be such a bitch. Her entire *raison d'être* was building the company – at any cost. Hallie knew

Grace had loved sales, but just before Rosie had arrived, Yaraslava had moved her to this newly created role as a 'relocation specialist', looking after clients' needs. The job seemed to involve everything from booking the movers, to registering new buyers for council tax and finding chauffeurs and chefs. Whatever was needed. Which could be a challenge.

Grace was brilliant with people, as chatty as they came, but some of the requests and expectations were trying even Grace's patience. As she'd said after the most recent request – to find a personal trainer who specialised in somatic yoga – she would have gone into human resources if she'd wanted to hire household staff.

Hallie kept her voice light. 'If Grace is with Rosie, it's a great opportunity to get some good photos. Rosie says her posts get even more traction if she's actually in them, but she wants them to look professional, and it helps if someone else is taking them, even if they actually look like selfies.'

'Precisely why I have hired her.' Yaraslava looked smug, as if she was the one who had plucked Rosie from the obscurity of Paris and built her account, follower by follower. She strode over to her office door, opening it as she continued. 'She is our secret weapon. Everyone at

Hunt Properties – and their clients – is following her.' If it was possible to look any smugger, Yaraslava had just managed it.

Hallie bristled, but Yaraslava had a point. Everyone at Hunt Properties had been seething since Rosie had arrived at Sterling & Co with her Irish charm and two hundred thousand followers – not least the owner, Yaraslava's previous boss. Yaraslava had left after a spectacular row, walking right out of Hunt's and into Sterling & Co, Hunt's arch-rivals, and had been smashing sales targets ever since. Even Hallie had to admire her for that.

Yaraslava pushed open her office door, threw her coat over a chair, and stalked out again to look at them. She was dressed in a figure-hugging black knitted dress, thick black tights and high patent heels. She always wore black, reminding Hallie of a panther. When she was with clients, she had that sort of sexy big cat coiled energy. It was just in the office that she could be all claws.

'Be quick if you go. Double espresso.' Yaraslava paused. 'When Rosie and Grace get back, I want you all for a meeting. Hunt's are in talks about Caulfield's development beside Regent's Park. Fourteen prime apartments. This is not a joke. We need to bring Caulfield Properties to us.'

Yaraslava turned around and disappeared inside her office, slamming the door.

Hallie sighed, keeping her voice low. 'My God, sometimes she talks to us like we're children.' Obviously, it wasn't low enough.

'I heard.' Yaraslava's voice was sharp, even through the closed door.

Nick scribbled something on a piece of paper and held it up. It took Hallie a minute to decipher his scrawl, but then she felt a grin crack. 'SHE'S GOT US BUGGED' was about right.

Nick rolled his eyes, then his expression changed.

'I've been thinking about Rosie and this Michael guy. He sent her a photo of her front door today, I mean, that's pretty pointed, but then he sent her an email about meeting for coffee and asking about that secret room in the Kensington house.' His brows knitted. 'I mean, how does he know about it? It's not on any of the listings, or in the photos. I didn't want to say it to Rosie, but he must have been inside.'

Hallie felt a surge of alarm. 'Like he's viewed it as a potential buyer, or—'

'Or ...' Nick screwed up his face. 'Like he's used it? I mean, if he's a full-on stalker, maybe he was in there watching whoever was in the bedroom.'

From the tone of his voice, Hallie could tell Nick's imagination had been in overdrive. They'd all had theories about the secret room off the master bedroom, but the full-length two-way mirror, shackles in the ceiling and the pole in the centre had been a bit of a clue. It had made for a lively discussion.

Hallie closed the lid of her laptop, just in case Yaraslava came out of her office while she was getting the coffee and realised she hadn't been hard at work for hours. Refocusing on what Nick was saying, she grimaced. 'That property has been listed with about three different agents, though. Loads of people must have been around it. That doesn't help Rosie – or us – work out who he is.'

'When Rosie went out with Grace, I had a quick look at our database and we've got three Michaels listed.' He turned to his laptop, scanning the screen. 'None of them have seen Kensington through us, but right after our night out Rosie asked me if I'd noticed anyone hanging about, listening to us. I didn't twig at the time, but I reckon she thinks he was there in the restaurant.' He looked around at Hallie. 'Maybe this is mad, but I was thinking of calling their offices – the three Michaels we have, I mean – and saying I've just realised I might have picked up their jacket by accident. See if they were there that night.'

Hallie nodded slowly. 'I can't see it would hurt. If we can find out who he is, she can report him.'

'Exactly, or we can go and have a chat with him.' Nick looked at her seriously. 'And if it's not one of our Michaels, can you reach out to the other agents who handled Kensington, to see if they've got anyone called Michael registered? You know loads of people in this game.'

Chapter 6

IT WAS JUST after twelve when Rosie and Grace finally got back to the office. Every minute that Rosie had been out, she'd been nervy. Even with Grace for company, she'd been looking over her shoulder constantly. After six weeks of being bombarded by chatty texts and emails, the photo of her front door had shaken her more than she'd expected. It was as if he couldn't get her attention before, and now he'd suddenly run out of patience.

'Hi, guys, anything strange?' Ahead of her, Grace pushed open the glazed office door and slipped off her coat.

Following Grace in, Rosie felt a surge of relief as she walked around the long table they all worked at, and took off her own jacket. Michael might know where she worked, but at least if he barged into the office, she wasn't on her own.

She dumped her bag onto her chair. It was dark grey suede, a gorgeous riot of tassels and silver chain that she'd picked up in a vintage designer store in Paris on almost her last day there. It was the exact shade of the paint on the walls, and somehow made her feel as if she fitted in.

Hallie had made a slightly withering comment – at least, that's how it had sounded to Rosie – about the decor being something 'else' Yaraslava had changed when she'd arrived at Sterling & Co. Rosie didn't know what it had been like before, but the whole place was ultra-sophisticated and minimalist now: pale wooden floors with lots of glass and steel and gold downlighters, and dark grey panelling everywhere.

Well, most of it was very tasteful. The row of five huge textured glass deer heads, which dominated the wall beside the main door, had been a bit of a surprise when she'd walked into the office the first time. And Yaraslava had another one in her office that lit up when the light levels dropped outside. Hallie had made it very clear in that same conversation that she didn't understand the need to put dead things on the walls, and fake dead things seemed even more ridiculous. Her wide-eyed look had made Rosie laugh.

Rosie sat down beside her as Hallie answered Grace from her station at the table. 'I was about to ask you two that very thing. Any sign of the strange Michael?'

Rosie shook her head. She hadn't been able to talk when Hallie had texted earlier, but she'd really appreciated her message, had sent back a heart emoji with the promise that she'd fill Hallie in as soon as she could. Perhaps she should have told her sooner. Perhaps she should have told them all sooner.

Grace was fixing her hair in the mirror on the inside of the coat cupboard door. Glancing over her shoulder, she answered Hallie. 'Nothing. We kept looking to see if anyone was following us on the Tube, but the problem is not knowing what he looks like.'

Nick tapped his phone on the table. 'If he was following you this time, he'll probably send a photo of you both on the Tube platform. He's looking for ways to creep you out.'

Rosie sat down and flipped open her laptop, taking a breath before she spoke. 'When you google stalking, the first result is from an organisation called the Suzy Lamplugh Trust. Get this – she was an estate agent who disappeared.' Rosie kept her voice level, trying to hide the shock waves that had been running through her since she'd opened the search page. Up to now she'd been trying to pretend that this wasn't really happening, that Michael would probably go away, but the photo of her house changed everything.

She'd felt physically sick when she'd read about Suzy Lamplugh: about how she'd disappeared after an appointment to show a house in Fulham. Rosie could remember feeling her chest tighten; she thought she'd left this fear of stalkers behind in Paris. Now she kept her eyes firmly on her screen so she could avoid looking at them. 'She disappeared in 1986. That was years before I was born, and they still haven't found her.'

And she was almost the same age as me.

Just like Sandrine Durand.

She didn't say the last bit out loud, tried to hide the shadow she felt pass over her, but Rosie could see from Hallie's reaction that she had seen it. Suzy Lamplugh had been twenty-five when she disappeared. The estate agent who had vanished in Paris was twenty-six, like Rosie.

'We won't let that happen to you, chick. Until you know who it is, one of us will go out with you, so you're not meeting anyone on your own.'

Before Rosie could reply, behind Hallie, Yaraslava's office door opened. Poised in the doorway, she glared around the room. Hallie had her back to the door, but Rosie could see she was watching their boss in the huge gilt mirror over the fireplace on the wall opposite her.

'My office – meeting now. Everyone. We need to talk about the Caulfield development.'

Hallie rolled her eyes.

It took them all a few minutes to reorganise the chairs and settle down in Yaraslava's office, a few minutes during which she glowered at her desktop screen, her dark eyes narrowed. Nick brought his chair in from the main space and set it down behind Grace and Hallie, then closed the door firmly behind him. He threw a wary glance at Rosie behind Grace's and Hallie's backs. Whatever was up with Yaraslava, she was giving off angry vibes, as if someone had plugged her into the mains.

'Thank you, everyone. Now, Regent's Park. Hunt's *will not* take this listing.' Yaraslava paused to let her words sink in. Rosie could see now why she was mad. There must have been some sort of a shift that she'd missed; she'd been sure that Caulfield's were planning to sell the whole development through Sterling & Co.

Yaraslava continued. 'Hallie, Conor Caulfield is Irish, but his wife is Australian. I want you to find out everything about her. Where she shops, where she goes to the gym.'

Hallie tried to hide a look of confusion. Rosie wasn't fully seeing what Conor Caulfield's wife had to do with anything either, but Grace clearly did.

'Oh, *clever*. So we get to Conor Caulfield through his wife – perhaps send her a care package? Focus on attention to detail.'

Sitting between Grace and Rosie, directly in front of Yaraslava's desk, Hallie winced slightly as she spoke. 'Isn't that a bit … sorry, Rosie … stalkery?'

Grace cut in before Yaraslava could answer. 'No, I think it's nice. It shows we'd research prospective buyers in the same way – so we can get a good match and a quick sale. Obviously, we need to say something like that in the card that goes with it, just to be *totally* clear.'

Yaraslava opened her mouth to speak, but Grace was in full flow. 'I think we need to take them out for dinner first, or maybe the races. There's horse racing on every weekend somewhere. A limo or helicopter to collect him, and a slap-up lunch. Find out what his favourite dishes are and have them on the menu, and his preferred wine, obviously. It's all about the details. Everyone likes to think you've taken trouble over them, that they are special. And all Irish developers love racing.'

There was a moment's silence while they all absorbed this. Behind her, Rosie could hear Nick shifting in his seat.

Yaraslava looked impressed. 'Excellent, Grace. You liaise with Hallie and see what you can find out. Talk to his people, see where he has been photographed and if his wife was with him. I will see if Sebastian can join us. He will like the horse racing, too, and he is a man. Caulfield will talk to him.' She said it as if all men were stupid and would only talk to other men. There were times when Rosie was sure she was right. Yaraslava paused. 'Now, I need an update on your Instagram, Rosie. Your post about the stalking issue this morning. Nick told me you had a photograph.'

Rosie felt her face flush and glanced sideways at Grace. Could you get sacked for getting stalked? The way Yaraslava said it, she made it sound as if it was a whole company problem. Edging forward in her seat, her palms starting to sweat, Rosie updated Yaraslava quickly.

'I wasn't sure about posting about it, but I only did it a few hours ago and there's been a deluge of likes and comments. It seems to have hit a nerve.'

Yaraslava pursed her lips, obviously absorbing the news. 'And you have no idea who this Michael is? You have noticed no one around?'

Rosie shook her head decisively.

Yaraslava took this in, obviously thinking for a moment. 'We need to be alert for anyone who should not be here. I will talk to the tenants downstairs – and upstairs, too – tell them to watch out for strangers. Do we need some security on the front door?'

Rosie looked at Yaraslava in surprise. She hadn't expected anything like this level of concern. She cleared her throat. 'Well, if we did have a guard or a doorman, it would mean someone would be watching the street. They'd see if I was being followed.'

'Yes, or if anyone is appearing frequently. I will organise it. It is imperative that staff and clients feel safe and comfortable coming into the building.'

Out of the corner of her eye, Rosie could see Grace and Hallie were just as surprised as she was. Looking over their heads, Yaraslava switched her attention to Nick.

'I have just had a chat with the vendor at Park House. They need a quick sale, so they have dropped the price to nine-three. I feel that is negotiable – that they will take nine million.'

Rosie could feel, rather than hear, the collective surprise in the room. There was always room for negotiation at this level – they all expected it – but to reduce the asking price by so much in such a short period of time was huge. Park House hadn't been on the market that long.

Yaraslava continued. 'Major and Mrs Bradford would like to see it again. Saturday at 11 a.m. is good. Major Bradford asked for you personally, Nick. A quick sale is a priority.' She smiled, her brown eyes flashing at him as if he was her golden boy. 'We will celebrate when you get an offer.'

Nick began to nod, then screwed up his face. 'Crap, I've got football training on Saturday, and I've booked the car in for a service. I'm going to get dumped off the team if I keep cancelling.'

Yaraslava smiled at him sweetly. Well, perhaps Yaraslava thought it was sweetly, but to Rosie she looked more like a wild cat eyeing up its prey. 'I will make it worth your while, Nick. This deal is *very* important to our client.'

Grace swivelled in her chair. 'Park House is right around the corner from the Tube, you'll be grand.' She grinned. 'Just think of the commission – you'll be able to buy a new car. And you might even beat Rosie on the leader board this month.'

+447480788409

Hey Rosie, how's Marmalade? He's such an orange cat. Your photos of him are adorable. Love Mike x

12:22

+447480788409

Can you believe this weather? What's happened to spring? I bet you'd love to be back in Paris when it's miserable here. Every time I smell coffee I think of Paris and of you, I'm so glad you came to London and we could meet. You're so special Rosie I'd hate it if you went back. Mxx

14:50

+447480788409

God I've had such a day, some people just moan nonstop don't they? It's exhausting listening to them. Sometimes I just want to say if they don't like it, they can just use the door and work somewhere else. Win–win. Hope yours was MUCH better. Love M x

17:00

Chapter 7

'HOW ARE YOU getting home, Rosie?' Nick shut his laptop lid and stuffing it into his bag, did up the buckle on the leather flap.

Rosie looked over at him as she pulled on her coat. 'I think the Tube tonight. I was going to walk to Russell Square rather than go to Holborn. I've been mixing everything up – buses, Tubes, taking different routes. I was just wondering about waiting for Grace, but she's ages at that viewing.'

Nick unhooked his Barbour from the hanger in the cupboard and wrapped a stripy scarf around his neck. 'I can walk you. Text her to tell her not to worry about coming back to the office. I will be your knight this evening, fair lady.' Heading over to the door he opened it and bowed, rolling his hand like a Shakespearean actor.

Rosie laughed. 'Thank you, kind sir.' Coming around

the table, she quickly knocked on Yaraslava's door and stuck her head in. 'Nick and I are just off.'

Yaraslava glanced up from her screen. 'I will lock up. Goodnight.'

Outside, the street was busy. Tired workers poured out of the surrounding offices, many already beginning to gather outside the restaurants and the pub they passed on their route to the Tube station. Rosie glanced around nervously as they crossed the road. She seemed to be constantly searching faces these days, always looking to see if there was one she'd seen before.

'This guy has really spooked you, hasn't he?' Reaching the pavement, Nick slipped behind her so he could walk on her outside, between her and the road.

Rosie glanced at him, touched that he was taking protecting her so seriously. 'The texts were bad enough, but that photo of my front door … It's been on my mind all day. I mean, I was worried about him following me, so I've been careful, but obviously not careful enough. It's just so scary that he knows where I live.'

Nick stuck his hands in his pockets. 'So he's been texting, emailing, sending gifts—'

'And voice messages, but he's stopped doing that, thank God, they were utterly pukesville. He's got this sort of nondescript accent, not one you can pinpoint to a region – not that I'm much good on UK accents.' Rosie pulled out her phone. 'Look, here are the last few from today.'

Nick took it from her and scanned them, scrolling through to see the rest. 'That's a lot. And they are a bit personal, about your cat and your family.'

'He's not even my cat, he's the house cat. But Michael talks like he knows me, that's the creepiest thing.'

Nick passed her phone back. 'The police said they could trace these messages?'

Dodging around a woman who had stopped right in the middle of the pavement in front of her, Rosie nodded. 'Once I file a report formally. I'm not sure how fast, though. I mean, he's not threatening my life or anything. The policewoman I spoke to on the phone said I need to go into a station and talk to them. But they're always saying on the news the police are overworked and undermanned, and whatever about protecting someone from a violent spouse, trying to find an anonymous stalker is a whole different problem.'

'But you *are* going to report it?' Nick looked at her, his face serious. 'I'll come with you if you're worried about it.'

Rosie could feel herself blushing. She was seeing a whole different side to Nick this evening. He was charming and caring, and really bothered by all of her problems.

'Thank you. I think I'll be grand, but yes, I need to make it official. Especially after that photo.' Rosie rolled her eyes. 'I'm starting to wonder if I should try and engineer a meeting with him, and organise for my brothers to be waiting for him.'

Nick grinned. 'I'm here, if you need an army.'

'They live in New York and Dublin, so it might take a bit of organising.' Rosie knew that Eoin and Fiacra getting arrested wasn't going to help anyone, but they'd be here in a heartbeat if she needed them. 'I need to find out who he is first, to know what to do. Not knowing is the bit that's driving me mad.' She glanced at him. 'I don't know who to be frightened of.'

They reached the Tube station and stepped inside, off the pavement. People milled around them, heading for the barriers and the ticket machines. Rosie had expected Nick to say goodbye here, but he didn't look as if he was about to. He frowned, his face serious.

'I know someone who might be able to help. Guy called Iain. He's a data scientist, works with an international agency in cybersecurity.'

Rosie felt her eyebrows shoot up.

'Don't look so surprised.' Nick grinned. 'We were at school together, I did computer science and maths with him. He went on to do literal rocket science, and I went and did politics and philosophy and lasted about a year. Essays are *not* my thing. I got a job in property while I figured out what I wanted to do, and discovered that, actually, that's my thing.'

'I had no idea you'd been to uni and dropped out. It's weird how people end up in jobs. I ended up in property by accident, too, except I was rubbish at school.'

'But you can sell, Rosie Kinsella. I know it feels easy to you, but it's a real gift.' Rosie felt herself blush again, but he frowned as he continued. 'Let me walk you to the platform.'

'Aren't you going the other way?' Rosie was dying to ask Nick about his friend tracing the emails; she suddenly felt like hugging him. He looked so concerned, and he'd already gone out of his way to make sure that she got to the station safely.

'I am, but you are, too. We can change at St Pancras.'

Predictably, the platform was crowded when they got down to it and could continue their conversation. Rosie hadn't felt comfortable talking in the relative silence of the lift, but now she leaned in closer to him, keeping her voice down.

'So, tell me about your friend. Do you think he can help?'

'I'm sure he can. You know you can trace emails to their IP address, the internet service provider. That gives you the general area, and, with a few tools, that, let's say, wouldn't be available to the mainstream user, you can get closer. Iain might be able to get an address for you.'

Rosie looked at him. 'Are you serious? Do you think he could do that? I keep thinking if I even had a clue where Michael …' Rosie paused, suddenly wondering whether saying his name out loud was a good idea, but it was too late. '… worked or lived, I might be able to figure out who he is.'

'Iain definitely can, he's got access to some top-level software. Forward the emails to me, and I'll get them over to Iain. He'll definitely be faster than the police. If this guy is clever, he could be sending them from public libraries or coffee shops or something, but if he's sending them late at night, he could be at home.'

Chapter 8

ROSIE LEANED ON the counter in her kitchenette and looked down at the end of her burgundy scarf sticking out of the swing bin. Michael's text was still burning in her head. She hadn't been able to get the scarf off fast enough when she'd got home, but part of her mourned its loss. It had only been £5 in Primark, but she'd liked it. After Nick's being so concerned, Michael's message had arrived like a punch in her side, just as she'd got off the Underground at Waterloo.

> Rosie! We missed each other again, the tube was so busy! I love that scarf on you, that burgundy colour is fabulous on you and it looks so soft and warm, like you could curl up in it. I was surprised to see you with that Nick guy, I don't think he's what he seems. Say hi to Grace

from me, she's a good friend. It's always good
to have someone from home in your circle.
Love Mike x

Well, Michael was right about one thing – Nick wasn't all that he seemed. He ran a whole lot deeper than Rosie had given him credit for.

Rosie closed her eyes for a moment. Michael's latest message topped off what had been a *very* long day. The comment about her scarf just felt so personal, as Nick had said. It had been the same with her perfume. She'd binned that, too, after he'd mentioned it in his very first email. She'd had no idea what was going to follow then, but it had made her skin crawl.

Across the room she could hear Grace talking to Marmalade. A flat that came with a cat had been the biggest selling point when she'd been hunting for somewhere to live. He belonged to the landlord, who lived on the ground floor in the garden apartment, but Marmalade spent more time up here than downstairs.

Everyone loved cats on the internet, but whenever Michael referenced a photo in his messages it made her freak out a bit. Knowing he was reading her posts and his commenting on them were two different things. She wouldn't be putting up photos of Marmalade for a bit, that was for sure.

'He's so cute.' Marmalade was lying on his back on the sofa, all four paws in the air as Grace rubbed his belly rigorously.

'He's just as dopey as they say orange cats are. But he manages to come in and out through the bathroom window, so he's smart enough when it suits him.'

Grace reached for the mug Rosie passed to her as she sat down. 'Decaf, right?'

Rosie nodded in answer, but her mind was elsewhere. 'I've decided I'm going to keep posting about it. About Michael, I mean. I need to. And the reaction has been amazing.'

Grace took a sip of her coffee. 'You don't think that will encourage him? Isn't the attention what stalkers need?'

Rosie shrugged. 'I think it's my attention he wants.' She paused, standing up again to look out of the window behind the sofa. There hadn't been any net curtains when she'd first moved in, and she'd loved being able to sit and look out at the lights of the city. She was on the fourth floor, and could see the tip of the Shard above the bare trees and the buildings on the opposite side of the busy road.

The day the umbrella had arrived at the office, with its icky handwritten note, she'd got home and suddenly realised that someone might be able to see in from one of the buildings opposite. She'd ordered nets and the thickest possible curtains she could find – heavy denim – to be delivered the next day.

Rosie had closed the curtains when she'd come home, and now twitched one aside so she could peek out into the darkness. She couldn't see anyone lurking, but it didn't make her feel any better. She'd tried to work out exactly where the front door shot had been taken from when she'd got home. He could have used a zoom, but it looked much more as if he'd been just inside the gate.

Much too close.

She turned around and sat down in the purple velvet armchair she'd found on Facebook Marketplace when she'd first moved in. 'Sorry, I'm starting to get obsessed with checking – out of the window, behind me. I can sort of feel him watching me sometimes, even when I'm in the office.' Rosie let out a sharp breath. 'This is so crazy. I'm sorry to be such a drama queen.'

Grace shook her head. 'Don't be apologising, we all want you to feel safe.' She leaned back on the sofa. 'What did the police say when you rang?'

'They said to keep a diary, record everything, save all the messages, take screenshots.' Rosie looked over at Marmalade; she could hear him purring from here. 'That website, the Suzy Lamplugh Trust, has lots of advice about changing passwords and things. I'm starting to think maybe he found me through my Instagram account, so it makes sense to do that.' Rosie drew in a ragged breath, thinking of the estate agent who had gone missing when she'd been working in Paris. Sandrine Durand's disappearance was much more recent than Suzy Lamplugh's, but Rosie had got such a shock when she'd googled stalking and Suzy's name had turned up in the search results, with a huge website and a ton of resources dedicated to her. Rosie had felt as if Suzy was talking to her somehow – warning her.

'That's a *very* good idea. How will you remember it, though, if you change passwords?' Grace gave the cat another tickle. 'Unless you use "Marmalade" and, like, your date of birth or something.'

Rosie smiled at Grace; sometimes she could be truly hopeless with technology. 'I use this thing called Dashlane. It stores all my passwords and then I only have to remember one to get into it.'

Grace's eyes widened, impressed. 'Can you show me how to use it? I *so* need to sort out my accounts.'

'I'll show you tomorrow. And I think I'll get my phone and laptop scanned, just in case there's some sort of malware on them and he's using that to follow me.'

'Is that a thing? Wow, that's creepy.' Grace hesitated. 'You need to make sure someone knows where you are all the time – and like Hallie said, don't go out to a viewing on your own. I can come, or Hallie. Even Nick.' She rolled her eyes and smiled. 'Although he could drive you mad. He thinks a lot of himself. He's the only lad I know who gets his nails manicured.'

Rosie felt her heart fill for a moment. 'Nick's such a sweetie. He walked me right to the Tube this evening, he even waited on the platform with me.'

Grace sat back, cradling her coffee. 'Sorry I got held up, that viewing took ages. Nick's really worried about you.'

'He's got a friend he thinks can trace the IP address of the emails. He's asked me to send them to him.' Rosie pulled the cushion up on the chair behind her, as Grace raised her eyebrows.

'I didn't realise he was a tech genius under that posh boy exterior.'

Rosie laughed. 'He said he did computer science, maths and politics. Who knew? Anyhow, he's going to forward the emails to his friend, so we'll see what he can find out.'

Grace took this in, her brow furrowed as Rosie continued. 'And I'm going to go to the police station and report it all. I should have done before, but somehow it felt like I could have misunderstood him, or maybe led him on somehow. But that photo …' Rosie drew in a breath. 'He was making a point.'

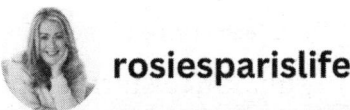 rosiesparislife

#stalker UPDATE

[Image: the words #stalker UPDATE, bold white lettering centred on a black background. UPDATE is in capital letters]

So Michael, or Mike as you sign yourself off now, I know you're reading this. I know you're reading this because you are watching everything I do. Maybe you found me through this account. I don't know. Did I overshare? Perhaps. We all tend to forget there are people we don't really know following us on social media.

When I first came to London, I thought those #askforAngela signs on the back of the loo doors in restaurants, pubs and clubs were brilliant. I didn't think I'd be the one to go to a member of staff to ask for Angela, to ask for help. But now I might be that person. If you, my stalker, show yourself.

A lot of you have been asking in comments what's actually happened and suggesting that maybe I've just seen the same guy twice on my way to work and I'm jumping to conclusions. The guy that asked if my skirts are too short and if I dress provocatively? Maybe read the room?

This all started with flowers, then an email arrived. Then more emails. He was in the same restaurant as me and my work colleagues. Then he started leaving voicemails. His tone is super friendly, like we've known each other for ages, like we're close friends. Like we have some sort of a relationship.

He's stopped leaving the voicemails now because I stopped listening to them, they seriously creeped me out.

Since it started I've been looking at everyone I meet differently, I've been reading things into what they say, looking for clues. And I'm constantly looking over my shoulder. My boss is taking it all very seriously and getting a security guard for the office so there will be someone whose job it is to watch what's happening in and outside the building.

I'm jumpy, every time my phone pings with a message my anxiety spikes.

And before you suggest I change my phone number, I'm trying to find a solution to that. I need to be in touch when I'm at work, I need to be in touch *with* work, so I need a phone and people need to be able to get hold of me.

But (Michael) I won't be showing properties on my own any more. And my colleagues know exactly what's happening. And soon the police will too.

#stalker #metoo #womensaid #nomore #askforAngela

Chapter 9

HOLBORN POLICE STATION was just around the corner from the office, and seemed the best place to go to talk to someone. Rosie got there early, hoping she could get everything reported and not be too late for work.

At the top of the steps she pushed open a glazed door to find the waiting room empty, the floor a surprising sky blue. The man on reception, separated from the room by what looked like a bulletproof glass panel, didn't seem to be a police officer. He couldn't help her much either.

'You need to go to Islington or Canary Wharf, to talk to them.' He held up two A4 sheets of paper encased in plastic with the addresses of the stations printed in bold black type.

Rosie looked at him in disbelief. How was she going to get across London and back to the office for 9.30? And what if Michael had seen her come in here, and she never got to Islington Police Station?

She shook the thought from her head. Michael could have grabbed her just about anywhere in the past few weeks, she was sure. Instead, he seemed to enjoy watching her. A shiver ran up her spine.

The question now was: should she go over to Islington this morning and risk Yaraslava's wrath, or wait until tonight? But Yaraslava had taken this seriously enough to suggest security at the office, so getting it done now felt like the most sensible thing to do.

She'd come this far, and she'd been nervous enough about making this whole thing official. Part of Rosie was still hoping it would all go away, that somehow she'd imagined it, or that Michael wasn't a creep – that it was all some sort of misunderstanding. Reporting it made it real.

Rosie fired Grace a quick text asking her to cover for her with Yaraslava.

Outside, it was threatening to rain, but as Rosie headed down to the pavement she saw a black cab, its yellow light as bright as her relief at spotting it. Sitting in the rear, anxiously playing with her phone, Rosie checked her email.

And wished she hadn't.

Michael had sent another photograph of the house.

This time, unmistakably, he'd taken it from just inside the front door.

Inside.

How has he got *inside* her house?

Rosie closed her eyes, terror running through her veins like ice water. After all these weeks of constant intimidation, did he not think he'd scared her enough? These photographs were so threatening – and worse, because they came with no message. They were like a bald statement that he could get close to her if he wanted to. She rubbed her face. It was definitely the right decision to report this now. She couldn't wait, not with this new photo arriving. Yaraslava would understand that.

Islington Police Station was an enormous red-brick building. Rising over Rosie didn't know how many floors, it seemed to fill the whole block. But at least, finally, she was in the right place.

In a small windowless interview room, the police constable who sat down in front of her was only a few years older than Rosie, her brunette hair in a pony tail, her white uniform shirt crisply ironed. Perhaps it was the strain on Rosie's face, but she brought Rosie water and now opened an A4 notepad, her pen poised.

'My name's Polly Amwell. Tell me what the problem is.'

Rosie began to run through everything, adding as much detail as she could.

'And do you have screenshots of the texts?'

'I deleted the first few but I've kept the rest. And I'm sorry, but I deleted all the voicemails. I can't listen to him. Even knowing they were on my phone made me want to vomit.'

'Could you tell anything about where he was from, from his accent?'

Rosie bit her lip. His voice played like a continual soundtrack in her head. Every time it rained she could hear him saying, 'My God, the rain today, I was so worried you'd get soaked …' It was as if he was haunting her.

'He sounded confident, warm, and very English. Not London, but a bit northern, maybe. I'm not great on British accents, but it definitely wasn't like the guy in our office, Nick – not so posh.' Rosie frowned. 'It was perfectly smooth, measured. I know this sounds a bit strange, but melodious, like he knew how to speak. Between his voice and the theatre tickets, I wondered if he was an actor.'

Polly frowned as she made notes. 'Does he leave many voice messages?'

Rosie shook her head. 'Not now. There were quite a few – from a private number – at the start. He's sending more emails now, and WhatsApp messages – but every time I block him, the number changes. Honestly I've given up now, it doesn't put him off.' Rosie bit her lip. 'And part of me needs to know what he's thinking in case he decides to turn up somewhere.' She picked up the plastic cup and took a sip of water. 'The policeman I spoke to on the helpline said that it's likely he's using a burner phone.'

'Sounds like it. And he was probably using a burner app to generate those new numbers.' Polly grimaced. 'But if you get any more voice messages, we can play them back. You won't have to listen to them.'

'Thank you for taking me seriously.'

Polly leaned forward earnestly. 'Stalking or harassment offences come under section 2A of the Protection from Harassment Act 1997 and section 42A (1) of the Criminal Justice and Police Act 2001. We don't rely on *intent* to classify actions as harassment, but on the impact. It's a summary offence that's tried in the magistrates' court, so you don't have to worry about a jury or big courtroom scenes. Harassment carries a penalty of a maximum fifty-one weeks' imprisonment.'

Fifty-one weeks didn't sound very long to Rosie, but if they could get to that stage, it would be fifty-one weeks of peace and getting her life back to normal, and, with luck, would stop him.

'Can I get a barring order or something to stop him contacting me?'

'Absolutely. It's called a restraining order here. But our first task is identifying him. If you can send me all the emails, I can get them over to our cybersecurity team for them to trace the IP address. We'll talk to the retailers he's used, and see if we can identify him from the transactions for the flowers and—'

Rosie interrupted her. 'I'm not sure they will help. They were Interflora, and I binned everything – I wasn't thinking. I've no idea which florist sent them.'

'Don't worry, the umbrella and the theatre tickets should give us an opportunity to trace him online. There could be CCTV if they were bought in person. I need you to keep a detailed diary of any interaction.'

Rosie let out a breath that she hadn't quite realised she'd been holding. 'And the pictures of my house ... Is there anything you can do about that?'

'Talk to your landlord and the other tenants to see if they remember anyone hanging about or trying to get access, perhaps pretending to be a friend of yours. Let them know this is happening, and to be careful about who they let in.'

'I'm going to tell my landlord tonight. I probably should have done it earlier.'

Polly put her head on one side and held up her hand. 'You're doing everything right, Rosie, honestly. You didn't ask for this and you've reported it now. You just need to concentrate on keeping safe.'

 rosiesparislife

[Image: the words #stalker UPDATE, bold white lettering centred on a black background. UPDATE is in capital letters]

I'm stunned there were so many comments on my last post about similar experiences of stalking you've all had. Research says that 91% of women have felt unsafe walking home at night – feels like it should be even higher. I've been checking this out, mainly to try and find out the ways other women either caught or identified their stalkers. It looks like a lot of people know who their stalkers are – ex-boyfriends or husbands, previous work colleagues, or other students at school or university.

Apparently there are different types of stalker (who knew?) Here's the list:
Rejected stalkers; resentful stalkers; the predatory stalker; the intimacy seeker; the incompetent suitor; the erotomaniac stalker who think their 'love' is being reciprocated; the political stalker; and the morbidly infatuated. (Another list I read had 'hitmen' in this last place. 'Morbidly infatuated' feels a bit different, but you get the picture.)

Some of these are words I had to look up. They aren't words I ever wanted or need in my vocabulary.

So which one are you, Michael?

The police have told me stalking is defined not by the intention of the perpetrator, but by the IMPACT of their actions. Any normal person should know that if you text someone multiple times a day for weeks and don't get a reply, then maybe they don't want to talk to you. That's harassment. But it's more than just texts, isn't it? I'm not going to go into all the details here, but it's much more.

I've made the first report, so the clock is ticking now, Michael.

#stalker #metoo #womensaid #nomore #askforAngela #notavictim

Chapter 10

WHEN ROSIE FINALLY got to the office, Hallie was the only one there.

'You're late. I was starting to wonder if something had happened.' Hallie's face was full of concern. Rosie dumped her bag on the floor beside her chair and leaned on the table for a minute, gathering herself.

'I went to the police, to report Michael.'

'Grace said. She's gone to get some decent coffee, she'll be back in a minute. How did it go?'

'The policewoman was so nice. I've given her all the details, and they're going to see if they can trace his location from his emails. But she didn't know if they'd be able to work out who he is. I mean, if I don't know …'

'That's a great start, though. This is what they do – find criminals. There's amazing technology these days.' Hallie had her head on one side and was looking at Rosie across the table, her voice calming. 'Sit down, you look done in. Nick's showing one of the Canary Wharf apartments and Yaraslava's out somewhere. You can relax.'

Rosie smiled gratefully and collapsed in her chair, reaching for the pocket of her coat to find her phone. Hallie was right: explaining everything had been exhausting, on top of not sleeping properly, on top of … well, everything.

'I think I just need a few minutes of total distraction.' Rosie glanced at Nick's empty chair and grinned. 'Some of Nick's dating chaos or …' She put her phone down beside her. 'A morning of mindless scrolling.' She woke her phone up and opened Instagram to see how the post she'd written in the cab on the way was doing, but the first post in her feed showed the tanned smiling face of one of the guys she followed. 'Or sexy lads hanging off cliffs.' She held up the phone to show Hallie and grinned. Hallie's eyebrows rose appreciatively.

'Wow, he is fit. What's his story?'

'He's called Jago, he's lovely, actually. Well, I don't know him properly, only from Insta. We DM quite a bit.'

'I'd sure be DM'ing him too.'

Rosie grinned, some of the tension she'd been feeling dissipating. 'He travels all over the world, rock-climbing.

His photography is amazing. But he's really into ecology, and the wildlife that lives on the cliffs.' Rosie clicked on the account and scrolled to find a selfie of Jago hanging from a rope, a black and white mountain goat beside him, looking at him with bemused interest. Jago was grinning, his skin tanned, hair bleached and flopping into his face. 'See.' She turned the phone around so Hallie could see.

'What's his Insta? I could do with some of that in my feed.'

Rosie laughed. 'That's what Grace said – she's following him, too.'

Hallie reached for her phone and opened her Instagram as Rosie gave her Jago's account details. Rosie opened her mouth to say more, but in that second a text arrived from a number she didn't recognise. She felt her stomach clench. She glanced up at Hallie.

'What, chick? You've gone pale. It's not Michael again, is it?'

Rosie bit her lip and opened the text, her finger shaking. She hoped to God it wasn't Michael. She felt a rush of relief as she scanned the message.

'No … No, it's not.' Rosie paused, absorbing what the message said. 'You won't believe this. It's from *Good Morning Britain*.'

'Seriously? What does it say?'

It took Rosie a moment longer to process it, and then she read it out to Hallie. 'I'm a researcher for *Good Morning Britain*. We saw your posts on being stalked are getting a lot of comments, we wondered if you were free to come in to the show on Friday morning. Could you ring me asap on this number? Elsa Kendall.' Rosie stopped and looked at Hallie in disbelief. 'That's mad.'

Hallie laughed, shaking her head. 'Only a bit. You've got a huge following, and I guess they've looked at your stories and stuff to see what you'd be like on camera. You should do it, you've obviously hit a nerve.'

As Hallie was speaking, another text came in.

Her eyes wide, shaking her head in disbelief, Rosie turned the phone around so Hallie could read it.

Hello, is that Rosie Kinsella? I work for Delphine magazine, I saw your post on being stalked and I wondered if we could have a chat. We want to do a feature on the 40th anniversary of the Suzy Lamplugh disappearance in July and we'd love to talk to you about your experience. My name's Natasha Piper, you can get me on this number or email me at natashap@delphinemagazine.com

'Wow, isn't that the Suzy girl you were talking about yesterday?'

Rosie nodded slowly, then frowned. 'How are they getting my number?'

'They're researchers, they're paid to connect with people. But I bet they called the office and the phone went through to Yaraslava. It's been deadly quiet here all morning.'

'And she just gave it to them?' Rosie frowned, suddenly wondering if Yaraslava had had something to do with Michael getting hold of her phone number originally. She hoped not, but then, if a client wanted to call her, Yaraslava wouldn't hesitate to pass the number on. That was part of the job. It *was* the job.

'What are you going to do? You need to call them back. The magazine can wait, but the TV is big.'

As Hallie spoke, her own phone rang and Rosie saw the name 'Ben' flashing on the screen. 'Oh, I'd better take this. I'll go into the hall.' She pointed towards Rosie's phone. 'Call them now.' Hallie stood up, the phone still ringing in her hand. 'Go on … At least see what they want to talk about. Think how big this could make your Instagram. You could give up property completely.'

Rosie pursed her lips and looked at Hallie cheekily through one eye. 'You tell me who Ben is, and I'll call.'

Hallie blushed hard. It took her a moment to think about it. 'OK, but it's top secret. Seriously secret. Call them, and I'll tell you later.'

Hallie answered her phone, glancing at Rosie, half laughing. Keeping her voice low, she headed for the office door and the hallway.

Rosie watched her go, still a bit stunned from the text. But Hallie was right – not so much about making her Instagram huge, but about spreading the message. Rosie had had hundreds of replies to her post. There were so many other women in the same situation; she owed it to them to get the conversation going around safety – online and offline.

Rosie glanced out of the glass door. Hallie had closed it behind her so Rosie couldn't hear her, but she could see Hallie was leaning on the wall beside the lift, and whatever was being said, she was glowing.

Rosie picked up her phone and hit the call button.

Chapter 11

'**OH MY GOD,** you're going to be on *TV?*' Grace was standing just inside the door of the office as if she was glued to the spot, the cardboard tray of coffees in her hands, her eyes wide open. '*Honestly?* How did that happen?'

As Rosie started to reply, out in the hall she saw Hallie suddenly finish her call. Whoever Ben was, she'd been on the phone the whole time Rosie had been talking to the TV researcher.

A moment later Hallie came in through the door, rolling her eyes. Right behind her was Yaraslava, wrapped snugly in her fur coat. Rosie wasn't sure why, but she felt herself blush, as if she'd been caught doing something she shouldn't have.

'What is happening?' Taking in Grace standing in the middle of the office and, from her reaction, Rosie's scarlet cheeks, Yaraslava stood waiting for an answer. Hallie sat down hastily on the opposite side of the table to Rosie and pulled a face. There were times when she behaved as if she was closer to Rosie's age than her own, and she *really* didn't like Yaraslava. Rosie tried hard not to laugh; this was all getting so ridiculous, and Grace was still a picture of astonishment.

'Rosie's going on TV, she just got called. About the stalker thing. I mean, that's mad.' Still aghast, Grace turned around to look at their boss.

Yaraslava raised one dark eyebrow in question. 'Tell me more.'

Rosie cleared her throat, trying to get a grip on what was happening. 'I've been contacted by *Good Morning Britain*, and *Delphine* magazine. They want me to go to the TV studio tomorrow. It feels like a real opportunity to get the conversation going about what's happening to me – and all the other women.'

Yaraslava's dark eyebrows stayed arched as she waited for Rosie to continue. Rosie sat up in her seat, one hand on her phone. Yaraslava was still looking at her. She felt she needed to fill the silence. '*Good Morning Britain* want me to go in tomorrow. Maybe that level of publicity will scare Michael off.' Grace was still standing, holding the coffee, as

Rosie continued. '*Delphine* are doing an anniversary piece about Suzy Lamplugh.' Yaraslava looked at Rosie blankly. Rosie continued hastily. 'She was an estate agent who disappeared. Her parents are incredible. They established a whole charity for stalking victims that gives information and support if it happens to you.'

'But *Good Morning Britain*? That's *so huge*.' Finally Grace realised she was still standing in the middle of the office and, moving over to the table, slipped the coffees onto it, pulling her own out of its cardboard tray and pushing the other one towards Hallie.

Rosie flicked her a smile. *Huge and nerve-racking.*

'This is very good. You must mention Sterling's, obviously.' As Yaraslava spoke, Hallie froze, her coffee halfway to her lips, obviously biting back a response.

As if Grace hadn't heard Yaraslava, she sat down in her chair heavily, her face still stunned. 'What are you going to wear? And you'll have to get your hair done.' She pulled her laptop towards her, waking it up to check the clock. 'It's only two o'clock now, you've got ages. Do you need me to help? Will they send a taxi in the morning? What do they want to talk about?'

Rosie winced; she was only processing the conversation she'd just had herself, and wasn't ready for the inquisition.

But Grace was looking across at her, waiting for the answers, her eyes huge.

'They were really interested at the number of comments on the stalker posts, all the stories people are sharing. It's like some of the women have never said anything about their experiences before. They are so raw.'

Hallie nodded. 'I read some. Who knew, honestly? It is a bit mind-blowing.'

'I was sure I'd lose followers because the content was so different. But it's good in some ways. I mean, it's brought people together and given them a chance to share. That's what the researcher was saying – once people share the first time, it gets easier to talk about. When they see other people in the same situation, it gives them permission to reach out properly.'

Grace put her coffee down. 'For, like what … therapy?'

Rosie shrugged. 'I suppose so. That's what they want me to talk about, anyway. They are getting someone from Women's Aid on, too, and someone else who was stalked by an ex.' She suddenly broke off. The girl who they'd said would be on the show with her had been all over the papers when she'd had acid thrown in her face. Rosie had been in Paris then, but she'd seen the reports. When the researcher had told her that bit, for a moment Rosie had almost backed out. She didn't need the thought of Michael throwing acid at her to add to her nightmares.

As if Grace had read her mind, she pursed her lips, her face deadly serious for a moment. 'Do you think it's a good idea? I mean, for real? What if this Michael sees it and gets mad? What if it makes him worse?'

Chapter 12

IT WAS SIX o'clock by the time Rosie heard her landlord, Maurizio, come home. She'd been keeping an eye out, watching for him. She would normally have left her front door open so she could hear the rattle of the street door as he closed it, but under the circumstances, she'd decided that wasn't the best idea.

Giving Maurizio time to get his groceries unpacked, Rosie found herself pacing around the living room. Since she'd got home from the office, she'd been thinking about what Polly, the police officer, had said about talking to her housemates.

Whatever happened with this TV thing – *particularly* because of the TV – she needed Maurizio, and the two Davids who lived downstairs, to know about Michael sending photos of the house. If they were all on the lookout, perhaps one of them would spot him hanging about.

Finally, Rosie couldn't wait any longer. Grabbing her keys and phone, she pulled her front door closed and ran down the stairs to the ground floor. Maurizio's own door was at the rear of the hall. As well as covering the whole ground floor, his flat included the basement, where French windows at the far end of his kitchen-cum-living-room opened into the tiny back garden. It was an upside down apartment, with his office on the first floor at the front of the house getting the morning sun, and the patio getting flooded with light in the evening. Rosie loved it.

Ringing his doorbell, she could hear Marmalade's plaintive mews and then the creak of the stairs as Maurizio came up. He was slightly out of breath when he opened the door, scooping Marmalade into his arms as he did so. He was still wearing his battered leather jacket, but had taken off his shoes; multicoloured stripy socks stuck out from his jeans. Rosie wasn't sure how old he was – about fifty, she thought; his closely cropped dark hair was greying at the temples. He was a graphic designer, working from home with his business and life partner Marco. She'd loved them both from the moment she'd stepped in the door to view the flat.

'Rosie, how are you? Come in, it's supper time for cats. Marmalade is furious with me for being out all day.'

Turning, Maurizio vanished inside, leaving Rosie to follow as he continued, his voice disappearing down the stairs. 'Marco's in Vienna until Tuesday, so our orange friend is feeling neglected. He thinks I don't know that when I'm out, he spends half his time with you and the two Davids.'

As she arrived at the bottom of the stairs, Maurizio was already spooning cat food into a dish on the counter. Marmalade was stretching up, trying to catch it with his paw. Picking the dish up, Maurizio held it aloft as he wove around the table and past the huge sofa dominating the sunny end of the room, putting it down on a mat beside the French doors.

'Now, tell me how I can help. The boiler is behaving, I hope?' Bustling to the counter, Maurizio shed his jacket onto the sofa en route and turned his huge coffee machine on. It looked more as if it should be in a restaurant than a home, and he used it at every possible opportunity.

'Sit, sit. Talk to me. I barely see you at the top of the house. You are like a little mouse up in the attic.'

Rosie laughed. His Italian accent was so strong, and he was so theatrical: he'd whispered 'leetle mouse' as if it might give Marmalade ideas.

'I'm good, thanks. The boiler is working brilliantly now, there's tons of hot water and no leaks.'

Picking up mugs from the sideboard, Maurizio looked at her seriously. '*That* is a bonus.'

He said it with a flourish that made it sound as if she'd won the lottery.

'It's something else.' Rosie felt herself blush. Part of her was embarrassed, as if it was her fault this was happening. Why was this so difficult to talk about? 'Well, you know I work for an estate agent.'

'I do – a *very* smart one, I believe.'

She smiled at the expression on his face. 'The thing is, I seem to have found a stalker … or rather, he's found me. At least I think he's a stalker. It's all a bit weird.'

The coffee machine clicked behind Maurizio and he put a mug under the spout, turning it on.

'It's a bit late for coffee. Would you like some proper Italian hot chocolate? It sounds like we need it for this.'

Comforted by the smell of the chocolate and the warmth of his reception, Rosie sighed. He was being so nice. She could feel herself welling up, but she couldn't get emotional now; she needed to explain.

A moment later Maurizio had slid their mugs onto the table with a jug of hot milk.

'Good hot chocolate, it makes everything well. Now, tell me about this stalker. He's a man you know?'

Rosie reached for a misshapen sugar cube from the bowl in the middle of the table and, dropping it into her mug, stirred it slowly.

'I've no idea who he is. He's called Michael and he seems to think he knows me. He started texting and emailing just after I started at Sterling's. Flowers and gifts. He bought theatre tickets and thought I'd go with him.' Rosie put down the spoon and took a ragged breath, her eyes fixed on the steaming froth in front of her.

She felt Maurizio's hand on her arm.

'You are upset. I don't like that. Tell me how I can help.'

As she looked up at him she felt her eyes filling. 'Thank you. I don't know what anyone can do. I went to the police station this morning … The thing is, he's sent me some photos of the house.' Rosie reached for her phone to show him. 'The first one was outside, but look … This one came yesterday and it was taken inside. Right inside.'

'*Mio dio*. This is not good. How did he get inside the hallway? Inside my house?'

Rosie shrugged. 'I wondered if you knew anyone called Michael, if he could have been visiting? I haven't been to talk to the two Davids yet.'

Maurizio waved his hand. 'I will do that, and impress on them the need to not allow anyone they don't know inside.'

Rosie smiled gratefully. 'I don't know if the door was open and he just wandered in by chance, or what …'

Maurizio looked at the photo again. 'David One's bike is there, so he must be in. Which means it's more likely to be morning or evening. I'll ask him if he's had any days at home.' He looked thoughtful for a minute. 'I've had a plumber and tilers in. A week or so ago, when we replaced the shower. It's possible they left the door open while they were bringing in equipment. They know the other floors are rented, but they wouldn't know who by.'

'Perhaps that's it, and this was taken before David One went to college. I was just a bit …' What should she say? Sick? Terrified? 'Maybe he'd been a previous tenant, or knew one, and had a key.'

Maurizio's eyes opened wide. 'That is a horrible thought. But the two Davids have been here for two years. And Fredrik who used to live in your apartment has gone back to Norway. He is very, very sensible. I doubt he would have given the key to anyone.'

'It sounds like he could have come in when the plumbers were here, then?'

'I think so. Maybe. But we won't take a risk. I'll talk to the others and get the front door lock changed. You said you've been to the police?'

Rosie nodded and burst into tears.

 rosiesparislife

[Image: the words #stalker UPDATE, bold white lettering centred on a black background. UPDATE is in capital letters]

We've all heard about stalking, through the media – it's usually the stories with the terrible outcomes that hit the press – or through friends, or maybe you've been followed home at night yourself.

The charities who compile statistics say that in the UK, the US and Australia, stalking happens to about one in five women and about one in 20 men.

Which makes it *very* common.

Stalking is basically anything that involved unwarranted contact that makes someone fear for their personal safety. It can be:

* Repeated calls, texts or contact through email or social media (lots of those)

* Being watched/someone showing up at your home or work

* Unwanted gifts (er, hello, Michael)

* Property damage – like your car getting keyed, or windows broken

* Having your stuff stolen – like your washing or personal property

* Being tracked or someone following your daily routine.

I can tick almost every box here. But all the articles I've found online talk about victims: 'Showing up at the *victim's* work.' I hate the word 'victim'.

I won't be a victim.

But what do all stalkers have in common?

I've been listening to a brilliant podcast by an American girl called Lily Baldwin. She was stalked for THIRTEEN YEARS. I keep rerunning one line in my head: 'What they all have in common is that they persist. They don't stop. They just keep going and going and going.'

Well, Michael, you might think you're going to keep on going, but I won't be a victim.

#stalker #metoo #womensaid #nomore #askforAngela #notavictim

Chapter 13

THE TV STUDIOS weren't one bit like Rosie had imagined them to be. After the huge open reception area where she'd signed in, had her bag scanned by security and had been given a visitor's badge, the corridors were endless: bland grey carpet and white walls, doors positioned at regular intervals. It felt a lot like being inside a rabbit warren.

The driver who picked her up had been far too chatty for that time on a Friday morning. If she'd been going to the airport on holiday or something, Rosie was sure she'd have been more friendly, but between the lack of sleep caused by her head racing all night, and her stomach churning with nerves, she'd had difficulty stringing a sentence together to answer him.

Which did not bode well for live TV.

A researcher called Willow, who was wearing impossibly

skinny jeans, huge Doc Martens boots, and whose long blonde hair was perfectly super-straight, met her at reception with an ultra-efficient-looking iPad in her hand. Rosie was now following her down miles of mysteriously identical corridor. Willow had a habit of flicking her hair over her shoulder every time she asked a question, which happened with alarming regularity as they headed into what felt like the bowels of the building. There was a lot of hair flicking.

'Here we are. This is the green room. You'll be called in for make-up first. I'll come and get you for that, then when they're ready for you, I'll take you through to the studio. You can leave your things in here safely.'

Willow swiped her badge on a keypad to access the room, and pushed open a heavy door. The 'green room' wasn't in the slightest bit green; it didn't look unlike the corridor, all pale grey and white. There was a low round black ash table with biscuits and pastries in baskets on it, and a coffee machine on a counter in the corner. The walls were lined with several huge soft grey sofas.

At one end was a massive TV screen showing the breakfast show. They were doing the weather forecast, and although the sound was turned down, Rosie could see from the cloud symbols that there was a storm coming in from the west.

At least on this station, the weather map showed Ireland beside the UK; on the BBC forecast, the Irish sea was mysteriously empty of all life. Rosie had always found it utterly bizarre – it was like leaving France off the map of Europe. Who on earth would do that?

She glanced back at the screen. It would be twelve degrees in Cork today. She felt a tug. Should she go home for a bit and see if that got rid of Michael – give him space to fixate on something else, perhaps? She sighed to herself; she wished it was that easy. Even if she did get a similar job in Cork, she'd have to live at home for a bit, and that would be a nightmare.

'Can I get you anything? There's coffee, and water in the fridge under there. Help yourself. And there's a bathroom through that door.'

Willow hovered in the doorway while Rosie took this in and realised she needed to answer. 'That's grand, thanks so much.'

The door clunked closed as Willow vanished, and Rosie made straight for the coffee machine. She needed to get her brain in sync with her body or this was going to be a disaster.

Although part of her already felt as if it was a disaster. *Why had she said yes?*

Well, she knew the answer to that: you didn't get invited to appear on national TV many times in a lifetime, and the exposure would get her message out to even more women.

She'd loved posting when she'd lived in Paris: it had been fun, and all sorts of opportunities had opened up as a result. But the increase in her follower count since she'd started to write about her stalker was starting to make her Instagram account look like something significant – and it had obviously attracted the producers, too.

Which left her unbelievably conflicted. Deep down, Rosie had a bad feeling about somehow benefiting from what was actually becoming a terrifying situation.

Grace was constantly commenting on the build-up in her follower numbers, but that wasn't in Rosie's mind at all as she wrote each post. It had become like therapy – a place for her to rationalise and share – and that had clearly hit a note with women all over the place. If more women saw it, and followed, surely that was a good thing for them all?

She just wanted to make sure that in the interview, she spoke about the therapy aspect: about how the women following her account gave her, and one another, the strength to continue.

Rosie put a paper cup under the coffee machine spout and pressed the latte button.

It was all going to be fine.

With a bit of luck, Michael wouldn't be watching at this time in the morning, and if he was, perhaps discussing him on live TV would show him the impact he was having on her. Rosie didn't really understand how he could think any of his contact with her was normal.

The coffee machine stopped gurgling and Rosie realised her cup was full. She didn't think she'd ever needed a coffee more.

Chapter 14

'SO, ARE YOU going into the office today?' Hallie could feel Ben's eyes on her from the other side of his white marble breakfast bar. She'd pulled on his navy and white striped towelling robe after her shower and twisted her blonde hair up into a knot. She'd licked on some mascara and a hint of blush, lip gloss, trying to improve her early morning look without looking as if she was wearing make-up. She needed to get tips from Rosie on how those girls on Instagram managed to look so gorgeous straight out of bed. They set impossible standards for the rest of womankind.

But it was probably all fake. Like everything these days. If you went far below the surface, things were very different on the inside.

Standing at the end of the counter, chopping fruit on a chunky wooden board, Ben glanced up at her again. His caramel hair was sticking up and tousled; he'd pulled on navy and grey check pyjama bottoms and a grey marl T-shirt that stretched across his broad shoulders and toned chest.

Why did some men get more sexy when they were a mess, but women just looked so *wretched*? Hallie faltered inside, realising she was using one of Rosie's words. 'Locked' was another word that charmed Hallie when Rosie was talking about people who were drunk, and in Ireland, occasionally things were 'savage', which always made her smile.

Poor Rosie. And now she had this TV thing to deal with. She was right to do it, but Hallie knew she was terrified.

Thoughts of the TV brought her back to the kitchen. Ben had switched the screen on so they could watch while they were having breakfast.

'Yes, I need to get ready for this viewing in Chelsea next week.'

'She has you working every weekend. You need a break. That woman's some piece of work.' Ben cut with force into the apple he was holding, the sound of the knife on the board loud, even over the TV. Hallie glanced at it again. Rosie had thought she'd be on about nine o'clock;

they only had another few minutes to wait. Hallie could feel her nerves for Rosie increasing with every increment of the clock.

With her concentration fixed on the TV, Hallie didn't reply to Ben. What could she say, anyway? He was right. The breakfast show switched to a competition segment and she turned to him.

'She's got a real bee in her bonnet about Conor Caulfield's development. She was expecting to handle the whole thing, but …'

'But a rival company might have stepped in?' Ben had started on a cucumber and shaved off a slice, eating it off the back of the knife, a broad grin on his face.

'Don't do that, that knife's lethal. I faint at the sight of blood.'

He narrowed his eyes sexily and did it again, more slowly, flicking the slice off the knife with his tongue. He was trying to distract her, Hallie was sure of it.

'Do you know anything about Caulfield, by any chance, Mr Hunt?' She looked at him hard as she said it. 'I'm supposed to be wining and dining him at the races if Grace can set everything up.'

'I'd have thought Grace would want to do that if she's going to the trouble of organising the hospitality.'

Hallie waited a beat to see if Ben would make any comments about his company muscling in on the Caulfield project, but his attention was back on his breakfast prep. Hallie sighed inside. She hated secrets; she needed him to be honest with her.

'Yaraslava said she wants Rosie to go with me. Grace would be great, but she doesn't have Rosie's—'

'Sparkle? See, it's not just me seeing it. Yaraslava might have her faults, but she's very shrewd when it comes to business. You and Rosie will be a formidable team.'

'I hope so. I need to increase my sales.'

'The commission will be sweet on that development. It's dog eat dog out there.' Ben picked up an orange and started work on peeling it, the scent making her hungry. She loved his fruit, yogurt and home-made granola.

'Don't I know it? That's precisely why Yaraslava is so mad about Caulfield exploring the opposition.' She looked at Ben pointedly. 'We're the fifth most successful agency in London, after the big international brands and Hunt's. She wants us to knock you down the ladder, so Sterling's can be number four, and she'll do anything to get to that position.' Hallie glanced at the TV again and then back to Ben, but he seemed to be enjoying the thought of Yaraslava getting mad.

He opened his mouth to speak, but before he could, Hallie caught sight of Rosie on the TV screen.

'Oh my God, she's on.'

Chapter 15

AS IT TURNED out, despite her nerves – or perhaps because of them – the whole interview went by in a blur. In the green room, Rosie had been introduced to the two women she was appearing with, and then they were all led into the darkened rear of the set.

Huge doors opened into what felt like a narrow area, but Rosie quickly realised it was curtained off from the main studio. The whole space was painted black, the curtains black, too. Cables ran across the floor, and those black cases with steel edges that you see in music videos were stacked everywhere. On the other side of the curtain was the brilliantly lit sofa, raised slightly on a dais and surrounded by huge cameras on wheels. Operators in headphones were focusing on the action as the presenters did a link to what Rosie realised must be a pre-recorded piece.

The set was smaller than Rosie had expected, and when you could see around it, it didn't look anything like the cosy living room that appeared on TV. She glanced nervously around at Tiffany, a girl who had had acid thrown at her, but she was mouthing something to Christine from Women's Aid, a wonderfully warm lady in an expansive floral dress who looked as if she should be serving tea at a village fete. They'd both done this before and seemed to be incredibly relaxed.

Willow the researcher led them to the sofa, where two sound technicians swooped in and wired them up, clipping mics discreetly onto their clothes, the battery packs hidden behind them. Rosie had had a long conversation last night with Hallie about what she should wear, and had gone for a navy blazer with smart narrow jeans and high-heeled boots. She'd pinned her hair up, and with a cream silk blouse, the whole outfit was simple and smart but still casual.

As they sat down, the two anchors glanced up and smiled warmly, but went back to their notes while a piece about travel or something was obviously being shown to the public. Getting comfortable on the sofa, Rosie realised she could see a screen showing their sofa, the three of them sitting side by side, and another dark blue screen with huge white type on it. The presenter suddenly looked up and started reading what was rolling on the screen, stopping abruptly and repeating it. She was nodding to someone somewhere else who, Rosie realised, must have been speaking in her ear.

And then they were on.

'For many more women than we often realise, stalking is a very real and terrifying issue. Whether they are stalked by someone they know, or a complete stranger, the impact is devastating. Joining us today are Rosie Kinsella, whose RosiesParisLife Instagram account has documented her job as a luxury property agent and taken us all on a joyful ride as she found her feet in a fabulous city. But Rosie's recently moved to London, and when she became the victim of a stalker, her Instagram account took on a whole new dimension ...'

Afterwards, Rosie wasn't even sure what she'd said, but she'd definitely mentioned how she felt supported by all the women who had shared their stories. Tiffany had talked about how for anyone who had been in a relationship, stalking was a form of coercive control, forcing contact. And Christine from Women's Aid had talked about keeping a diary of any behaviour and reaching out.

Rosie hadn't needed any of the research she'd done at three o'clock this morning on the identification of de Clérambault's syndrome in the 1800s or the papers suggesting that people who stalk have real difficulties in forming and maintaining intimate relationships. Not that that was a surprise. There was clearly something very dysfunctional with anyone who thought stalking was the answer to their problems, but discovering that stalkers often had a terror of abandonment had sort of made her feel bad for Michael. For about thirty seconds.

Michael's issues weren't her problem to solve, no matter how much she felt they were. In her wilder moments, Rosie had convinced herself that if she could get him fixed, perhaps he'd leave her alone.

But that all depended on knowing who he was.

'Thanks so much, ladies, that was a brilliant piece.' The female presenter turned to them and put her hand to her earpiece. 'My producer says the phone lines and social media have lit up. It's already getting a great reaction. Perhaps we can get you in again, Rosie, if there are any developments?'

Rosie smiled, but the presenter's attention was already taken elsewhere. *The last thing she wanted was any developments.*

The sound technicians removed their mics, and the next minute, Willow was showing them back to the green room.

'Thanks so much, that was great. I think the balance with Tiffany's stalker being jailed and you not even knowing who yours is, Rosie, was great. I looked at your posts. Some of those houses you see are incredible. It's a gorgeous account. I'm following now.' She said it as if her follow was the highest compliment anyone could receive.

Rosie made her face work as it was obviously expected to, and smiled appreciatively. 'Thank you so much.'

As she reached the end of the sofa where she'd left her bag, Rosie could hear her phone pinging with messages. She pulled it out; her notifications had gone mad. But there, in the middle of them, was a message from a private number. With another photo attached.

She sat down heavily, and opened it.

'Are you OK, my love?' Christine ambled over to Rosie and sat down beside her. 'What's happened?'

'Michael's messaged me. He must have seen ...' Rosie put her hand to her forehead, part of her feeling so sick she could barely speak, and the other half feeling as if it was in free fall, as if she'd just jumped off a cliff and there was no going back. *She'd been so sure he wouldn't see it – he'd be in work by nine o'clock.*

'Oh dear, what did he say?' Christine put her arm around Rosie, pulling her towards her. 'He's not here and he can't hurt you, you know that.'

Rosie glanced at her, her eyes full of tears.

'He's sent me another picture. It's my hallway.' She could see the black and white tiles, the rear wheel of David One's bike leaning against the wall, and Marmalade loafing two-thirds of the way up the stairs.

She enlarged the photo Michael had sent on WhatsApp and showed it to Christine.

'He had to have been inside the house to take this picture. A long way inside, almost at the bottom of the stairs.' Rosie looked at it again. 'The worst thing is these photos don't have any message with them. I don't know why he's sending them, just that he's getting closer.'

Chapter 16

'YOU WERE SO good on TV. Was it amazing?' Grace pulled her knees up as she sat on Rosie's sofa, curling up like a cat, and looked at Rosie over the top of her mug.

Outside the rain was beating against the windows, each gust of wind sounding as if someone was throwing gravel at the glass. It had started as the cab had dropped Rosie at the office from the studio, but after the adrenaline high of live TV, and the crash of the photo arriving, she hadn't been able to settle to getting any real work done.

Sitting at her laptop, her head full of … well, everything, the only thing Rosie had been able to concentrate on had been the rain. 'Pathetic fallacy', Fiacra called it in a script when the weather mirrored the action on set. 'Pathetic' was right, and 'fallacy' summed up Michael perfectly.

Whatever he thought he had with Rosie was very much mistaken.

She sighed, not sure how to answer Grace. 'I think it might have been brilliant under different circumstances, but ...' She sighed. 'Anyway, it's done.'

'God, yes, of course. But you explained it all really well, and that other lady – Christine, was it – came across brilliantly. Tiffany seemed a bit full of herself, talking about all the advocacy work she's done. Was she a bit of a diva?'

Rosie's eyebrows went up as she reached for a chocolate digestive from the tin on her coffee table between them. It was only five o'clock, and if she ate too many she knew she wouldn't be hungry later, but right now she needed a sugar fix. They all had appointments tomorrow so they'd left work early, thank goodness, but even at home, Rosie still felt listless. Taking a bite of her biscuit, she tuned back into what Grace had said.

'Tiffany was incredible. She's been through a lot, but she's done loads of TV so that's probably why she's so confident. The presenter – she's so well known, but I can never remember her name – was really nice, too. She was really concerned, asked about what the police were doing and how I was protecting myself.' Rosie closed her eyes. Michael had been watching – he must have been. The photo had arrived the minute they were off air. It made her sick to think about it. She needed to change the subject.

Rosie sighed. 'I've got viewings lined up half the day tomorrow. I don't know how I'm going to concentrate.'

'Do you want me to come with you? You can't go on your own.'

Rosie shook her head. 'I should be fine. Yaraslava said I could get a cab between them.'

As well as keeping in touch with Grace, Hallie had insisted that Rosie give her a list and check with her when she left home, when she got to each viewing appointment, and when she'd finished each one. Knowing someone knew where she was made Rosie feel much better about being out on her own.

Grace raised her eyebrows. 'That's not very Yaraslava, is it?'

'I know, but I suppose after being on TV, if I get murdered on the job it'll make Sterling's look bad.'

Grace rolled her eyes. 'True. Maybe it was Sebastian's idea. I heard her on the phone to him this afternoon. She was telling him what's happening …'

Grace left the sentence hanging there. Rosie wasn't sure what she should say. She looked at Grace expectantly, waiting to see if there was more.

'I couldn't hear his end, obviously, but he sounded concerned. I think he's coming in next week. He saw you on TV.'

Rosie sighed again. That hadn't been exactly what she wanted to hear. When she'd met Sebastian at her interview she'd found him a bit leery. Perhaps it was the ridiculously posh accent and the handmade suit, but he made her feel deeply uncomfortable. Their boss making a rare appearance wasn't the bonus to her TV moment that she had anticipated. She'd been half hoping someone else would recognise Michael's pattern of behaviour and be able to identify him. That would have been a real win.

'Nick will be there, though, won't he? I mean, when Sebastian's in.' Rosie shifted in the chair, moving the cushion up behind her. She was going to need an early night tonight; she was exhausted. Rosie knew Grace meant well, coming home with her, but she needed some time on her own. The thought of Sebastian in the office just added another layer of anxiety that she needed to process.

'Yes, of course. Did he say anything about his friend looking at the emails? Has he been able to trace them?'

Grace put her mug on the coffee table. 'I know the police are looking, too, but they could take ages. They're always saying on the TV about reduced resources.'

'I'm not sure yet. Nick said he was seeing his friend tonight for a drink. We're going to meet for a late lunch after he's shown the Bradfords Park House tomorrow.'

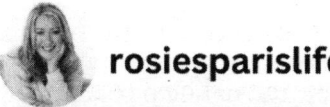 rosiesparislife

[image: the word #stalkerUPDATE, white lettering centred on a black background]

Some of you may have seen me on GMB TV this morning with Tiffany Taylor and Christine Hughes from Women's Aid. Many of you will know about Tiffany's horrific experience when she was stalked by her ex and attacked on her way home from work.

Christine is an amazing woman whose personal experience led her to Women's Aid, where she is now CEO. She knows first-hand the complexities of an abusive relationship. Huge thanks to the team at GMB TV for airing our stories, and to all of you who have supported me through this.

Tiffany wanted to say hi to all of you and Christine said to remind you, if you are in this situation, to keep a diary of everything. Take photographs, write down dates and times, report it all to the police.

You can now report stalking online, so you don't even have to go into the police station. This is vitally important if you feel you are being followed. Look at the Metropolitan Police website and click through – whether you are in a relationship and need to report domestic abuse, or if the intimidation has only occurred once.

The form takes about 5 to 10 mins, so make sure you're safe for that long. If someone walks in, use the 'leave this site button' – it'll close down and open Google automatically, but remember your form won't be saved or sent to the police. You'll need to start it again.

Once it's done, your report goes to the police's 24/7 contact centre and it'll be reviewed within a few hours. You'll hear back within a max of 24 hours, or at the time and in the way you've asked. There's a box on the form to say if you feel safer to talk to them at work, or at a friend's house.

The police won't send you an email acknowledgement as they know this could be a problem.

I'm feeling increasingly threatened and unsafe, but I know the police are looking into what's happening – at everything – email trails, texts, and the photographs Michael sends me.

My stalker is delusional, that's very clear from his messages, and research shows this type of harassment can persist for years. But I'm not going to wait years.

Everything sent online leaves a trail.

#stalker #metoo #womensaid #nomore #askforAngela #harassment #notavictim

Chapter 17

ROSIE FELT MARMALADE'S paw on her face and, barely waking, lifted the duvet for him to come in beside her. He slithered in under the pink polka dots, cold, wet, and exactly what she didn't need at this time on a Saturday morning. She opened one eye and, pushing her hair out of her face, looked at the blood-red digital display on her alarm clock: just after six a.m.

What was it with cats? They slept for hours and hours, went rushing about, and then woke everyone up way too early. She pulled the duvet up over her shoulder. The heating wouldn't be on for another hour and the room felt chill. That was the only disadvantage to an old house. It looked super-pretty, with its high ceilings and original features – even up here in the attic there were little cast-iron fireplaces – but the draughts were something else.

Marmalade snuggled in beside her and started purring,

and Rosie instantly forgave him for waking her up. It was Saturday, and she had a full day ahead, starting in Kensington at 10.30, so she needed to be up and about soon, anyway. She'd got up horribly early to wash her hair for the TV yesterday, but with all the rain afterwards it had gone frizzy. She'd grown out her layers into a long bob in Paris, so she could slick it back and tie it up on bad hair days, but even so, the amount of personal grooming that went into looking the part in this job took time to happen.

Even on days when the last thing she wanted was to look attractive.

Resentment began to flare inside her again. How the heck was this her life? Changing her routes to and from work had to help, but she still ended up in the same building every day at about the same time, picking up a coffee around the corner from the office on her way in. She felt as if she was always looking over her shoulder, scanning the road, her senses on hyper-alert, looking for the same face to appear more than once.

Maybe that was it? The coffee shop? Was that where he'd seen her, and heard her name called when she'd ordered her latte? Trying not to disturb Marmalade, Rosie turned over onto her back. How had she not thought of that before?

Anyone who had seen her pick up her morning coffee that first week could have followed her around the corner straight into the Sterling & Co offices. Their building was a Victorian town house, shared with a charity on the top floor and an insurance company downstairs, but she was the only Rosie in the building. It wouldn't take a genius to work out that she worked at Sterling & Co, and then get her email address – and her phone number. She was on the website, for God's sake. With a link to her Instagram account.

Rosie pulled her arm out from under the duvet and rubbed her face, a dark, heavy feeling of anxiety creeping through her. *That was it. That had to be it.* Once he knew where she worked, Michael could follow her from the office just about anywhere: to the gym; to a restaurant, like the other night; to her front door. She always got public transport, and London was so busy, melting into a crowd on the bus or Tube was easy.

Rosie let out a sharp breath, causing Marmalade to stick his claw in her side. She ran her hand down his back apologetically. He'd fully stretched out beside her, taking up the warm bit of sheet she'd been asleep on.

If the coffee shop *was* where this had all started, she could go in and ask them if there were any Michaels who came in around the same time she did. And wait for him, and damn well ask him what he thought he was playing at.

Or maybe not. Maybe that was something she should leave to the police.

Rosie heard her phone ping with a text, and closed her eyes, her stomach clenching. She hadn't quite told the others in the office the full story when she'd shown them that first photo on Wednesday. She'd told them about the texts and the email about the restaurant, but not that there were sometimes eight or ten texts a day, and random emails at all times of night. Michael seemed to get more intense after about eleven o'clock, probably after a few jars, when alcohol had dulled his senses.

Her phone pinged again.

It had to be him. Who else would be messaging her at this time in the morning? Snaking her hand out from under the duvet, Rosie reached for her phone. 6.15. Oh, joy.

She could see two notifications from WhatsApp. Maybe one of them was one of her brothers. Unconvinced, she opened the app and could see immediately the messages were from a private number. Rosie closed her eyes and steeled herself to see what they said – to what *he'd* said this time. She needed to get into the habit of just archiving them without reading, but part of her had to be sure it was him. What happened if a new client was putting in a huge offer by text? A lot of the people she dealt with withheld their personal numbers.

Rosie took a breath and opened the message.

Photos. Two of them.

But not of the front door, or of the hallway.

These were photos of her landing from the top of the stairs. The fourth-floor landing. He'd got right inside the house. And in them both, Rosie could see her flat door was open.

He must have been right there while she was inside.

Rosie could feel a surge of fear and anxiety and emotion, tears pricking at her eyes. After she'd spoken to her landlord, Maurizio, she'd been so upset she'd come home and written a fighting post.

But now this? She was starting to feel as if she'd run out of fight. She took in a sobby breath, as she looked at the second picture.

It was a step closer to her door. Her open door.

Rosie suddenly felt the fear consumed by anger. Why the hell was he trying to frighten her? He wanted to be friends with her – he thought he was friends with her – but then he sent these photos?

This was about control. He wanted to control her life. And he was starting to succeed, but she wasn't going to give in now. She needed to zap all these defeatist feelings. That's what Michael wanted, and she wasn't going to let him win.

She was meeting Nick later. If his friend Iain had found out where the emails were being sent from, it would be a huge gain. Knowing who Michael was would change the whole equation. He held the balance of power at the moment, but she was damn well going to get it back.

 rosiesparislife

#stalker UPDATE

[image: the word UPDATE, white lettering centred on a black background]

Welcome new followers, and thank you for following. I don't usually post so often, but I wanted to say thank you. Every time I switch on my phone, it's hopping with notifications across my social media, you are all so supportive.

And SO many of you have experienced something similar, I've been crying reading the comments. I'm starting to feel as if this account is gathering energy, it's becoming a place for you to find each other, to offer support to me and to each other. My follower numbers have more than doubled, and for that I am truly thankful.

According to a Crime Survey for England and Wales I found online, an estimated 1.5 million adults were stalked in the twelve months ending in March 2021. I'm sure that's even bigger now.

One of the reasons I'd started thinking about leaving Paris was because of an estate agent who was murdered. It turned out she was attacked by a serial killer who preyed on women with red hair, but it was terrifying for a while, not knowing if your client could be a killer. It really shook us all up in the office. We changed all our safety protocols to make sure we always checked in when we arrived at and left a property. Anyone who registered for a viewing had to provide their identity card, which we kept a copy of on file in the office. The killer was caught, but it was about then that I was starting to think about my next move.

1.5 million. I know many of you made up that number. Many more of you didn't report it, or found ways to deal with your stalker, so go unrecorded.

I'm going to keep posting here to try and raise awareness of this issue – it's huge and, honestly, terrifying. You are giving me strength, and if any of you are reading and think maybe this is happening to you too, start keeping a diary of events – texts, voicemails, emails, moments when you don't feel safe. Female intuition has developed over thousands of years – if you can sense danger, it's there.

This needs to stop being an issue we suffer in silence.

#stalker #metoo #womensaid #nomore #askforAngela

Chapter 18

WHEN SHE'D STARTED working in the boutique at home in Cork, straight after she left school, Rosie had got used to working weekends. They'd been open Sundays, too, so she'd rarely got two days off together.

But Rosie liked working weekends.

The mornings were always a bit quieter as people stayed in bed later. One of the things about London, and Paris, too, that had surprised her when she'd moved there, was the sheer numbers of people moving around all the time. It could be a bit overwhelming when you just needed time to think and a bit of peace and quiet without traffic noise, sirens or crowded pavements. Especially where she lived, close to Waterloo Station.

Getting out early on a Saturday morning was actually bliss.

Pulling her front door behind her, Rosie looked up and down the road. There were shops on either side of Maurizio's four-storey Georgian terraced house: on one side, a barber's that never had any customers, and on the other, a convenience shop. The barber's puzzled her – how could someone run any sort of business in central London that never had any customers? The rents had to be huge. Still, that wasn't her problem. Making sure there was no one following her, was.

The house was set away from the pavement, which gave her extra time to scan the road as she went down the path, her house keys ready in her hand, and with the safety of the front door behind her just in case she needed to dash back in.

The barber's was closed, its steel shutters down, and as she swung out of the gate, she glanced at the convenience shop. They had so much stuff piled in the windows that she couldn't see in, but she jumped as the door opened and a tall guy in a tracksuit and headphones emerged and jogged off down the road ahead of her.

Rosie put her free hand in her coat pocket and gripped her phone. How long could she keep this going? Lily Baldwin, the girl who had made the podcast she'd listened to, had been stalked for so long. *Years.*

Grace had said she'd listened to it, too, and she had been just as aghast.

Her head down, Rosie hurried along the road to the Tube station. She was glad that her appointments today were all with women, agents she'd met before, who were looking for property on behalf of big clients. When you got to the level that a lot of their purchasers were at, dropping multi-millions for second or third homes, or a pad for a university-going child, or an investment to lease, it seemed as if you didn't do anything yourself. Not even look at the property.

As she reached the Tube, Rosie felt her phone vibrate and her anxiety spike in perfect synchronicity. She waited until she got inside the station to pull it out, her hand shaking as she checked the screen.

This time it was Nick. Being a sweetie.

> Howdy Rosie, I've only got the Park House viewing today over in Hampstead at 11, should be done for 1pm, lunch then? I've got news. We'll catch this creep. Not all heroes wear capes 😊

He had news? Rosie could feel every cell of her body cheering. Desperate to ring him, she looked at the time. She needed to get moving to her first appointment, and he'd be heading to Park House soon. She could wait.

She was going to have her first stress-free morning in ages, and she was going to enjoy every minute of it. They could celebrate over lunch. Rosie smiled at his winky eye emoji as another message arrived, this time from Grace.

> I've nothing on today, just have to collect dry-cleaning, so if you need company, shout! I can drive you instead of waiting for taxis. Text to say when you're leaving xx

Rosie smiled. Everyone was being so supportive. She was glad now that she'd told them. She shivered. He was just there all the time. Sometimes it almost felt as if he'd listened to that Lily Baldwin podcast, too, and had been taking notes.

Maybe he'd studied psychology or something. Or maybe he was just a total fruit loop, as Grace said, and honestly thought he and Rosie had a relationship.

It didn't matter really. She'd reported it now. And Polly, the PC she'd spoken to, had been reassuring. And Nick had news.

Rosie quickly messaged Grace back.

> Nick says he has news!!!!!! Meeting him for lunch at 1pm, stand by!! R xxx

Rosie hit *send*, her mind racing. When they were able to identify Michael, would she recognise him? Was he someone she passed every day, or the driver on the bus, or the man in the convenience shop next to home? When she'd thought about it before, so many faces popped up into her mind that she'd felt totally overwhelmed, as if she was suffocating.

But now, maybe things were about to change.

She fired off a message to Nick, just as another one came in: Hallie this time, telling her to call if she needed anything.

Telling them had definitely been the right thing to do. Even Yaraslava had been concerned, which had surprised everyone a bit.

As soon as Rosie got one clue as to who this Michael was, she was going to get a restraining order. And then she was going to talk to her brothers.

Her phone vibrated again. WhatsApp.

+447480788409

Hey Rosie, I saw your post and oh my God, I'm so angry someone is still frightening you like this. I googled that estate agent in Paris, so terrible. I can see why this is upsetting you so much. You need to look after yourself, really look after yourself. I still can't believe he's calling himself Michael, I feel personally affronted. I'm here if you need to talk, about anything. Text any time and I can call, or I can meet you for a coffee. Love Mike xx

Rosie read the message again, anger building inside her. He was delusional – utterly delusional. How could he be so disconnected that he didn't realise she was talking about him?

Chapter 19

'EMERGENCY, WHICH SERVICE do you require?'

'The police, I need the police. And an ambulance. As fast as you can.' Grace's voice shook as she held her phone to her ear. She could feel Major and Mrs Bradford looking at her from the safety of their car as she paced across the gravel drive in front of Park House. The Bradfords' Bentley was pulled up at an angle in the sweeping drive. They looked pale and put out.

Not nearly as pale and put out as she felt.

Grace turned and glanced up the steps to the open front door again. Everything had been so normal when she'd arrived. Except for Nick not turning up, of course. She'd told the Bradfords to have a potter around the neighbourhood while she got her shit together and drove over to meet them. She didn't put it quite like that, obviously, but this was the third time they'd viewed the double-fronted Georgian property set in its own gardens – the mews for the staff and the pool for the grandchildren had pushed it up their list apparently. And now the price drop was making it very attractive. They were moving out of their own house in less than a month, so needed to make a decision.

Which was just as well. Grace had picked up a definite undercurrent in their last meeting. Yaraslava would go apeshit if Sterling & Co lost this sale.

More importantly, if Grace closed the sale instead of Nick, she'd have a very strong claim on the commission. Which would be rather nice and make the disturbance to her Saturday very well worth it.

Yaraslava had set up their appointment for 11.00, and when there had been no sign of Nick by 11.15, the Bradfords, unimpressed and crotchety, had tried Grace's mobile. Part of the substantial pay rise she'd got when she'd moved into her new role was for being available for clients pretty much 24/7. Which had been partly brilliant (Fiat 500, mint green) and partly horrendous (business hours in Dubai were the middle of the night in London), until the wife of an outrageously demanding Iranian businessman had passed her an envelope stuffed with cash. Stuffed. That had made things much better.

But no amount of cash was worth this stress – this *horror*. Grace didn't even have the words.

The call finally connected. *She knew the emergency services were under pressure in this country, but holy God, could they not do things a bit faster?*

'Police. Can you give me your name and phone number?'

Grace reeled off her details.

'And what's the problem?'

'It's my colleague Nick Armitage, he's an estate agent. He was supposed to be showing a house, but he wasn't here when the buyers arrived, so I came instead. Something terrible's happened. He was here all along, but he's lying in the living room, and there's all this blood and I think he's dead.'

The words tumbled over themselves as she tried to explain. She took a deep breath. 'I'm sorry, I think it's shock. I went into the living room and that's when I saw Nick … well, his foot anyway, sticking out from behind the sofa.' Grace could feel herself starting to hyperventilate. 'Please come, please come fast.'

Grace could feel herself shaking as she gripped the paper cup of tea. She had no idea where it had come from, but someone had passed it to her as she sat in the passenger seat of a police car and watched an officer roll out crime scene tape.

The detective who seemed to be in charge had got the details from her, then talked to the Bradfords and let them go. Now Grace was on her own with him in the driveway. If 'on their own' counted in an area filled with emergency vehicles.

'So you called Nick this morning?'

Grace nodded in response to the officer. She'd forgotten his name already, but he seemed nice. He was actually very good-looking and a lot younger than she'd expected, and he had excellent taste in suits. Before she could answer, behind him, another van pulled into the driveway – a big white one. The ambulance was still here, not that the paramedics could do anything. She'd been right. Nick was dead.

Grace suddenly realised she hadn't answered. 'Sorry, yes ... Well, I messaged him to wish him luck with the Bradfords. The Bradfords had mentioned needing a bedroom on the ground floor, and I realised with all the Rosie drama, I'd forgotten to tell him – there isn't one here, but there's a den that would convert brilliantly, and sometimes you need to say things for people to realise.' Grace took a sip of her tea, trying to slow down her mind. She knew she was telling the police officer a load of stuff that he probably didn't need to know, but she just couldn't stop herself.

'Nick messaged me back to say he'd got here early – he's always too early, it's one of his things – and then he rang to say he thought he'd seen someone in the garden, and he asked about the gardeners. That's when I spoke to him. The house backs onto the heath and there's a fence, but I don't know how secure it is.' She took a sip of her tea. 'That must have been about 10.30, I'm not sure, but he was fine then.'

Leaning on the roof of the car, the detective jotted down everything she was saying. Finishing, he took a step away to look at her again. 'And then what happened?'

'Then, about 11.15, the Bradfords called. They'd arrived and couldn't get in. They'd tried Nick's phone and got no answer, so they called me. I tried him, too. I mean, I knew he was here, or had been. When I couldn't get him, I came over straight away. It was weird he'd vanished, but I didn't have time to think about it. I mean, I thought he must be here *somewhere*, but they just couldn't find him.

'I didn't have a set of keys, but I didn't want the Bradfords to feel like they'd had a wasted trip. I was getting a coffee when they called, so I said for them to look at the neighbourhood while they were waiting for me. There's a little park down the road that I thought would be great for walks with their grandchildren.'

Grace closed her eyes, trying to get everything that had happened into the right order. It was important to get it right.

'When I arrived Nick still wasn't answering his phone, but the gates were open. I tried his phone again and I thought I could hear it ringing. He's got this awful music as his ringtone.' Grace opened her eyes, pausing to see if the detective would interrupt, but he seemed to want to hear the rest.

'The front door was locked, so I went around the back and realised the garden door was open. I thought Nick must have gone out to open up the pool house or something. I went inside, so I could open the front door when the Bradfords got there.'

'So you arrived here at what time?'

'About 11.30, I think.'

'That was good going from home.'

'I was already out, I was collecting my work stuff from

the dry-cleaner's. They sounded really cross, I didn't want to keep them waiting and lose the sale. I took all the side roads to get here. I might have driven a bit fast.' Grace waved in the general direction of the gates. 'I parked along the road so I could throw on the jacket I'd got cleaned and arrive looking a bit together.' She suddenly remembered her tea again and took another sip. It was hot and sweet – exactly what she needed.

'And what happened then?'

'Like I said, the gates were already open, but the Bradfords hadn't come back yet. I heard their car on the gravel from inside, so I went down the hall to open the front door – that's when I saw the keys were in it, on the inside. That was the first thing I noticed. And then I saw this rock thing, like a big paperweight or a sculpture or something, in the doorway to the living room, just lying there on the floor in the hall. It was like a spiky chunk of black rock with a polished base. I picked it up, to put it on the hall table, and realised it was wet.' Grace shuddered and, unwrapping her hand from her cup, looked at her fingers. She had traces of black ink under her nails – the police had taken her fingerprints to eliminate her because she'd picked up the rock – but she could still see the blood.

'I … I sort of thought it was paint or something.'

'So you put it down on the hall table?' The detective's voice was calm and encouraging.

Grace looked up at him. She could feel her eyes filling again. 'I was going to, but then I twigged the living room door was open. The property's been empty for ages, and I came with Nick to look at it with the Bradfords last time. They had loads of questions about wall space for their paintings, and the size of the wardrobes I needed to check – but I remembered closing it. The living room door, I mean. I definitely closed it.' She rubbed her eyes with the heel of her hand and took another sip of her tea. 'He was there on the floor. I looked in quickly and I could see a foot sticking out from behind the far sofa. He's got these brown suede shoes that he wears with bright yellow socks. I knew it was him straight away. I still had the rock in my hand. I went in and looked, and there was all this blood. His head …' Grace put her hand to her forehead, trying to massage away the pain forming behind her eyes. 'I think I dropped the rock then. I'm sorry, I'm not totally sure.'

'Take your time. I know this is hard. You mentioned you messaged him earlier about the den. You said you'd forgotten because of "the Rosie drama". What was that?'

Grace tried to push the memories of Nick's lifeless body from her mind and answer the questions. She shifted slightly in the seat, and shivered.

'Rosie works in our office. She's been getting weird emails and flowers and stuff from this guy called Michael. We've all been really worried about her. He's started sending her these horrible creepy photos from inside her house.' Grace took a breath. 'She was on *Good Morning Britain* on Friday. She's got this huge Instagram and it's getting loads of new followers because she's talking about it. The stalking, I mean.' Grace paused, realisation dawning as if someone had switched on a floodlight. 'You don't think it could have been him, do you – this Michael? Oh my God, we need to call Rosie and make sure she's OK.'

Chapter 20

ROSIE SAT DOWN heavily on the sofa beside Grace and put her arm around her. She wasn't completely sure if she did it to comfort Grace, or whether she was actually holding on to her the way a drowning person grabs a lifebuoy.

Because right now, she felt as if she was drowning. Rosie's chest had been getting tighter since Grace had told her the news. She'd been sitting in the cafe waiting for Nick, wondering why he was so late for their lunch date. Shock had passed through her again like an electric charge. She'd literally stood up and gone out to the street to hail a taxi and come straight home, locking her door and putting a chair up against it.

She'd curled up on the sofa waiting for Grace, who had almost collapsed when she arrived, blurting out everything that had happened as if she couldn't hold it in any longer.

Nick was dead.

Nick was dead, and Nick had been going to meet Rosie to tell her what his friend Iain had found out about the emails – about Michael.

Perhaps the two events were completely unrelated, but Rosie had never been stalked before, and none of her work colleagues had ever been murdered before. So it felt as if the two things could, *maybe*, be connected.

What were the chances?

Finding him must have been so totally traumatic. Rosie knew she needed to be strong for Grace, but right now her head was racing, desperately trying to work out *why*. If they were connected, how could Michael know what Nick had discovered? How did he know Nick was even looking? And what did this whole crapshoot of events mean for her?

That's the bit that was making her stomach churn and her head feel decidedly lighter than it should, in a dizzy might-be-about-to-faint sort of way.

But she couldn't faint. That wouldn't help any of them now. Least of all Grace, who had barely been able to speak since she got upstairs and collapsed on the sofa.

'Oh God, it was so horrible, Rosie, and the worst thing is …' Grace sniffed loudly and, screwing up the damp tissue in her hand, turned to Rosie, her eyes wide. 'I know this is really bad, but I kept thinking, "what if it had been you?"'

Grace dissolved into tears again and Rosie passed her another tissue. Rosie herself was so tense that she could barely speak.

What if it had been her?

She felt horrible thinking it, that she was somehow disrespecting lovely Nick, but what the actual hell?

Was Michael so cross that she hadn't turned up to the theatre to watch *Hamilton*, and so jealous of Nick working in the same office as her, that he'd gone totally nuts and murdered him?

Was this her fault?

Rosie's stomach turned over again at the thought. That all seemed so crazy. Her fight or flight reaction was set to high alert right now, so maybe she was jumping to conclusions. Maybe Nick had disturbed someone who had broken in – Grace had said something about him seeing someone in the garden. People got attacked all the time in London: stabbed; their phones grabbed out of their hands as they walked along the street.

'Poor, poor Nick. I mean, I know he was a bit of an over-privileged twat, but he was fun. And he was only thirty-two, Rosie, that's two years older than me. He'd barely had a chance to do anything with his life.'

Rosie let out a breath. 'I know, I know.' *She needed to get Grace on to something non-Nick related, at least for a moment, so Grace could gather herself.* 'I thought you were the same age as me?'

Grace glanced at her sideways through her tears. 'I wish. No, I just look years younger than I am.' She forced a grin. 'I'm channelling Yaraslava. You know she's forty-seven?'

'Is she? Wow, she looks amazing. I thought Hallie was older than her.'

Grace sniffed. 'She's only thirty-five. I think she's spent a lot of time in the sun.' She sighed. 'I know it sounds mean, but I think that's another reason she hates Yaraslava.'

'Does she?' Rosie could barely concentrate on what Grace was saying, but she had stopped crying for a moment, and that had to be a good thing. 'I thought they just rubbed each other up the wrong way. Yaraslava can be pretty scathing sometimes, and Hallie has loads of experience in high-end sales.'

'She wanted Yaraslava's job, Hallie did. Well, she sort of had it. She was office manager before Yaraslava arrived, but Sebastian brought Yaraslava in over her head. Keeping on top of the milk order and making sure there's enough paper for the printers isn't quite the level of responsibility Hallie's used to. And she's been at Sterling's for years. She started way before me.'

The office gossip seemed to calm Grace, but Rosie was desperate to know what the police thought had happened to Nick. Across the room her phone was pinging with a stream of notifications, but she wasn't about to look at it now. She could pretty much guess who it was.

'Did you call Yaraslava to let her know about … about this morning?' Rosie wasn't ready to say the word 'murder' yet.

Grace nodded. 'The detective did. He wants to talk to everyone at the office tomorrow – even though it's Sunday. I said we worked Sundays too because we have to be able to show places when the clients are free. He said properties of that value can attract criminals, people who need to launder money, so they are looking at that.'

Everything Grace was saying seemed to be coming out tangled in a knot of emotion, but Rosie did a double take. 'Do they think Major Bradford is the head of some sort of cartel or organised crime group, or something?' It sounded ridiculous. Rosie's incredulity made Grace smile for a moment.

'I doubt it. They've got a sausage dog. I don't think crime bosses have sausage dogs, do you? I reckon they'd be more likely to have a Rottweiler or something.' Grace took in a shaky breath. 'They want to see who else was interested in the property, and who would have known Nick was going to be there. The appointment was organised at such short notice …'

Rosie closed her eyes, a feeling of doom wrapping its arms tightly around her.

'We were talking about it while we were waiting for the Tube on Thursday, right before Nick said we might be able to work out who Michael is if we could trace the email sender. He was worried the police might take ages. I think Nick might have said the name of the house.'

Grace pulled away from her, her eyes red and puffy.

'Oh God, Rosie, did either of you say his name – Michael's, I mean? Do you think this Michael guy could have followed you both? That he could have been listening?'

Chapter 21

PUSHING HER FRONT door closed behind her with her foot, Grace dropped her handbag onto the tiny kitchen counter. She was exhausted. Today had to be the longest day she'd ever experienced. It was certainly the most stressful and upsetting.

She reached for the kettle, then changed her mind. She needed a glass of wine and, more urgently, some fresh air.

Her bedsit felt stuffy. Grace corrected herself: 'studio apartment'. That's what it had said on the listing when she'd come to see it. One-bed flats where the rent wasn't extortionate were almost impossible to find in London, and it had taken her ages to find this one. This place wasn't ideal, but Grace didn't plan to stay here forever. And she liked the anonymity of it. Everyone minded their own business around here, and that suited her.

The Mercy Convent hadn't prepared its pupils for much, but at least it had taught them to be independent and survive on their own. The nuns' strategy to divide and conquer had been one of the ways they'd held on to control. But Grace didn't want to think about that now. She'd put school firmly behind her when she'd left Portlaoise as fast as she could – the town's main claim to fame was a maximum security prison.

Skirting the bed, she opened the small top window, pausing to look out at the garages in the lane beside her block. It was dark now, and two teenage boys, their hoods pulled up, were kicking a ball off one of the doors, taking it in turns. She'd heard them as she'd turned down the concrete path to the building's main doors, the rhythmic sound grating on her already frayed nerves. Thankfully they weren't anywhere near her garage or Milly, her gorgeous little car. Grace felt her spirits rise a notch. Milly was a bit like her first designer handbag, the LV Neverfull she used for work every day: another rung on the ladder. She might commit actual murder if anyone started bouncing a ball anywhere near Milly's beautiful mint green bodywork.

The thought made her shudder all over again.

Actual murder.

Today hadn't gone the way that she'd expected at all.

Picking up the remote from beside the bed, Grace put on Spotify and turned up the volume, hoping it would drown out the repeated sound of the ball rattling off the steel door onto the concrete, and back again.

Tossing the remote onto her unmade bed, Grace pulled the curtains closed. They were thin, but at least they made her feel safer. She was on the third floor, but she still sometimes worried that someone could see in. Around here there were always people hanging around the stairwells and along by the garages. She wasn't even sure what they were waiting for half the time, although she could imagine. Some things were better not to think about. 'Loitering with intent', the police called it on the 999 shows she watched.

This morning had been so deeply shocking that she didn't think she was ever going to recover from it.

Now there would be no Nick in the office, and every day she walked in she knew she'd see him lying face down on that parquet floor. And the blood. She didn't think she'd ever unsee the blood.

She'd loved Sterling & Co when she'd started working there, showing incredible houses that, growing up, she'd only seen in magazines. It had all been so perfect, like a dream. Then Yaraslava had blown in one day and changed everything – in a good way. Mainly.

Grace listened to the music filling the room as she sloshed wine into a glass. She loved the signature tune to *Big Little Lies*; it was haunting and melancholic and a bit creepy all at the same time. And it filled her head, stopped her thinking about all the blood.

She had had no idea that someone could bleed that much. As the detective had said, Nick couldn't have known what hit him; the pointy side of that rock thing had been really sharp.

It didn't make her feel any better.

Even after going over to Rosie's and talking it out, she still felt shaken and a bit sick.

Right now, going to bed early and watching mindless TV was starting to feel very appealing.

Should she call Rosie first to see if she was OK? She'd been really frightened by the possibility that everything that had happened to Nick could have been connected to Michael. Grace was sure Rosie felt a bit responsible for Nick's death; she'd seen it in Rosie's eyes the minute she mentioned it.

When Grace left, Rosie had given her an extra hug for good measure. Picking up her glass, Grace sat down heavily on the bed and kicked off her boots, reaching for her iPhone to message Rosie.

Grace hit *send* and took a slug of her wine. It was incredible how Rosie's Instagram account had grown – and then with the TV coverage, it had exploded. She'd had so many comments from people who had been stalked, or feared that it was happening to them. Grace had been amazed. She was sure the glossies would be next. It was unbelievable.

Grace watched her phone screen, waiting to see if Rosie would reply, but her phone was quiet. She switched to Instagram to check her direct messages and see if Rosie was still online. There was no green dot next to Rosie's avatar. Perhaps she'd turned her phone off.

Grace rested her chin on the rim of her glass.

The real question was: if Michael had seen Rosie on TV talking about him, and then this had happened, what would Michael do next?

+447480788409

Hey Rosie, hope you had a great day and sold lots! Really they should give you some weekends off. It would be lovely if you had a Sunday off – if you're free tomorrow and need a chat we could meet up for a coffee and a walk, maybe go to Hampstead Heath, it's beautiful in the spring. I've had a crazy day, feet up now, exhausted. Thinking about you Mxx

19:25

+447480788409

Did you see the news about that estate agent? 'Serious injuries.' They didn't say the name of the company but there's so much violent crime these days. It's getting like America. It makes me worry about you Rosie, especially when you're on your own at appointments. Just because it's a property worth millions doesn't mean the people will be nice. When people have money or go to a posh school they think they own you. It makes me really mad. They think you're just a piece of shit on their shoe. You need to look after yourself Rosie, you don't know what could happen at one of these viewings. M xxxxxx

22:23

+447480788409

I'm glad you've got Grace as a friend, she's the best. Some of the others in that office?? That Hallie is a bit washed up. I bet she just wants to get married, she's not getting any younger. And she hasn't been on a date in months. Perhaps she was shagging that Nick. He had his eye on you too, you know, but he wouldn't have looked after you like I would. I'd treat you like a Princess, you know that don't you my love? M xxxxxxx

23:07

Chapter 22

YARASLAVA PACED ACROSS the wooden floor of her bedroom in the town house she was currently living in. Outside the window, the road was empty of its usual traffic: Range Rovers mainly, the occasional low-slung Ferrari, and a constant stream of black cabs. From here she could see the lights in the Battersea Power Station shopping centre, empty now of everyone except the cleaners.

Focusing on the phone in her hand, Yaraslava willed Dimitri to pick up. She was wearing black jogging bottoms and a cashmere sweater, her feet bare on the warm floor. The minute the police had called she'd offered to go over to Hampstead, but they'd organised to come into the office in the morning to talk to everyone. There was too much happening at the house, with the forensics and officers calling to talk to all the neighbours.

She wished them luck with that.

Nobody in properties the size of the one in Hampstead ever noticed what was happening with their neighbours. The houses were all down long driveways, which didn't help, but they were far more interested in obsessing over what was going on in their children's posh schools: who had got the lead in the play, or who was getting private tennis lessons with the gorgeous new American coach.

Dimitri suddenly answered, his voice raspy. 'What? Have you got news for me? The sale?'

Yaraslava cleared her throat, focusing on keeping her voice steady. One of them, at least, needed to keep calm.

'I've got some news, yes, but not the sort you want.'

She heard her brother exhaling rapidly. 'Go on.'

'Have you heard from the Grigori brothers? Have they got any reason to be upset with you?' Yaraslava could feel the nervous tension increasing in her neck as her muscles began to cramp.

His retort was loaded with vitriol. 'You mean, apart from the fact that we invested millions of pounds of their money and they want it back, plus interest?'

'Don't be so smart. Remember I told you I was putting one of my top agents on to it? That I was sure he'd close the sale?'

Dimitri's voice was guarded as he replied, 'Yes.'

'Well, he's dead. Someone murdered him this morning.' It came out with more of a hiss than she'd intended.

There was silence at the other end while Dimitri figured out what she was saying. She saved him the bother.

'So now the police are all over the house. They want to know everything. They are already wondering why a shelf company registered in the Caymans, owned by a shelf company registered in Switzerland, is selling a house in London, and why I didn't think of making a Suspicious Activity Report.' She paused and swallowed. 'I've told them when I met the vendor originally she seemed completely bona fide. I'd seen her at a Versace show and half recognised her. If they ask again, I'll explain we met for coffee in the park, and she said she was looking for a property like Park House to buy. I think I already told them about her husband relocating – I didn't have any reason to think the money was suspicious ... Then when she decided to sell, we were the obvious choice.'

'Which park?'

She paused, thinking. 'Regent's? But I'll say I'm not sure. There's CCTV around it, but I don't think *in* it. I can pretend I got the wrong park in the heat of the moment, if needs be.' Yaraslava closed her eyes and worked through the story in her head. She'd already had to think super-fast on the phone to the police officer to make it sound as if she absolutely believed that this woman was the real deal. 'I told them the fashion show was in that hotel in St Pancras. It'll have a guest list, and I'll be on it.'

'They'll check the list. Make sure you say she mentioned that she'd taken a friend's place. You told them her name was Irina?'

'Obviously. That's the name on the documentation, isn't it? I'm not stupid, Dimitri.'

He let that pass. 'How did they get all this information so quickly?'

Yaraslava sighed. She had no idea, but obviously they'd asked who was selling Park House, and when she'd said a Russian name …

Dimitri interrupted her thoughts. 'What happened to your sales guy?'

'He was whacked over the head. I didn't find out what with, but there was a lot of blood, apparently.'

'Heads do that.'

'Do what?'

'Bleed a lot.'

'Thanks, Dimitri. The point is that we can't sell the house until the police vacate, which doesn't look like it'll be any time soon, and we can't exactly rush the buyers. I mean, who wants a house where the guy who was showing it to you was brutally murdered? I think the vendor will have to drop the price again.'

'The police might want to see your emails from this woman you "met in the park" – about dropping the price.'

'I know. I'm covered, I told them she used WhatsApp. She was selling the house so she could leave her husband, and needed to be very discreet. The number is a burner. I set it all up when we purchased the house originally.'

She heard Dimitri exhale. 'Our biggest problem is the cash flow issue. I'm going to have to see if I can find the ten million somewhere else.'

Yaraslava ran her hand into her thick hair and pulled at the roots. 'We'll need to sell a different property, discreetly, and use the cash. Then when whichever client owns that property needs to cash in, we'll sell Hampstead. Hopefully the heat will have died down by then.'

They currently had four high-end properties in play via a variety of shelf companies. Yaraslava wasn't sure that selling any of them quickly would be all that easy, but it felt like their only option.

'That's not the biggest problem here, though. Dimitri, is there something you're not telling me? Are the Grigoris trying to take me and Sterling's down to threaten you because you've pissed them off?'

'What makes you think that?' Her brother sounded genuinely mystified. Yaraslava could have screamed at him.

'Because Nick is dead, Dimitri, and if I was trying to send you a message, I'd start by getting some heat on your closest associates. And I'd leave a calling card, like a dead body, right where you can see it.'

'But I can't see it.'

'Dimitri, I can see it. I work for Sterling's – and on top of that, one of my girls is being stalked, by someone who calls himself "Michael".' Yaraslava put the emphasis on the last word.

There was a pause. 'You mean like Mikhail Grigori? That's ridiculous. It must have been an intruder who killed this Nick. Didn't you say he'd been brained with something? That's not their style.' He made a humphing noise. 'And pretty girls attract unwanted attention all the time. It's a coincidence.'

'But what if it's not?' Yaraslava paused her pacing at one side of the floor-to-ceiling sash window and, twitching the net back, looked out. 'What if it's not, Dimitri? What if the Grigori brothers don't want to alert the police to their involvement with a bullet? What if they are closing in on you – on us? What will they do next?'

Chapter 23

'ARE YOU SURE you're OK, Rosie? I read your posts. This sounds serious.' On the phone, Rosie could hear the American twang her brother Eoin had picked up. He always lost it as soon as he started talking to the family in person, but right now he sounded like someone on the TV.

But that's what living in New York for over a decade did for you. Maybe she'd start to sound a bit English if she stayed here long enough. Which was an issue that had been very much on her mind since Grace had left.

Sitting up in bed, Rosie stroked Marmalade and yawned. It was emotional exhaustion, as much as the fact that it was after midnight. Not that she'd been able to sleep. When she'd looked at her phone, of course there had been a pile of messages from Michael.

Eoin was right: the Michael situation was serious, and

he didn't know the half of it. Rosie fought to keep the wobble out of her voice, hiding it in another yawn.

'Sorry, it's really late here.'

'I know. I had to catch you before Mam sees your posts about being stalked. I know she doesn't use social media, but someone might say it to her and she'll have a nervous breakdown and want you to come home. Or for me and Fiacra to come and get you, more like.'

'I was going to call her … but some stuff happened.' Rosie paused, her words catching in her throat as a tear fell down her cheek. Thank God it wasn't a video call. As if Marmalade knew there was something wrong, he stood up and began rubbing his face against her chin.

At the other end, she could hear suspicion in Eoin's voice. It was like a laser pointer, getting straight into the heart of what she didn't want to say.

'Like what, exactly?'

Rosie sighed. It was no good trying to hide things from her big brothers, and although she didn't really want to tell Eoin about Nick, there was no way she was going to tell her mother. Eoin was dead right that she'd need her brothers to help keep their mother calm.

'Stop stalling, tell me what's happening and you can go to bed. That'll give us time to get the story straight.'

Rosie half smiled. When she was little, she'd often covered for the boys when they sneaked out at night, or ran into their rooms to hide bottles of Jameson or cigarettes when their mother was on the warpath. She seemed to work longer hours than was humanly possible at the hospital, relying on them all to get themselves to school, and after their dad left, relying on Fiacra, the eldest, to make sure the household ran smoothly.

Over the years they'd all had moments. Fiacra called it 'constructing the narrative', but he worked for RTE in TV production now, and spent his whole life constructing narratives. He'd been bamboozling their mother with his long words and complex vocabulary since school.

Rosie wiped away another tear. 'OK, so this is it … And I've been to the police, before you ask. I was there on Thursday. Before, before … Well, anyway, like I said in my post, there's this creep called Michael who seems to think he knows me. He's been texting and emailing and sending flowers and stuff and …' Rosie cleared her throat. 'Then he sent me a photo of my front door.'

'OK …' Eoin drew it out. He knew her well enough to know there was more coming.

'And just after I went to the police, he sent me a photo from inside the house.'

'Does he know one of your housemates? Those guys with the same name?'

'The Davids? I don't think so. I honestly don't know. I've told my landlord and he's checking with them. But it freaked me out a bit.'

'*Sleeveen*.' Eoin said it with feeling, as if he had something nasty on the tip of his tongue: the Irish word for a sly or cunning creep; 'obsequious', as Fiacra would say. 'What did the police say? They can trace emails, you know.'

Rosie almost rolled her eyes. She loved her brothers, but they still treated her as if she didn't know how to use Google half the time.

'The officer I spoke to was great. They'll see if he bought any of the things he sent online. They have to go through every purchase and look at the delivery addresses to see which was mine. She said the flowers and the theatre tickets might be easier. Even if he bought them with cash, they can find the retailer and the time, and then look at the CCTV – assuming the shop had any, of course.'

'Well, that's good. Looking at the news, though, British institutions like the police seem to be a bit thinly spread. Do we need to call anyone, speed things up?'

Eoin worked in banking, and was part of the American Irish network that reached into every corner of the country. There were Irish everywhere, and as with the Italians, nationality was important to them; brotherhood was important. When two people from home met, even if they were total strangers, the first part of the conversation was always spent working out who they knew in common. Things happened in Ireland because of who you knew: contacts were everything.

'I don't think so. I think maybe we need to let them do their job.'

'Point taken. So what's happened today to change things?'

Rosie paused for a moment. She was just going to have to say it. Her mother didn't watch the British news, so she'd probably never know this bit, but she needed to tell her brothers everything. That's how this worked. 'One of my colleagues was showing a house today and someone bashed him over the head with a rock.'

'What?' Eoin's reaction was as explosive as she'd expected. 'Is he all right?'

'Not very … He's dead.' Another tear rolled down her face. 'He was so great, E. His name was Nick.' Saying it in the past tense cut right through her. She sniffed loudly.

'I've no idea if it was connected with this Michael thing, but ...'

'Bloody hell.'

'Yes, that about sums it up.'

'Jesus, Rosie. But the police will be on to it now – on to this Michael. Do they think it's connected?'

'I've no idea, but I'm talking to them tomorrow, I'll know more then.'

 rosiesparislife

[image: the word #stalkerUPDATE, white lettering centred on a black background]

Hello everyone, and huge thanks for all your brilliant comments about my stalking situation. As I said before (do check back on my previous posts), I HAVE reported this, the police are looking into everything. They have asked me for screenshots of the text messages, and I have forwarded emails so their cybersecurity team can investigate.

The police have advised me to get a Ring doorbell so all approaches to where I live will be recorded. My landlord has agreed to get one on the main door and I'm putting one on my own door. I've put up another safety chain and I have a brilliant personal alarm that makes a deafening noise and flashes a super-bright light.

I'm varying my route to work, and am contacting a friend when I leave the house and reporting my movements at all times. None of us should have to change our lives to feel safe, but that's the situation I'm in now.

Something awful has happened to a friend of mine and I might not be able to post for a few days. I'm going to speak to the police more, but I am OK. Your support means so much to me and is helping me through this. Thank you xx

#stalker #metoo #womensaid #nomore #askforAngela

Chapter 24

HALLIE PULLED THE cream Egyptian cotton pillow up a bit further and reached for her wine, looking out beyond the bedroom window at the city lights twinkling in the darkness. You could see the London Eye and the swing of the river from here, floor-to-ceiling windows wrapping around the entire apartment, the blinds rarely drawn. One day the residents of the block were going to find out there was someone with binoculars and a telephoto lens in one of the buildings on the other side of the Thames, and all hell would break loose.

Beside her, Ben put his phone down and turned to her.

'Sorry – work. It never stops. Even on a Saturday night.' He squinted at his watch. 'That should be Sunday morning. The joy of having clients in Los Angeles.'

Hallie smiled and kissed him. 'Tell me about it.'

'So what's going to happen about Nick, then? What the actual hell?'

Hallie shrugged. She'd been so shocked when Yaraslava had called this evening to tell her, she'd come straight over to Ben's apartment, but they hadn't ended up talking much.

Ben continued. 'I can't believe Yaraslava didn't call straight away when it happened this morning, but that's her all over. She has to be in control of everything.'

'She said he had terrible head injuries.' Hallie snuggled into him. At least up here, on top of the world, curtains or not, she felt safe. 'It's horrible. Poor Grace found him.'

Ben kissed the top of her head. '"Poor Grace" is right.'

Hallie leaned back to look at him. 'What do you mean?'

He shrugged. 'Nothing. She's nice, but she doesn't have much charisma, does she?'

'Ben, that's a horrible thing to say. She's brilliant at relocations, she's good with people.'

Ben grimaced, the greying stubble on his chin prickling her shoulder as he pulled her towards him. 'If you say so. She's not like … what's her name, Rosie, though, is she? She's a girl you'd cross the road for.' He obviously didn't feel Hallie stiffen beside him as he turned around and reached for his whisky. The soft light from the bedside lamp reflected in the sides of the heavy cut glass; the ice clinked as he continued. 'How's she doing at Sterling's? Did she enjoy being top saleswoman in her first month?'

Hallie narrowed her eyes. She didn't like the way Ben was talking about Rosie at all; it was as if he was mentally undressing her. 'She wasn't, actually – *I* was. The team dinner just happened to coincide with her closing on that penthouse in Greenwich, so it turned into a bit of a celebration. It wasn't about her specifically – Yaraslava's plan was for a team-building night.'

He crooked an eyebrow. 'At Park Chinois? I think she's got shares in that restaurant. Mayfair's not exactly handy for anyone, is it? Typical Yaraslava.' He took a sip of his whisky, the rich odour of alcohol blending with his aftershave and her perfume. 'But … Nick – what's the story there?'

Hallie shook her head, her eyes filling again. Nick had been fun to have in the office. Between his dating antics and his total excitement when he made a sale, it was like working with a giant puppy. When he landed a deal, it was as if he'd personally conquered the world: he'd be on the phone, his free arm outstretched; his fist punching the air as an offer came in; his victory swagger as he strolled in to give Yaraslava the good news … Utterly hilarious.

He'd been a man-child, but Hallie had liked him a lot. The past tense made her feel worse. She sniffed. He'd been part of the team, and she was really going to miss him.

'It's terrifying, it could have been any of us. He's …' She corrected herself. 'He was a fit guy. I don't know how it could have happened.'

Frowning, Ben looked at his glass. 'They definitely think it's foul play? It's a weird way to off someone. I mean, you've got to get close to cosh someone over the head.'

Hallie did a double take. 'I don't think the *how* is the issue here, the *why* and *what the hell* are bigger.'

As Hallie spoke, her phone rang with a distinctive tone. 'Oh crap, that's Yaraslava. I'd better take it.' She put her hand out to pick it up from the polished walnut bedside table.

'Does she know you've got that ringtone for her?' Ben smirked into his whisky as he took another sip.

Hallie put her finger to her lips and answered. As usual, Yaraslava didn't bother with pleasantries.

'Sorry to call late. I was going to leave a message. The police have just called to confirm they can be at the office at nine tomorrow. Can you come in early? They need to know where everyone was yesterday and everything we can tell them about the Bradfords.'

'Of course.' Hallie elbowed herself up in the bed. 'Major Bradford and Glynis?'

'Obviously. How many Bradfords do we have who were at the scene of our staff getting murdered?'

The sharpness of Yaraslava's tone took Hallie's breath away for a moment. 'He was, then, definitely … murdered?'

There was an impatient intake of breath at the other end. 'I doubt he bashed *himself* with a blunt instrument. Anyway, you showed them a few places, didn't you, the Bradfords, before Nick took over?'

It look a moment for Hallie to find her thoughts. She'd been more than annoyed when Major Bradford had called into the office and bonded with Nick over his ridiculous vintage sports car. Parking next to it in their basement garage, the major had come up gushing about it being the same model as his first car, and, unbelievably, the same poisonous shade of yellow.

There'd been no room for Hallie and Grace after that. They'd been working on Park House as a co-listing, at Yaraslava's insistence, because the client wanted a quick sale. Nick had taken over as if he was the Bradfords' new best friend.

But regardless of Hallie's reaction to Nick's taking their client, when she'd heard the news of his death from Yaraslava, her first stop had been the bathroom, where she'd emptied her lunch into the toilet. It could so easily have been her showing the Bradfords Park House.

Her mind back on the call, Hallie answered. 'Yes, yes, I got to know them pretty well. Grace did, too. Well, Glynis, anyway. The major's a bit handsy, I tried to keep clear of him.'

'Did Mrs Bradford give you any hints about where the major's money came from? The police seem to be very interested in that.'

Hallie rubbed her forehead. 'Family? It's not the sort of question I'd ask someone like him. They have proof of funds and their house has already sold.'

When she'd been selling superyachts, the origin of funds had been a constant issue. Interpol and the French police had regularly called about individuals they believed to be involved in organised crime, who might be trying to move funds. It hadn't bothered Hallie in the slightest; all their customers had been charming and polite, the commission had been amazing, and the tips when she went the extra mile substantial. Where they got their money wasn't her problem.

Yaraslava's voice brought Hallie's drifting mind back to the phone. 'Well, you're going to be asked tomorrow, so have a good think about everything you know about them – every detail. We cannot afford to be caught up in a news story.'

Yaraslava hung up, leaving Hallie thinking for a moment that she'd been cut off. She looked at the phone to see if it still had a signal.

It was pretty inevitable they were going to get caught up in a news story. Just what that turned out to be was the million-dollar question.

Ben put his chin on her bare arm, both eyebrows raised in question. It took a moment for Hallie to refocus on him. 'The police are coming to the office tomorrow. They are interested in Major Bradford's funds.' She rubbed her forehead. 'I can't see Major Bradford involved in—'

'Money laundering?' Ben made it sound practical.

'I was going to say "anything shady", but yes, that's probably what they mean.'

Ben shrugged. 'Always a possibility in this game. Especially with prime and super-prime property. You've been there, done that.'

'Yeah, and bought the T-shirt. But you sort of expect it with boats. I mean, they are portable. And there are lots of ways to use up cash, they need constant maintenance. Change the cushions or the hot tub and it costs a couple of million, before you even get to the engines or the water toys.'

'Or the full-time crew.'

Hallie slipped her phone onto the bedside table again and reached for her wine. 'Exactly. Major Bradford, though? That just sounds ridiculous. What do they think happened? The major let something slip about where the money was coming from, and someone hired a killer to keep Nick quiet?'

Grace work

Just checking you're safe and sound. I've had a bottle of wine, just going to bed. I'm locking all the doors and I'll keep the phone near me. Hope you can sleep. See you tomorrow xx

00:10

Hallie work

Rosie I hope you're OK. It's just so awful, I'm devastated, I can't sleep. I'm dreading tomorrow. Sorry to text in the middle of the night but
Nick really liked you, he was always saying that.

I wanted you to know. I guess I'll see you in the office in the morning. H xox

02:13

Polly Police

Hi Rosie, this is Polly from Islington Police Station. I've just come on shift and there was a message about your colleague. The detectives who are looking after that case will work alongside the team who are working on yours. The incidents may be totally unconnected, so I don't want you to panic, but we need to be thorough. If you need me, please don't hesitate to call on this number. Polly Amwell.

07:05

+447480788409

I've been thinking about Nick all night. Oh my love, I'm so worried about you. What on earth could he have done for this to happen? Take care of yourself and don't take any risks. Call me if you need me, you know I'm always here for you. Mike xxxxxxx

07:32

Chapter 25

ROSIE TIMED HER exit from the house to within seconds, so she could run down the road and jump on the bus. It wasn't her usual bus – it was, in fact, going in the opposite direction – but she figured if she caught this one, changed outside the fancy hotel that she could never remember the name of, and doubled back, she'd avoid any chance of bumping into Michael, or of him getting on the same one. She didn't know if he'd be expecting her to be heading for the office on a Sunday, but she wasn't about to take any risks.

It meant she had to leave early each morning to allow for the extra time, but if she didn't know what route she was going to take to work each day, Michael wouldn't be able to anticipate it either. He'd mentioned seeing her at the bus stop or in the Tube so many times, she'd become convinced he was monitoring her movements.

Predictably, the bus was almost empty and she swung upstairs to find a seat. Reaching the top, she held on tight as it lurched, peeking out over the rail, praying it would be empty upstairs as well. Seeing that it was, her sigh of relief was almost audible.

Moving to the front, she sat down in the very first seat. From here she could see who got on. Not that it would help, because she didn't know what Michael looked like, but from his tone, and from the messages he had left her, she was sure he was white, in his thirties, and probably from London. And obviously he was a man. *So that narrowed it down to half the population.*

Pulling her bag onto her knee, Rosie twisted so she could see the top of the stairs and almost yelped as a sharp crack filled the upper deck. The bus had hit a tree branch right beside her head, the impact like a gunshot. She closed her eyes, her heart racing.

When would this stop? When would she feel relaxed and comfortable on public transport?

But at least this extended trip also gave her time to think. When she'd woken up this morning to see another bunch of texts, she'd known at least one of them had to be from him. But what was puzzling her was how the heck Michael knew something had happened to Nick.

Rosie had assumed from Michael's text that it had been in the headlines last night, but when she'd checked this morning, Nick's name hadn't been mentioned.

As she'd sat in bed looking at her phone screen, a dark hole yawning in her stomach, Rosie had started to wonder if there might be some sort of spyware in her phone. Could Michael have been reading her messages and pieced together what had happened? Or overheard her talking? Grace had called her yesterday, and then she had come over to Rosie's flat.

Maybe her flat was bugged? Had he come into the building, pretending to be fixing the Wi-Fi or pretending to be a phone engineer or something? Rosie's mind was starting to race. But Maurizio would have said. And how could he have got inside her flat?

Sitting on the bus, thinking about it, made Rosie tense up so tightly that her jaw started to ache. Could he have left something outside that had a bug in it – something she'd brought into the flat? Rosie thought hard. She had loads of Amazon deliveries and sometimes kept the boxes to store things in. Was that it?

Swivelling around in her seat, Rosie rested her forehead on the cool window glass, looking down at the damp pavements below, compulsively scanning them, looking for a face she might have seen somewhere else.

The idea that was worrying her most was that Michael knew about Nick because he'd had something to do with it.

As if he'd heard her thinking, her phone vibrated. Rosie closed her eyes. *Would he ever leave her alone?* He was WhatsApp-ing mainly now, rather than emailing or leaving voice messages, thank God. It was probably because he couldn't tell if she'd read an email, but he could see the two blue ticks on WhatsApp, so he always knew then she'd read whatever nonsense he'd sent.

The problem was, if she didn't look, the curiosity about what he'd said ate away at her. A tiny part of her hoped there would be a message signing off. *Hi Rosie, have to go away with work, I won't be around for a bit.* Or *Hi Rosie, I've discovered I'm terminally ill and I have to go into space. There won't be a phone signal so I won't be able to text.*

Some hope.

She felt her phone vibrate again.

She pulled the phone out of her coat pocket.

Hi Rosie, this is Dermot from News Daily, I saw you on GMBTV and your posts on the stalking situation. I've just heard about your colleague. I'd love to talk to you about it this morning if I could. You can get me on this number. I'll try your office too.

At least it wasn't Michael, but Rosie wasn't sure if *News Daily* was much better.

Chapter 26

GRACE LEANED ON the counter in the office kitchenette and crossed her arms, waiting for the kettle to boil again. She'd never met anyone who drank as much tea as these two detectives. Every time she showed someone in, or checked to see if they needed anything between meetings, their mugs were empty.

Sebastian Sterling was in the conference room with them; the burble of voices was indistinct, but clearly they were having a deep conversation. When she'd met him in the lift this morning, he'd come straight from the airport, was wearing pink canvas trousers and a navy blazer over a white polo shirt, the collar open, his skin tanned and glowing. Grace thought he was about sixty; his thick black hair, swept back from his face, was greying slightly at the temples. She knew he travelled a lot, but he was in the office whenever he was in London, making sure he sat in on everyone's interviews and their team meetings. He dripped class and money, which was sort of annoying, but a bit of Grace half hoped some of it might rub off.

When they'd arrived, Sebastian had gone straight into Yaraslava's office, followed by Hallie, when she came in.

Grace peeped out into the office space. Rosie was sitting in her usual spot now, her head down over her phone. She looked as if she was checking Instagram – probably answering all the comments on her stalking posts. It was unbelievable how that had blown up.

Grace had been first to be interviewed, going over her statement from the previous day to see if she could remember anything new, running through her day, and her chat to Nick as he'd arrived at Park House. Then the Bradfords' call when she'd been getting her coffee. Grace closed her eyes, running through it all again.

She was sad about Nick. She'd liked him a lot, had thought he might be interested in going on a date at some stage, but hadn't been brave enough to ask him herself. Talking about him to the detectives was sort of comforting. They'd listened sympathetically as she'd reeled off for the second time everything that had happened.

Who knew, when she'd got into her car on Saturday morning, that the day would play out the way it had?

She'd burst into tears, of course, but they'd been ready with the tissues.

Grace sniffed. She would be starting again if Hallie didn't get back quickly with the sandwiches they'd ordered from the deli around the corner. She couldn't function when she was hungry. As if Hallie had heard her name, the office door opened and she came in, a huge tray wrapped in silver foil in her arms. Glancing in through the kitchen door to Grace, she smiled glumly and slipped the tray onto the table as Rosie finally looked up.

'They've done loads. Wraps and sandwiches, and they're sending up someone with the coffee. They were all so upset when I told them. I didn't say what had happened, but …' Hallie caught her breath. 'Nick was mad about their chocolate brownies, the ones with the walnuts, so they sent a tray of them, too.' She lifted off the top layer of foil as she spoke, revealing a smaller tray filled with rich dark brown slabs of cake.

Coming out of the kitchen, Grace put a pile of plates and paper napkins down on the end of the table.

Hallie continued, keeping her voice low. 'They said they're going to rename them "Nick's Brownies".' Hallie shook her head. 'I still can't believe this is happening. Honestly, it's the type of thing you read about.'

As Hallie spoke, Yaraslava's door opened. Pausing in the doorway, Yaraslava pointed wordlessly to the conference room door, mouthing, 'Is he still in there?'

Rosie nodded in response. Glancing at the firmly closed conference room door, her black patent stiletto heels clicking on the wooden floor, Yaraslava made her way over to the table. She leaned on the edge of it as if she was bracing herself. 'It might be about to get worse.'

Grace felt her stomach drop. Her shock must have been reflected in her face. Yaraslava glanced at her as she continued. 'A journalist has called from *News Daily*. He's seen Rosie's Instagram posts about this stalker.' She raised one eyebrow, as if she was questioning why Rosie was posting about it at all. 'And somehow he knows all about Nick, and he's asking if everything is linked, if we feel the company is being attacked somehow.'

Grace could feel her eyes widen. 'He thinks someone is trying to shut us down?'

Hallie looked up sharply at Yaraslava. 'Do you mean we could all be in danger?'

Yaraslava didn't answer for a moment, but pursed her red lips as if that was exactly what she thought, but couldn't say it. 'I think they are trying to make a story, and there is a lot of interest in this company suddenly. It is very important that if the press try to talk to you, that you refuse to comment.' She spoke slowly, her tone deliberate, as if she was choosing her words carefully. 'I am going to talk to Sebastian and we will see if we need a PR company to help. Crisis communications is not a job for Tootals. We need a specialist in reputation management.'

'It sounds like we need that security guard.' Grace crossed her arms.

Yaraslava inclined her head. 'Indeed. We will have one tomorrow. This might blow up online, not just with the press. If someone is targeting us, they could troll or spread disinformation. Be very careful what you say. Do not answer messages unless you know who is sending them, and remember, you could be quoted.' She stood up straight. 'Anything you say could splash across headlines.'

Chapter 27

SITTING AT HER station on the team table, half listening to Yaraslava, Rosie rested her forehead on her fingertips. She was getting a stress headache and the day was only starting. The whole office felt stark and empty without Nick or his laptop, his battered leather manbag slung over the back of his chair.

Rosie glanced at the closed conference room door. She was dreading explaining everything again, but anything she could say that might help the police with what had happened to Nick would be worth it. Rosie could feel tears welling up as she thought about him. She might be frightened, but she couldn't imagine how Nick had felt in those last moments; it was beyond words.

He'd told her once he wasn't worried about dying, because he knew when he got to Heaven all the pets he'd ever had would be waiting for him. He didn't even really believe in Heaven, but he'd smiled as he'd said that he could see them rushing towards him, all flying ears and wagging tails, and he was sort of looking forward to that.

But he'd thought he'd be about a hundred, and ready to go. Rosie curled up inside at the thought.

This *News Daily* thing was the icing on a very rotten cake; it was a scaremongering red top that would sensationalise Nick's story – and hers – and she didn't want anything to do with it.

Rosie could have kicked herself for not telling Yaraslava about the text from the *News Daily* journalist sooner. She'd planned to, when she'd arrived this morning, but she just hadn't had a chance. Now that he'd got in touch directly, it sounded as if everything was blowing up.

At the other end of the table, Yaraslava was still talking about the media, as if somehow this was all Rosie's fault. She hadn't actually said that the publicity would undermine client confidence, but that was exactly what she was implying. When she'd suggested it, Rosie had had a strong suspicion that getting a security guard was more about their clients than it was about her, and now she was sure of it.

The pain across Rosie's forehead was increasing as Yaraslava continued talking. She wasn't even fully listening; instead she found herself praying that the detectives appeared and took her away from this conversation, and into the conference room where she could find out what was happening about Nick.

'Rosie's been getting massive attention since she did the TV.' Rosie looked up sharply as she heard Grace say her name. Grace was looking down the table at her, her brow creased. 'Is it safe for her to keep posting?'

Rosie could feel Yaraslava's eyes on her like lasers. 'We work with some very big clients, and where there is big money there is always a possibility of bad actors. We already know Hunt's want the Caulfield Regent's Park development.' Yaraslava paused significantly. 'Perhaps they have stepped things up.'

Beside Grace, Hallie went pale. 'No *way*. Hunt's couldn't have killed Nick *or* be behind Rosie's stalker. That's just mad. There are much easier ways to poach clients. I mean … *murder*? And this Michael's been inside Rosie's house.'

'We don't know – this is my point. All of these things together …' Yaraslava turned to Rosie. 'How do you know he has been in your house, Rosie? Have you told the police?'

It took Rosie a moment to find her words. 'He sent some photographs, and yes, I've given them to the police. When I went to the station to report it all, they said they'd investigate, but that was before ... before Nick.'

Yaraslava crossed her arms. 'I do not think we can make guesses at this. But remember, be careful who you speak to and stay offline if you can.'

Something in Rosie seemed to snap. 'I can't do that. It's not just about me. There are so many women this has happened to ... They need support – not from me, from each other. Telling my story is showing them they aren't alone. I can't suddenly go quiet – people will think something has happened.'

Rosie could feel Grace looking at her, her mouth open, but she had to say it. Sterling & Co's reputation paled into insignificance beside the personal stories she'd read in the comments on her page. And Nick had liked loads of her posts; he wouldn't have wanted her to stop.

She needed Michael to understand that she wasn't going to take this harassment any longer – that he would be held accountable. And if he'd hurt Nick, too, it made her standing up and speaking out all the more important.

Who was he? Rosie had tried to go through every interaction she'd had since she'd arrived in London, through every meeting, every night out before she'd started at Sterling & Co. Had she sat next to this guy at the cinema, or on the bus? Or was he someone she'd shown a house to? Had she smiled at someone on the Tube? She had no idea, but the more she'd thought about it, the more Rosie was convinced that wherever she'd 'met' Michael, it had to be connected to work. He'd seen her laughing with Nick in the restaurant – he'd mentioned it specifically in one of his messages.

But that didn't bring her any closer to working out who he was. Her work was all about meeting people: viewing properties; showing properties; hosting open house events where hundreds of people might come through in a day. Michael could be any one of them.

Out of the corner of her eye, Rosie could tell Grace was holding her breath, waiting to see how Yaraslava would react to her outburst, but the door to the conference room opened before she could comment. Yaraslava turned as Sebastian emerged talking to the detectives, who were following him out of the conference room.

'Thank you, gentlemen, I know you'll do your best. If you need anything, this office is at your disposal.'

Sebastian spotted the food. 'Ah, lunch is here. Do please help yourselves.' He came into the office properly, his accent pure British public school.

'I need a quick word, Sebastian, before you go.' Yaraslava indicated her office. 'It is important.'

Chapter 28

ROSIE GLANCED AT the door of Yaraslava's office, still firmly closed. Sebastian had been in there for ages, and Rosie didn't have any doubt that they were discussing the media situation. She sighed, looking at the sandwich in front of her, already curling in the heat of the room. She was due in next, to talk to the police officers once they'd eaten, but right now she just wanted to get out of the office and get some fresh air.

Hallie sat down heavily at the head of the table, opened her mouth to speak, seemed to change her mind, then changed it back again. She glanced at Yaraslava's office door as she finally found her words.

'Are you going to keep posting, Rosie? And talking to the media about it? What happens if that makes this Michael angry? He could be properly dangerous.' Aware that their voices travelled, Hallie was keeping hers down. 'And Yaraslava could be right – I mean, not about Hunt's, but about someone who wants to close down the company. Maybe targeting you is a way to threaten the business, too? Perhaps Sebastian has pissed someone – someone big – off.' She didn't say 'someone criminal', but Rosie was pretty sure that's what she meant.

'Maybe Nick heard something …'

Rosie could see Grace glancing across at Hallie. 'How do you know it's not Hunt's, Hal? Yaraslava's right about that Regent's Park development, and didn't they handle the house in Kensington with the secret room? I've been wondering how Rosie's Michael could know about that.'

'He's not *my* Michael.' Rosie looked pointedly at Grace as she said it.

'Sorry, you know what I mean.'

Hallie glanced between them. 'Nick was wondering about that, too, about how he could know about the secret room. He checked our database for clients called Michael, and I've asked in the other agencies. There's a bit of a list, but I haven't heard back from Hunt's yet.'

Rosie's eyes met Hallie's. 'Thank you for that. Really. I never even thought of asking the previous agencies if they had details of who had seen the house.'

'Michael is a pretty common name.' Grace paused, looking thoughtful. 'Which sort of makes you think Yaraslava could be right – he's actually not a real stalker, but part of something bigger.'

Rosie moved up to their end of the table, bringing her plate with her. 'I'd love to think he's a troll, Grace, but he's ticking all the boxes for a stalker. I don't think, if this was fake, whoever is doing it would have delved into the psychology of stalkers so deeply. I mean, his behaviour is almost textbook. He's behaving just like that Lily Baldwin's stalker.' Rosie turned to Hallie to fill her in. 'Lily Baldwin's this American dancer who did a podcast about being stalked.' She looked at Grace. 'And the gifts – why would they have sent a super-expensive umbrella?'

'Rosie's right.' Hallie looked more confident, as if some of her shock at Yaraslava's suggestion about industrial espionage was subsiding. She turned to Grace. 'If he was a troll, I think his messages would have been more obvious – you know, the sort of creepy sexual messages you expect when you hear about a stalker. Everything's Rosie's had has been weirdly friendly.'

Rosie picked up the sandwich and took a bite, finding it a lot tastier than she'd expected. Beside her, Grace grimaced. 'But it's still a huge coincidence, isn't it? I think someone needs to check to see where all Hunt's employees were on Saturday, just in case, *and* get a list of who looked at the house with the secret room. We don't even know Michael's his real name.'

Hallie did a double take. 'I don't think one of Hunt's team killed Nick. Do you, honestly? Yaraslava used to work there. And she's got a point that there could be big money involved, but, I mean, it could be something to do with Park House. How much do we know about who's selling it, or who lived there before?'

What Hallie was saying was true. Rosie picked up her phone, needing a moment to process the information. The thought that Nick's friend had found something out about who had been emailing her was nagging at her. It was the first thing she was going to talk to the detectives about. She just wished they'd hurry up with their lunch.

'Have we heard anything from the Bradfords?' Rosie glanced at the conference room door again as Grace shook her head.

'I'm going to call them today. They love that house, but I think the vendor might have to drop the price even more now. DC Owens said they will probably have to replace that wooden floor in the living room.'

Hallie let out a breath and closed her eyes, paling as Grace spoke. Rosie knew Grace was only being practical, but hearing about Nick's blood on the floor made her feel sick, too.

As if she'd realised what she'd said, Grace added, 'We need to keep going. That's what Nick would have wanted. He wanted to sell that house. If we can do that, his family will get all the commission. Yaraslava said so this morning when I arrived.'

Hallie sniffed, her eyes glistening with tears. Grace leaned over to rub her arm. 'Eat something or you'll be ill. And we don't want this to all go to waste.'

Only half listening to what they were saying, Rosie saw a notification flash on her phone screen. An email from Outlander. She felt her whole body sag. Why couldn't he leave her alone for just one day? Part of her didn't want to look, but part of her needed to.

Opening her phone, Rosie clicked on her Gmail. He'd sent another photo with no message. What was it this time? Rosie could feel her chest getting tight as she opened it. She gasped involuntarily, her hand shooting to her mouth.

Across the table, Hallie leaned forward. 'What is it? You've gone as white as a sheet.' Out of the corner of her eye, Rosie could see Hallie glance at Grace.

Rosie didn't answer; instead, she sat staring at her phone, paralysed. She suddenly felt horrendously dizzy and closed her eyes. When she opened them, they were burning with tears. In her peripheral vision she saw Grace glance at Hallie again, as if for reassurance. Getting up, Grace came around the end of the table to look at Rosie's screen.

'What the actual hell?' Grace put her hand on Rosie's shoulder. 'He must be using AI, he has to be.'

Rosie took a deep breath and held up her phone to show Hallie the photo she'd just been emailed. It was a picture of a long, narrow wooden-floored hallway, an orange cat disappearing through a door opening into a bright living room, the wing of a high-backed purple velvet chair just visible. Whoever had taken it must have been leaning on the wall inside the front door – the angle took in another open door on the right. Rosie's bedroom.

Chapter 29

'ARE YOU READY for a chat, Rosie?' On the other side of the office, the older detective – DC Owens, Rosie thought Grace had called him – appeared at the door to the conference room.

Rosie stood up shakily. *She was so worn out with this, so devastated about Nick. What did this guy Michael think he was doing? He'd been inside her flat – inside her home.*

'Yes, yes, I'm definitely ready.'

In the L-shaped conference room, the two detectives had pads of lined paper and a pile of brown manila files positioned on the glass table in front of them. Rosie took the chair at the end facing the window, her back to the door. It was a big room, light and airy. Inviting buttery leather sofas and a low coffee table at the end of the long arm provided a more relaxed space to chat with clients.

DC Owens sat down opposite Rosie. 'Have a biscuit, these are very good.' He pushed a plate of heavily coated chocolate biscuits towards her, and Rosie smiled despite herself. Grace had obviously been looking after them.

She reached for one. She still felt dizzy, urgently needed a sugar boost.

'I'm Detective Sergeant Tristan Nandy.' The younger detective, who had taken the chair at the round end of the table between them, smiled at her encouragingly. He was British Asian, and as she turned to acknowledge him, she realised he was very good-looking, his dark skin glowing beside his distinctly pasty Welsh colleague. And he was very well dressed, gold cufflinks peeking out from the cuffs of his pure white waffle cotton shirt, his suit an inky blue.

He grinned reassuringly. 'We've been briefed by Polly Amwell. It sounds like you've had a bit of a tough time of it.'

'It feels like that.'

'Anything more from this Michael character since you spoke to Polly?'

Rosie nodded, pulling out her phone. 'I've had a bunch of WhatsApp messages and he's emailed photographs.

It's like he's getting closer and closer.' She felt a chill as she said it. She took a deep breath. 'This just came, it's been taken from *inside* my front door.' She took a shaky breath. 'He knows about Nick. He messaged to say he'd heard the terrible news and ask if I was OK.'

DS Nandy's voice was guarded. 'Any ideas how he could have got into your home?' He paused. 'Or found out about Nick? Very few details were released to the press.'

'Lots on both. Not all of them rational.' Rosie could feel her anxiety levels rising sharply. She'd been on edge when she'd been talking to Polly Amwell in Islington, but now … Now she had a dead colleague and a lunatic creeping up her stairs. She bit her lip.

Where did she even start?

'I've been wondering how he knows where I am, if he's put some sort of tracker in my phone. And then when I got the message this morning about Nick, I started wondering if my apartment was bugged. Grace came over yesterday afternoon to tell me what happened. She wouldn't give me all the details on the phone.'

Nandy tapped his pen on his notepad. 'Did she mention talking to anyone else about it? On the bus on the way over, perhaps, could she have been overheard?'

Rosie shook her head. 'I don't think so, she came in her car. She left Hampstead and came straight over to mine, I think, and went home about 11.30.'

'I think PC Amwell's already explained how we can trace this Michael's emails?' Nandy cocked an eyebrow. 'We're going to work as quickly as we can. Your case has been escalated because of recent events.'

'Michael was horrid about Nick in his texts. I think he was jealous. And when we were in the Tube station on Thursday, Nick was talking about how a friend of his could find out where Michael's emails were sent from.'

Nandy put his forearms on the table, his voice low. 'We wanted to talk to you about that. Did Nick say anything about tracing the emails himself?'

Rosie frowned, thinking. 'No, he asked me to forward everything to him for his friend. I did it as soon as I got home. The photos, too. He was wondering about the metadata or something.' Rosie paused. 'He did seem to know a lot about how to do it, though.'

'That's great, Rosie. If we need to come back to you on any of that, can we give you a call?' Nandy nodded to Owens, who picked up his pen, flicking open his notebook.

'You run the RosiesParisLife Instagram account?' DC Owens smiled at her encouragingly.

'Yes, I started it when I worked in Paris. I should probably change it to RosiesLondonLife now.'

'And you have sole access to it?' DC Owens' tone was warm and friendly.

Rosie looked at him, confused, wondering where he was going with this. 'Yes, obviously—'

Nandy cut in. 'And how about the Sterling & Co Instagram account? Who has access to that?'

'It's run by a PR company, Tootals. We send them photos when we're at properties, plus personality and location shots, and they upload everything. Yaraslava asked me if I wanted to take it over when I started, but I've enough to do with my own account.'

'Did she give you, or anyone else, the password?' Nandy was making notes as Rosie spoke.

Rosie thought for a moment. 'She'll be able to tell you, but I think Tootals have only been doing it for a few months. Before that, Hallie said she did most of the posts. She might still have access.'

'And do you know anything about it being hacked?'

Rosie looked at Owens in surprise. 'No – has it been?'

Nandy pursed his lips before he spoke. 'Someone has been direct messaging Sterling & Co followers and trying to engage them in conversation. Ironically, it starts off warning them they might be contacted by Sterling & Co impersonators.' Rosie looked at him blankly as he continued. 'It looks like someone is targeting high net worth individuals who are following prime property agents, and telling them Sebastian Sterling or Yaraslava Kavalenko has something they'd like to discuss with them privately.' He paused. 'They are then encouraged to set up a Telegram account.'

'Oh, I see.' Rosie didn't know anyone who used Telegram. It was a heavily encrypted private messaging platform that enabled communication across different devices, but without having to register phone numbers. At least, it was private if you got the settings right. In her head, she'd always associated it with Russian hackers, although that could have been a leap of her own. Either way, it didn't sound like something any of their clients wanted to get involved in. If Sebastian or Yaraslava wanted to talk to someone, they'd organise lunch.

As the implication hit her, Rosie felt shock flood through her. 'Has someone been scammed?'

Was this why Nick had been killed?

Chapter 30

SEBASTIAN WAS STANDING beside the office window when Rosie put her head around Yaraslava's office door. Sitting at her desk, Yaraslava looked up from her laptop as Rosie spoke. 'You wanted me?'

'Yes, Sebastian does. Please come in – and Grace, is she there?' Yaraslava half rose from her chair. Rosie looked over her shoulder into the office and gestured to Grace, who was heading into the kitchen. She gave Rosie a 'Who, me?' sign and Rosie nodded, opening her eyes wide.

Hallie had told Rosie as soon as she'd come out of the conference room that Yaraslava wanted a word. Rosie had cringed inside. It was probably about the whole media thing, but Rosie was determined to keep going. Perhaps she was being disloyal to Sterling & Co, but sometimes you had to look after yourself, and there was a lot at stake here. If she could help one woman who was afraid – who was in a similar situation to her – Rosie knew she had to do it.

She hadn't meant to blurt it out earlier, but once she had, she knew for sure that getting her message out to as much of the media as she could was vitally important. And she was sure Nick would have wanted her to. As they'd got on the Tube last week and she'd told him a bit more about Michael's increasingly incessant and obsessive texts, he'd got increasingly mad.

Rosie slipped inside Yaraslava's door and headed for one of her guest chairs. 'Grace's coming.'

'Super. Sit down, please. How did you get on with the detectives?'

Rosie sat down, trying not to look like a balloon deflating. She hadn't realised how much emotional energy she'd used giving Nandy and Owens from CID the full picture while keeping calm and not breaking down completely. Every time she explained what was going on, she felt as if she was reliving the arrival of each message. Burying the fear and keeping the messages compartmentalised in her head, well away from the rest of her life, was the only way she had of coping with it all, and not hightailing it back to Paris or over to her brother in New York.

Not that hightailing it anywhere would guarantee to put Michael off. Rosie felt as if he was stuck to her like a burr, his hooks firmly embedded, so she'd never be able to simply shake him off.

Rosie realised Yaraslava was looking at her intently. 'Sorry … good. They were very nice. It's just … It's just, it's a lot.'

Yaraslava nodded, her face serious as the door opened and Grace appeared.

'Come, sit.'

Behind Yaraslava, Sebastian was leaning on the windowsill, his arms folded. Rosie could feel him looking at her and it made her feel distinctly uncomfortable. She definitely didn't want to look in his direction, so she looked around the office instead, realising she was probably taking it in properly for the first time.

Hallie was always saying that the whole arrangement of the main office space, with its long table, had terrible feng shui. Hallie, Nick and Grace had their backs to the conference room doors and Yaraslava's office, all because – Grace had told her – if the table was swung around the other way, Yaraslava thought they'd spend half the day staring out of the Georgian floor-to-ceiling windows.

But in here, the feng shui felt good; the atmosphere was completely different.

Yaraslava's office was a cosy, intimate room, antique walnut furniture complementing sleek panelling and modern lighting. The glass deer head looked down on them all from the wall above the angled desk.

Sterling & Co's awards were lit up in a Victorian trophy cabinet beside the door, and Yaraslava had put a stunning painting of the sea on one wall. Opposite the painting, a beautiful antique rosewood wardrobe opened up to reveal a mirrored interior with a champagne fridge and marble-topped cocktail bar, elegant glasses sparkling in the interior lights. It was the type of thing Rosie had seen in apartments in Paris and absolutely adored: a clever upcycle that dripped luxury.

'Now, I was telling Sebastian about your Michael troubles, Rosie. He is very concerned, particularly with everything that happened yesterday and with all this media interest. Nick's name has been kept out of the papers so far, but that might not last.' Yaraslava had her elbows on the desk and had linked her perfectly manicured fingers, the light catching her glossy dark red nails. Sebastian was still standing, but had moved to hover closer to her desk.

Rosie opened her mouth to speak, but Grace got in before her. 'I really think Rosie should move in with me for a bit. I don't have much space, but she can't be safe in her flat. Whoever he is, Michael seems to be able to get in. He sent another photo of her house this morning.'

Yaraslava's eyebrow rose. 'This is true?'

Rosie sighed and nodded. 'I've given the photo to the police. They are going to see what they can find out from it.' Her voice cracked. 'It could have been Michael – hurting Nick, I mean. They're worried that Nick might have traced the emails on his own, and had worked out who Michael is.'

She felt tears pricking at her eyes. *If this was all her fault, she didn't know how she could live with herself.*

Chapter 31

ROSIE COULD FEEL the walls of Yaraslava's office closing in on her for a moment. Sebastian Sterling's looming figure between her and the window, blocking the light, made her feel even more claustrophobic. She wiped away a tear that was threatening to fall. Living with Michael's voice constantly in her ear had pushed her as far as she thought she could bear, and now poor Nick. A feeling of panic began to rise inside her as she realised Sebastian was speaking.

'Given the circumstances, I agree with Grace that you need to think about your personal safety.' His voice made Rosie jump. She looked up. He was still lurking behind Yaraslava, but staring at her intently. There had always been something about him that put her on edge, but today … She rubbed her eyes and crossed her arms tightly as she replied.

'The police said they can put a flag on me on their systems, so if I call, someone will come straight away.' The possibility of what might precipitate a 999 call made Rosie shiver. 'But they did say they think he would have shown himself before now if he actually wanted to speak to me. This has been going on for weeks. It's like he's too shy or something to talk to me face to face.'

'I think he's living out some sort of fantasy that you know each other, but it's in his head. If he came face to face with you, he'd be too morto to actually talk to you.' Grace reached over and squeezed Rosie's arm reassuringly.

From across the desk. Yaraslava looked at Grace, confused. '"Morto"?'

'Sorry – mortified. Like he'd be terrified to actually meet her.'

'Let's hope so,' Rosie said under her breath as Yaraslava took in Grace's point.

'It's very concerning.' Sebastian frowned. 'There is a strong possibility the TV and media coverage could make this Michael individual angry. I feel you need to have a plan in place. If Nick's attack *is* connected to the company, or to what has been happening to you, Rosie,

I think it makes sense to take a week or so off.' Rosie looked at him, not sure what to say.

If Nick's death is connected. His words rolled around inside her head. Deep inside, she knew they had to be connected – that something had happened to Nick because of Michael. That night at the restaurant she'd done a reel: shots of herself and Nick – everyone else, too, but mainly of her and Nick. They'd been sitting next to each other, had got giddy laughing when Rosie started talking about shifting someone. She'd been utterly confused as Nick's eyes had widened in shock, quickly discovering that the word for a snog in Ireland meant something completely different in the UK. They'd had too much to drink, and laughed far too much. It had been a brilliant night.

And Michael had been there, watching them. Had her messing with Nick made him jealous? Had he been waiting for his chance?

'You are a very valuable asset to this company.' Yaraslava's voice broke into her thoughts. Rosie looked at her, trying to catch up. Yaraslava was smiling, apparently aiming for warmth, but falling a little short. 'We are very concerned for your safety.'

'Have you thought about getting out of London for a bit?' Sebastian's voice was serious.

Rosie let out a breath. 'I've thought about going home, but that's complicated.' Horrifying images of trying to explain to her mother why she was suddenly home jostled with images of being trapped in her teenage bedroom – assuming she could get in the door around Conor's drums. Rosie had been living on her own since she was eighteen; how could she return now? She cleared her throat. 'And I've only just got here, I don't have any leave …'

Yaraslava looked up. 'We will be closing the office for a week, out of respect for Nick's loss.'

Sebastian picked up the thread again. 'I have a house in Cornwall. It's beside the sea, in a village, but remote compared to central London. I think you and Grace should go down there together while the police get to grips with their investigation. Now is not a good time for you to be alone. There's a housekeeper, she'll look after you. The mobile phone signal is very patchy, so you'll get some peace and quiet. There's internet in the house, that can be a bit weak, too, but there's a pool and games room, so you won't need to leave.'

'What about the clients?' asked Grace. 'Don't we risk them defecting to Hunt's if we're not providing the level of service they expect?'

'Anything urgent, Yaraslava can look after. And Hallie will be here in London as well. And don't worry, we'll keep you both on full pay. Our paramount concern right now is Rosie's safety.'

Chapter 32

ROSIE PULLED GRACE'S neon baseball cap down low over her face as she pushed the release button on the street door. She'd tucked her hair into the back of Hallie's jacket. She wasn't sure if changing her clothes for theirs would confuse anyone watching for her, but if there was a chance Michael was hanging around the building, she'd happily put on a bear suit.

'Are you sure this is a good idea?' Grace followed her out of the wide front door, looking anxiously up and down the street. This was a side road and never very busy, unlike the road it connected to, with the coffee shop and deli.

Rosie deliberately turned away from her usual route to the coffee shop. 'I just have to get out of that office. All that grey was starting to come in on top of me. And I need to think about this Cornwall idea. What do you think of it?'

Grace looped her arm through Rosie's, and for a second Rosie was tempted to shake her off, but stopped herself. Grace wouldn't understand that it made her feel trapped – that if she needed to run, she'd have to waste precious moments untangling herself. Rosie's hand closed on her house keys in her pocket, adjusting them so the sharpest key was sitting between her fingers. When the first photo had arrived, she'd ordered a personal alarm online – it was attached to her keys. If she pulled the loop at the top, it let out a piercing wail and a built-in light started flashing with a high-intensity beam that was almost blinding. She never went anywhere without it.

Not waiting for Grace to answer, Rosie drew in a breath and, keeping her eyes on the wet pavement, began to walk, almost pulling Grace with her. She'd been lovely, insisting Rosie didn't go out on her own, but now, having Grace with her was making Rosie even more anxious. Michael knew what Grace looked like, so Rosie trying to disguise herself became a bit pointless. But at least he'd be less likely to approach her if she was with someone.

Maybe.

Rosie hoped so.

But nothing Michael had done or said so far had been logical, or rational, or in any way normal. He was behaving so like the stalker Lily Baldwin had described on her podcast, it was uncanny. But that meant he'd be classified as an erotomanic stalker as well, which was a word that made Rosie feel ill.

'Are you OK?' Grace was looking at her curiously. 'You've gone a bit pale.'

Rosie let out a breath. 'If we go down here we can swing around and cross the main road. There's that little square, Red Lion Gardens, we can talk there. They've got benches and coffee. I think I need both.'

Red Lion Gardens was a tiny square enclosed by high black iron railings and bushes. In the middle, a huge tree had been surrounded by planting and paving, curved wooden benches with their backs to the trunk, facing neat areas of grass. Beside the gate a little Elizabethan-style beamed hut had been turned into a coffee shop, with steel tables and rattan chairs outside it.

Rosie chose a bench well away from anyone who might overhear their conversation.

'I'll get the coffee. Latte, two sugars, right?'

Rosie smiled at Grace gratefully. She needed a few minutes to decompress. Sebastian's offer had come from nowhere and she needed to process it. She'd never been to Cornwall, although it looked beautiful in Jago's Instagram shots.

She leaned forward and put her elbows on her knees, running her hands into her hair and cradling her head. The headache she'd got earlier hadn't gone away.

A few minutes later Grace was back with the coffees. 'I put in your sugar.' She sat down on the bench beside Rosie and took the lid off her coffee as she continued. 'I think Sebastian's idea is a good one, don't you? I mean, apart from a free holiday by the sea – I bet his house is gorgeous – it means you can vanish completely, go off-grid or whatever they call it.'

Rosie took her own lid off and took a sip of her coffee. Hot and sweet was exactly what she needed right now. 'I need to think about it.'

She could see why Grace might think going away was a brilliant idea, but there was something safe about her own space. She knew where she was; she'd worked out all her escape routes if Michael turned up at her front door – where she could hide. She'd put an extra lock on the bathroom door, so she could lock herself in and then get out of the window. There was a ladder running up the rear of the building. She wasn't sure what it was for – it didn't exactly meet fire escape regulations – but she was sure she could swing around onto it and then down onto the roof of the extension on the building next door. Even as she thought about it now, she ran through the plan again. She had a spare pay-as-you-go phone charging in the bathroom, too – just in case she got cut off from her own phone.

With the extra lock, she reckoned she'd have enough time to grab it and get out of the window.

But in a house she didn't know, what would she do if Michael turned up? He could feel bolder if they were out of London and away from prying eyes. In the city there were street cameras everywhere. It was probably true that you could scream and people would keep on walking by, but at least there were people. Sebastian had said that the house was isolated. What if there were no neighbours? What if she went outside and he was there? What would she do then?

Rosie had googled erotomanic stalkers; the article she'd found had said that:

> Delusional thinking may be shaped by feelings of being unloved or even unlovable; narcissistic tendencies are overcome by fantasy. Cases in which erotomania is prominent are usually diagnosed as paranoid state or paranoid schizophrenia.

A line from Lily Baldwin's podcast came back to her like a snatch of music:

'It's not the ones that say they're going to kill you, that we worry about.'

Chapter 33

SITTING IN THE conference room, Yaraslava leaned across the glass table towards the two detectives, her hands locked around her coffee mug, and smiled sadly. 'It has been such a shock. Thank you so for coming into the office to talk to everyone. It has been very traumatic, and this is so much better than them going into a police station.'

DS Tristan Nandy acknowledged her point with a nod of his head. 'Do you mind if we record this conversation? Just so we don't miss anything.'

Yaraslava shrugged. 'Of course.'

Nandy checked the volume on his phone and put it carefully between the three of them. 'Tell us about Nick Armitage. What was he like?'

'Young, keen, reliable, a very good salesman. Everything you want. Sometimes he was silly, made people laugh. He came from a very good family. Perhaps he did not need to work, but he enjoyed it.'

'And he got on with everyone?'

Yaraslava glanced across at DC Owens. He was sitting away from the table, his arms folded, obviously watching her as she answered. Yaraslava flashed him a smile. 'Very much. He was a real team player, in the office and on the football field.'

'We're talking to his friends. He appears to have been universally liked. Which makes this attack even more random. His phone was beside his body, his wallet in his trouser pocket, so robbery wasn't the motive.' Nandy paused. 'Did you ever get any hint he could be involved in anything untoward – drugs, perhaps?'

Yaraslava frowned. 'Maybe at parties he might have tried … I do not know. But he was young, well off, so …' She shrugged again.

Nandy flashed her a smile, but the atmosphere in the room had tightened. 'Tell us about the appointment itself. We gather the Bradfords suggested 11 a.m. to meet Nick. Who else knew about that?'

Yaraslava glanced out of the conference room window over Owens' shoulder, as if she was taking a moment to think. It was at the corner of the building and overlooked a row of trees, their bare branches shuddering in a stiff breeze. She'd anticipated this question, but like the trees, it left her feeling exposed. She looked back at Nandy.

'The staff here, anyone the Bradfords told. Perhaps Nick mentioned it to someone. I do not know. It was not a secret. He said something about football training on Saturday, so perhaps he told his team.'

'And was the vendor informed that the Bradfords were going to view the house again?'

A moment too late, Yaraslava saw where the detectives were going with this. Her colleagues would have told them that the vendor had dropped the price and initiated the meeting. Yaraslava was going to have to think fast when they asked to talk to the woman selling the property. How had she not seen that one coming? She had too much on her mind.

'She was keen on a quick sale. The Bradfords had seen the property twice, but when they did not make an offer, she dropped the price. That is why the appointment.'

Nandy made a note on his pad. 'Tell me about her.'

Yaraslava shrugged. 'She is Russian. Her husband works in banking, I understand. Her name is Irina Ivanov, but I am not sure if she uses his surname. They bought the house as a London base, but she said he has been working more in Europe so they have not used it. They decided to sell here and buy elsewhere.'

It sounded convincing: not too much detail, but just enough. Don't over-explain.

'And when this Irina Ivanov came to the office to discuss the sale, she met Nick?' Nandy looked at her expectantly.

Yaraslava shook her head. 'We go to our clients. That is why we do not have a premises with a street front – we do not need it. Discretion is vital in this business. Clients do not often come here, but if they do, they can drive straight into the underground car park and take the lift to the office, so they are not seen.'

'So you met this Irina Ivanov where? At the property?' The other detective, Owens, leaned forward, his face impassive.

Perhaps this was her out.

The 'meeting her in the park' idea had sounded weak when she'd said it to Dimitri, and she hadn't come up with anything more convincing. He'd thought she'd pull it off, but he hadn't met Nandy and Owens. Yaraslava had a feeling they knew a lot more than they were saying, and it was making her nervous. She hated to be the one playing catch-up.

'Yes. I called to look at the property, to revalue it. We had sold it to her initially, but I needed to see if she had made any changes. That would have been the second time that I met her. She called whenever she needed news.'

'No emails?' Owens' eyebrows rose in question.

Yaraslava raised her own eyebrows, mirroring his body language, as if she was suddenly realising that yes, he was right. 'No, actually, now you say it. She always called.'

Nandy pursed his lips. 'And were you in any way suspicious? Did you consider that perhaps her story might not be totally true?'

'I had no reason to be. I work with this calibre of client all the time. She looked right, sounded right. There was nothing to suggest she was not what she said.'

'So you didn't check her identity?' Nandy sounded perplexed. 'Mr Sterling mentioned you have access to a system that cross-references about four thousand sources globally to verify identity, company credentials and the like.'

Yaraslava rubbed her face thoughtfully. 'You know, I honestly did not feel the need to. She came across as totally legitimate.'

Owens flipped a page in his notebook. 'Tell us about meeting her at the house. Did she show you around the property?'

'I would need to look in my diary for the date, but yes, of course, I went in every room, and then we sat in the lounge to have coffee and discuss what she was hoping to achieve. It was all very normal.'

'Did you touch anything while you were there?' Nandy made it sound like an offhand comment.

Yaraslava's brow creased. 'I must have done. But I cannot remember what. She had some fine ornaments, and we talked about her paintings.'

Nandy took this in. 'The thing is, Yaraslava, we're trying to work out how your fingerprints ended up on the murder weapon – the piece of rock Nick was hit with.'

Yaraslava felt her mouth dry as Nandy continued. 'Can you tell us where you were and what were you doing on Saturday morning?'

Chapter 34

AS ROSIE ROUNDED the last stair onto her landing, she felt very glad that Grace had insisted on coming home with her. Grace's chatter as they'd come up the stairs was comforting; she'd barely noticed that Rosie's responses had been getting fewer and fewer as she'd got closer to her own door. Part of Rosie was terrified of getting to the top of the stairs and finding Michael standing there.

'So what did the police say about that last photo?' Rosie put her key in the lock as Grace spoke, her hand trembling. *Part of why they were so scary, was because there was no message.*

Rosie pushed the front door open as she replied. 'They're still waiting for their cyber team to get to the emails, to see if they can identify him, or his IP address, at least. If it turns out to be Westminster Central

Library or something, it's not going to be a lot of help.'

'They could stake it out. Wait for him to send something and then catch him?'

Rosie wished it was that simple. Walking through to the living room, she put her bag down and looked around her. The only reason she could afford this place was because of the commission she was earning at Sterling & Co. She'd been able to save enough when she'd lived in Paris to tide her over for her first few months in London, but if this didn't stop, would she be able to stay here, and in the job she loved? She shook the idea from her head and turned to look at Grace as she came in behind her.

'Unless they can tie Michael to Nick somehow, I don't think they have the resources for stakeouts or surveillance.'

Grace flopped down on the sofa, her brows knotted. 'Do they really think the two are connected? They'll only know he had nothing to do with Nick if they track him down and eliminate him from that investigation, won't they?'

'*Eliminate?*' Rosie looked across at her and half smiled. 'You sound like you've been watching too many cop shows on TV.'

Grace grinned half-heartedly. 'True crime all the way. I'm an expert. Honestly, some of the people they feature are unbelievably stupid.'

'I hope Michael's stupid, but I've got a sort of gut feeling he isn't. He sounds educated from his texts … and stuff.' She'd been about to say 'and his voice messages', but she didn't even want to think about them.

'Did you tell them that?'

Rosie nodded; she'd told Polly Amwell in Islington station. Part of her still wished she hadn't deleted the voice messages. Maybe they could have matched his voice to someone, if she still had them. But keeping them on her phone had given her chills. Those messages brought him too close. Thankfully he'd finally stopped sending them. He must have guessed that she wasn't listening to them.

Grace sighed. 'The detectives asked me lots of questions about the Bradfords – about where their money came from. I mean, Glynis didn't tell me much, but I know they've two sons. One spends a lot of time in the Middle East – that's why they help with the grandchildren. He owns a load of companies, but she didn't say what they do.'

Grace had told her this already, but Rosie knew she needed to talk about it. She'd found Nick's body; she must still be in shock.

'Did Glynis say anything about her other son?'

'I think she said he was in finance, some sort of investor.' Grace pulled a face. 'I don't think the Bradfords could be into drugs or money laundering. They're too posh, and … like, Middle England. That doesn't make sense at all.'

Rosie turned towards the kitchenette to put on the kettle. Grace loved the hot chocolate she'd brought from Paris, and Rosie needed something comforting, too.

Someone had killed Nick, and if it wasn't connected to Michael, perhaps the reason *was* something to do with Park House. She closed her eyes for a moment, listening to the rain on the Velux window above the kitchen counter. It was possible that Nick had wandered in on a robbery; it was a fabulous house, after all, and it backed right onto Hampstead Heath. But he was a fit guy, and Rosie couldn't imagine that he would have turned his back on a would-be robber. Perhaps someone had been upstairs and, hearing him come into the house, had come into the lounge behind him.

'Have you thought any more about Cornwall?'

Grace interrupted Rosie's musing, and for a moment Rosie felt the glimmer of a smile inside. Grace's tone was a mix of 'I don't want to push you, but I really want to go'. Hopeful, but trying to sound nonchalant.

It was so lovely and caring that it made Rosie tear up for a second.

'Actually, I have.' Rosie didn't need to get into her TV station weather map moment: how running away home had suddenly seemed like a good idea – for about five seconds. The home bit wasn't going to work, but the running bit was becoming increasingly attractive. 'I'm not feeling very safe here – I don't know how he's getting into the house.' She sighed. 'Part of me doesn't want to go anywhere and give in to him, but part of me would like to get a full night's sleep while the police do their thing.' The kettle began to boil as she continued. 'So, basically, I'm starting to think it's a very good idea. How soon can you get organised?'

Chapter 35

HALLIE FELT THE warmth of Ben's enormous cat Winston as he wrapped himself around her ankles. Sitting at Ben's desk in his home office, she had her laptop open, but had spent most of the morning looking out of the window at the river. It wasn't the Monday she'd expected when she'd been sorting out her diary on Friday. And on top of everything, it was grey today, the sky heavy and overcast, about to spill with rain.

Her own flat had views of suburban gardens, which wasn't terrible, but she felt alive here, part of the city. Growing up in Melbourne she'd been able to see the sea, had taken her proximity to it for granted, but here in London, she missed it. When she'd first met Ben and come back to this incredible apartment, it was as if all her hopes and aspirations had come together. He was gorgeous, incredibly successful, he loved kids, he had a cat. And he was as mad about her as she was about him.

She just wished their relationship didn't have to be a secret; as time went on, more and more she wanted to go public. But that brought a whole bundle of complications with it.

As she watched one of the water taxis pass below, it struck her that actually, until now, she'd always lived in sight of water – at home, but in Cannes and then Monaco, too. She wasn't sure why she was only realising, at this stage of her life, that she craved this connection.

Being near water made you feel that you were part of something bigger, that there was a world out there that didn't revolve around your problems. It put things in perspective.

Although there wasn't a whole lot of perspective that could improve what was happening right now. There had been dramas in her life along the way – her father's death, her brother's spectacular divorce – but nothing like this.

Hallie glanced at the time. It was almost eleven, and she felt as if she'd done nothing all day. She'd sent all her urgent emails, and she'd had an offer in for a property she'd shown at the end of last week, which normally she'd be thrilled with.

But even earning a huge commission had lost its shine. She needed to get outside and go for a walk down the river, but that felt a bit scary, too. She was starting to be just a little afraid of going out. What if this Michael started following her, too? She'd read Rosie's posts and they had chilled her right through.

Hallie reached down to stroke the cat. He was ridiculously huge, the size of a small dog, with big pointy fluffy ears and a face like a fox. He started to purr, the sound like someone swirling gravel with a stick.

She pulled him up onto her lap and buried her face in his long fur. There wasn't quite enough room for both of them on the office chair, but his body felt warm and soft. And most of all, safe.

What the hell was going on at Sterling's?

Winston tried to rub his face against her chin as she reached for her phone. Ben had gone to work, and she felt as if she was rattling in this huge apartment. There were worse places to rattle in than a luxury three-bed, four-bath, £7 million river view apartment, but you could feel lonely anywhere.

Everything was such a mess.

Being with Ben meant she couldn't talk to anyone about a whole part of her life that was so important, and that was hard. The gossipy chats you had with your girlfriends – even talking clothes or hair dramas – had to be closely edited to make sure she didn't let anything slip. Hallie had always found Grace a bit distant, but she loved Rosie; she was so natural and unpretentious. The other day, when Rosie had seen Ben's name on her phone, Hallie had been tempted to tell her a bit – not everything – but she'd never had a chance.

It was Yaraslava who was the problem. It was always Yaraslava.

Hallie knew she needed to find another job – it was the only way things could move forward with Ben – but she'd negotiated a high personal commission rate with Sebastian when she'd first started. He'd been down in Monaco looking at boats, and had been so impressed with her that he'd offered her a job. Not only a job, but he'd paid for her move and her rent for the first three months in London while she found her feet. She'd never be able to negotiate another package like this one, and until it was looking as if things could be permanent with Ben, she couldn't move company.

There was more to life than money, but having it gave her independence and confidence. And she wasn't ready to give that up yet.

It was chicken-and-egg. They couldn't go public until she changed job, and she couldn't change job until she could be sure Ben was committed to a future with her.

Winston nudged Hallie's chin again, demanding more attention. Stroking him, she shifted him over on her lap and woke her phone up. She wanted to check in on Rosie and see how she was – and find out what was happening. Being on her own was starting to creep Hallie out; she could only imagine how Rosie was feeling.

Rosie picked up immediately.

'Hey, chicken, how are you doing?' At the other end, Hallie could hear Rosie moving around her flat.

'I'm good. I'm staying at home today, but Grace is coming over later, I think. I just can't get Nick out of my head.' Hallie heard Rosie sigh. 'There's just so much at the moment. Too much. Poor Nick and bloody Michael and the press. Did the police ask you about the Sterling's Instagram account being hacked?'

'About someone messaging a client pretending to be Yaraslava, and asking the recipient to set up a Telegram account to talk privately?' Hallie tickled Winston as he pushed against her. 'They did. But nobody uses Telegram – that's mad.'

'I know. I'd guess that was a bit of a big red flag for most people, but the police wanted to know if Nick had the Insta login details. Maybe someone thought he'd scammed them and got mad.'

'I don't think he had the login. I told them I have it saved on my phone, and Yaraslava has it, and maybe Grace. But Tootals do everything now, so we don't need to go near it.' Hallie thought for a moment, her brow furrowed. 'I'm sure they'll talk to Yaraslava. She'll know who had passwords.'

'That's what I told them. Grace said Yaraslava would probably blame Hunt's again. Grace says she's convinced they are trying to get our business.' Hallie heard what sounded like Rosie sitting down. 'Maybe she's right – they've definitely moved in on Caulfield's. I don't know how they even knew we were talking to them. Yaraslava was so careful.'

Chapter 36

'WHAT THE HELL is happening?' Dimitri's voice was hard-edged.

Yaraslava drew in a slow breath, closing her eyes and trying hard not to snap back in response. He'd called her, and she could tell from the testiness in his tone that her brother was getting mad. She let out a sigh; she'd got home very late the night before and had barely slept. She leaned her head on the deep wooden window surround in her living room, looking out at the rain. It ran down the glass in heavy tears.

'I was with the police all afternoon yesterday.'

'They called.'

Yaraslava swung around away from the window and padded barefoot across the room. She could think better when she walked. She needed to keep moving, always moving. Whenever her stress levels went up, she walked. Around the office, around the block. The bigger the problem, the more space she needed. She loved Hampstead Heath, with its wide open spaces, Hyde Park, Richmond Park. Anywhere she could breathe.

At the other end of the call, she heard Dimitri close his office door and she came back to the problem at hand. 'Are they asking about Landmark? About your Russian buyer?'

'They're asking about Irina, yes – how I met her, who she is. They haven't got to Landmark yet, as far as I can tell. But this is a murder investigation, Dimitri, they are being very thorough.'

'I gathered. But they'll find her listed as company secretary if they dig deeply enough. The paperwork is watertight.'

Yaraslava put her hand on her neck, trying to massage away the tension. She rotated her head. Dimitri had come through for her when she'd needed to confirm her alibi for Saturday, but he wasn't being nearly as supportive as she'd like now. She understood he was under pressure. Huge pressure.

But they both were.

'We need to move the Grigori business to Dubai.' He made it sound like a statement rather than a question. One that came with no room for negotiation.

Yaraslava closed her eyes. It was a risk bringing their money through London, one that had increased in recent years, but they got well paid for doing it, and when it came through one of the companies she worked for, she got the commission on the sale. Win–win.

It all added up to a significant amount of money. She reckoned she only needed a couple more deals and she could set up on her own: open in London and New York; run her own show. She already had a dossier on the individuals who she wanted to join her, to build her team, had been looking out for properties to lease as their headquarters.

But Dimitri was right.

London had been the centre for Russian money for a long time, but things were changing. Hong Kong and Dubai were rapidly becoming the two global centres for Russian investment now. As soon as the war in Ukraine had broken out, you could suddenly hear Russian spoken in the malls in Dubai. It was an ideal location: lots of high-end property, no detailed checks and no extradition.

London was becoming more and more difficult.

But Yaraslava wasn't about to move to Dubai. You might be able to get your morning coffee delivered, or your car filled up with petrol in the middle of the night, but it was a transient community, and she needed to put down solid roots.

Safe, solid roots. Leaving Belarus had been much tougher that she'd expected. She'd headed to London thinking she had enough saved and that she'd get a job easily. But she hadn't bargained – ironically, it seemed now – for the property prices, the rents. The tiny room she'd been able to afford in a house-share of hopelessness, where the rodent population was sharper than her housemates, had been her idea of Hell. She was comfortable now, but it had been a gruelling climb.

'It's a bit late to have this brilliant idea now, Dimi. We've got everything tied up in, what …? Four properties. We need time to sell.' She paused. 'And you can take the business out of here, but I live in London. I'm not ready to leave yet.' She let out a breath, like steam escaping. 'Plus it doesn't solve our immediate problem, does it?'

At the other end, Dimitri grunted. 'What do the cops think happened?'

'They don't know yet.' Yaraslava could hear the tightness in her voice, tried to relax.

'But they've identified your fingerprints at the scene. How exactly did that happen?'

'I was in the house, obviously.'

'Yaraslava, I'm not talking about you being in the house. I'm wondering why your prints were on file in the first place. Did they print everyone at Sterling's?'

Yaraslava pursed her lips as the silence grew.

'I thought not. We cannot afford for you to attract any heat, Yaraslava. Why would your prints be on the police database. What did I miss here?'

'Nothing, Dimitri, nothing at all.' She could tell his patience was wearing thin, but it was none of his business.

'I need to know everything that is relevant here.'

As he spoke, Yaraslava saw a car pull up beside the pavement outside, the driver and passenger doors swinging open as two men got out. She could feel her heart rate increase as she took a step away from the window.

'It's all fine. They'll get nothing on Irina. I've explained that she didn't raise any suspicions. Landmark was set up through multiple locations, it's safe. Our probl—' She corrected herself. 'Our challenge here is finding a buyer to free up nine million sterling to keep the Grigori brothers sweet.'

As she spoke, she heard the doorbell echo down the hallway.

'I have to go, Dimi, I'll call you later. It *will* all be fine. I know what I'm doing.'

Chapter 37

AT THE END of the phone, Hallie could hear Rosie tearing up. Rolling her chair away from the desk, she tried to scoop up the cat so she could move over to the sofa. Like all the rooms in this apartment, the wall overlooking the river was completely made of glass, but in the office, the other three were lined with oak bookcases, crammed full with everything from the books Ben had used when he was getting his pilot's licence to books on ancient China. He was a total history buff, and loved nothing more than wandering around the British Museum on a Sunday afternoon. The only problem, in somewhere so public, was that they had to pretend they weren't together.

The L-shaped black leather sofa at the rear of the office was calling her. 'Ben's Book Nook', she called it. Winston had a bright red cashmere blanket on one end, but he wasn't impressed at being moved and squirmed in her arms. He was too big for her to fight him, so she let him drop to the floor as she crossed the room. She needed to sit somewhere comfortable for this conversation.

'It will all sort itself out, chicken. You've got the full attention of the police now – well, poor Nick has. They'll find out what was happening, I'm sure.' She sat down heavily. Rosie sounded so strained, Hallie just wanted to reach out and give her a hug.

'I'm going to miss Nick so much. It's just so bad, Hals. I mean, how did he get caught up in this – in my mess?' Hallie heard Rosie sniff loudly. 'He was really sweet, and he wanted to help me with tracing those emails. He was so worried that things could get worse, and his friend was only around for a day or something. Nick said he was going off-grid hiking somewhere and wouldn't be home for a few days.'

'Nick was the best, Rosie. One of a kind. Will you see if Grace can come over early? It's better you're not on your own. If anything happens, make sure you call me, day or night – any time – OK?'

After Hallie said goodbye, she put her phone down slowly on the sofa beside her, her stomach turning over.

She'd called intending to have a proper gossip with Rosie, but she couldn't concentrate, could feel her own tears welling up. Breaking down on the phone wasn't going to do Rosie any good at all. But her mentioning the Instagram hacking had opened a dark hole of worry somewhere in Hallie's stomach.

Could Yaraslava be right – that Hunt's was trying to bring down Sterling & Co? She looked at her phone and, opening her Instagram account, tapped to go to her profile page. It was exactly as she had left it, set up so she could flick between her own account and the Sterling & Co account. She'd been posting a lot of the sales and interiors content before Tootals took over.

Hallie bit her lip as Winston decided to get over his huff at being moved. Padding over to her, he jumped onto the sofa beside her, looking for attention. She stroked his soft head absent-mindedly while she thought about what Rosie had said.

When Rosie first accepted the job, Yaraslava had called Hallie into the office to tell her, her eyes alight with excitement about expanding the team.

'Her Instagram has two hundred thousand followers from all over the world. Sebastian and I have had just a quick look and so many of them are exactly our type of customers. If she brings in anything like the business you do, it will push us up way ahead of Hunt's.'

Hallie had nodded as if she didn't know this already. Sometimes when Yaraslava got excited about something, it was as if she thought out loud.

'She'll be fabulous. Will she be generating her own leads? She won't have many contacts here apart from followers, and they might not be actual buyers.'

Yaraslava had picked up the sleek Mont Blanc pen on her desk and played it through her fingers. 'I would like to divide the strongest leads between you and Rosie. Nick has his own social contacts, from school and university. We know what works for him.'

'But what about Grace?'

'We will get her to look at the properties under two million, and I want to promote her to manage relocations. Hunt's do not have anyone who helps their clients move, gets them info on schools, the council tax, finds them good local staff. It will be like a concierge service.' Yaraslava leaned back in her chair, tapping the pen on her palm. 'Rosie's arrival will mean we can extend our revenue streams in all sorts of directions.'

Hunt's, Hunt's, Hunt's … It was all Yaraslava focused on. Hallie had known Grace wouldn't be hugely impressed with this 'promotion', but Yaraslava had a point about extending their services to look after their clients. And she'd always favoured a tight team who pulled their weight, rather than loads of associates who spent half their time shooting the breeze and gossiping.

Yaraslava had hoped Rosie would take over the Sterling & Co Instagram account, too, but she hadn't been keen. Instead, she'd found Tootals, who had started posting the content they all generated, but …

Hallie could feel a pain starting to build in her forehead. The Sterling & Co Insta getting hacked by scammers was a big problem. It had the potential to be a massive reputational issue that could cost them a lot of business.

Hallie felt her anxiety spiking. Was she the problem here? More importantly, was it her habit of waking up in the morning and checking Instagram, and leaving her phone beside the bed while she went in for her shower, that had caused this?

Had it given someone ideas?

She knew her phone went to sleep quickly, but Ben was always telling her off for using the same password for everything. And she still sometimes switched to the Sterling & Co account to post content, as she used to; it added colour.

Could Ben have used her phone to get into the account and DM their clients, just to cause trouble? He'd been the one who Yaraslava had rowed with when she'd left Hunt's, but did he hate her that much? Hallie felt sick inside. Her phone password was long and a mix of words and numbers, but it wasn't hard to remember if you knew what it stood for. It was the name of her dad's first boat, with her parents' house number thrown in for luck.

A few months ago they'd been curled up on the sofa and Ben had said he'd left his phone in the bedroom, so he'd ordered Chinese from hers.

And she'd reminded him of the password.

Chapter 38

ROSIE TURNED TO look at the window in her living room, every chink of light blocked by the tightly closed curtains. The thought of a whole week away without Michael constantly in her face – without unlocking her front door and hesitating on the landing, to make sure she wasn't going to meet him on the stairs – would be wonderful.

In her bedroom, Rosie found Marmalade curled up in a ball on her bed. She'd forgotten she'd let him in earlier. He looked so peaceful; he had his paw over his head and his little pink tongue sticking out. Rosie smiled and, opening her wardrobe, reached in for her suitcase. It was Samsonite, and probably one of her best investments ever – she'd got it in a sale in Cork before she'd moved to Paris. It had been expensive then, even half-price, but it was as light as a feather, and it had been all over the world with her. It was also a gorgeous ice blue, so it fitted with her denim aesthetic and stood out on the baggage carousel on the rare occasions she had to check it in.

Now it was going to help her put some distance between herself and Michael.

Unzipping the case woke Marmalade. She could feel him scowling sleepily at her as she gathered her clothes – thick walking socks and a nightshirt – throwing them behind her into the case. Pulling out sweatshirts and jumpers, she turned around to refold them, and discovered Marmalade had relocated and was now watching her studiously from the case itself, as if he was waiting for her to pack him, too.

She brought the pile of sweaters to the edge of the bed. As she'd pulled out each garment, she'd felt lighter somehow. This week would give the police time to narrow down their investigation. They always said on TV that the most progress was made in the early days.

Rosie reached for her phone and checked the time. It was late afternoon in New York. Her brother should be in the office, and he never had meetings on a Monday; it was one of his rules.

'Yo, Roses, what's happening?' Eoin answered the phone immediately, his fake Bronx accent making her smile.

'I've got some news.' It didn't take her long to fill him in on Sebastian's offer.

'That all sounds amazing. I know it's done and dusted now, but I'd be worried about your talking about this Michael on TV. It could make him mad.'

She didn't want to tell Eoin about the latest photo. 'But he doesn't think I'm talking about him, honestly. He thinks someone is using his name to threaten me. All his messages are like he's known me forever. Half his texts are just like chatting, sharing memes, like you and I do.' She bit her lip. 'There are just so many of them, and it's so creepy when I don't have the first idea who the hell he is.'

'Agreed.' Eoin paused. 'Any news on that lad in your office?'

'Nick?' She filled him in. When she'd finished, Rosie sighed. 'I'm starting to really hate this. But I love my job so much. I love property, I love meeting people, I love selling. I love getting out and being in this world of absolute luxury, of mixing with the people whose norm is just so totally different from how we grew up.'

'And you're good at it. Go to Cornwall. I've never heard of a boss look after their employee like that. They know your worth, Rosie – that's great.' Rosie glanced over at Marmalade as Eoin continued. 'Getting away will be good for you, and it's great Grace can go as well.'

'I know, I'd be mad not to. I was talking to Hallie about it and she came up with an idea about posting as if I'm still in London, so Michael will think I'm still here. She has a viewing next week in Chelsea – Cheyne Walk. We're going to pretend it's my listing.'

There was a pause while Eoin thought about this. 'That sounds like a good idea. You know your phone has a dual SIM, like mine. You can redirect the London number to the office and use another one for your personal calls. Give that number to a couple of key people, and I mean just a couple – me, and maybe your boss, but no one else. Then you'll have a week free of messages from this Michael creep … And will you get a "find my phone app" and put me in as the backup, so I can see where you are?'

'So if I get kidnapped, you can find me?'

'Well, I wasn't exactly thinking that, but …'

Rosie sighed. 'I know. As Mam always says – be prepared. I've still got my French SIM and you've all got that number. I can add credit and then it'll be good to go. Good plan.' She paused. 'And I like the idea of you knowing where I am. Will you tell Fiacra, too? If needs be, he can get to London in a couple of hours, assuming he's in Dublin.'

'I will, I'll tell him what's happening. He's been filming in Peru or somewhere. I think he's due back any day.'

'Thanks, Eoin, I'll add credit to that SIM. That's genius.' Rosie knew he'd be able to hear the relief in her tone. Suddenly being rid of Michael, even for a few hours, was becoming a real possibility.

'Text me when you have it working. When are you leaving?'

'As soon as possible. My God, I definitely need a break, and I can't wait to see the sea.'

Chapter 39

'AT LAST, GRACIE. I've been calling you all weekend, I left so many messages on your phone.' Leaning on her kitchen counter, Grace drew in a breath and rolled her eyes. Her mother was in the kitchen at home in Ireland; she could hear the Monday morning sounds of the washing machine and RTE's *Today with Claire Byrne* on the radio, both competing with Ninja's yapping. Some sort of Jack Russell cross, he was small but always vocal. Whenever her mother or father picked up the phone, he started.

'Sorry, Mam, I keep telling you I don't pick up voice messages. You need to text me.'

'And I keep telling you I can't get this bloody new phone to work for texting. You're my only child, I need you to call me.' She barely stopped to pause for breath. 'But listen to me ... Your Rosie was on the

TV on Friday.' She said it as if Grace didn't already know.

'Yes, Mam, *Good Morning Britain*. It's huge.'

'If you knew, why didn't you tell me? I could have recorded it. I only caught it by accident, and I love that girl that does the sofa with yer man. I can't remember her name.' Grace couldn't either, but it didn't stop her mother. 'But this stalker, Michael, what sort of *créatúr* is he to be plaguing her like that?'

In the background, she heard her father come through the back door, his 'Is that our Gracie?' just about audible over Ninja, who was clearly delighted to see him.

'Take that dog out, Derek, he never stops, and take off your shoes.'

Grace could see the scene in the kitchen. There would be bread baking in the oven, and her father would have been working in the garden or tinkering with his car, and would be coming in for his lunch. The whole house had run like clockwork since they both retired.

'Rosie doesn't know who this Michael is, Mam, that's the problem.'

'The poor lassie, and from Cork, too.' At the other end, Grace heard her mother tutting as she put on the kettle. Briege Cassidy didn't sit still for a minute. 'She was very good, mind, not nervous at all, I'd be terrified, worrying about who was watching and what I might say. Why didn't you tell me?'

Grace sighed. 'There's a lot been happening at work, Mam.'

'But you're still selling those big houses and making lots of money?'

'Yes, I got promoted to client relations. I told you, I'm the relocation specialist.'

'So you did. I like "specialist". That Rosie looks like a great girl to work with. It makes such a difference when you have nice people around you. Where did she go to school?'

'I can't remember, Mam. It wasn't Mercy, though, she's from outside Cork …'

'I do wish you'd call more often, I need to keep up with your news. And come home, maybe. Will you think about that? We haven't seen you for months.'

Her mother sounded incredulous that she hadn't been home for ages. She was right; Grace had been over in the summer and for Christmas, but then she'd got so busy in work, had had such a lot on her mind recently, that she hadn't had a chance to think about it.

'I might not be able to call next week. Our boss Sebastian has suggested we go down to his summer house in Cornwall for a week, me and Rosie, to see if this stalking thing blows over a bit.' She wasn't about to explain to her mother about Nick. The image of him lying on the floor in Park House leaped into her mind again, making her gasp involuntarily. She closed her eyes, trying to replace it with another image. Saturday had been such a terrible day. Just in case her mother had heard her react, Grace coughed. But she needn't have worried; her mother was rattling pots and moving around the kitchen, clearly focused on the washing-up.

'That sounds good – a week's holiday? I hope he's still paying you if he's the one telling you to take a week off.'

'He is, Mam. Anyway, Rosie is still deciding, but the phone coverage down there isn't great, so I might have to wait to call you again when I get back.'

Briege's mind had already moved on. 'I bet if it's your boss's house, it'll be nice. Has he got a pool?'

Grace rolled her eyes again. 'He said he did, and he's got a housekeeper who's going to make sure the fridge is full and we have everything we need.'

'That does sound fancy. I was just telling—'

'Mam, I'm really sorry, I have to go. I've got to get organised if I'm going to be away next week.'

'Of course you have, love. You get sorted, and when you see her, say hello to that Rosie for me. That Instagram of hers is amazing. Bridie in the post office said she follows it.'

'I will, Mam. Say hi to Bridie from me. Bye.'

Grace ended the call with a stab of her finger, her mother's inquisitiveness and Bridie's opinions grating on her. She was right to feel sorry for Rosie, though; whatever it was that people loved about her, it was drawing in Michael as well. And these photos going up to her door were terrifying; she'd gone completely white when she'd told Grace about the latest one.

Would the next one be inside her flat? How petrifying would that be?

Grace put down her phone and looked at her bed, where she'd opened up her cabin case and had laid out most of her clothes ready. Working out what to take with her was proving a challenge. Rosie always looked amazing, even when they'd met at the weekends and she'd been in an old sweatshirt and jeans with no make-up on.

Grace ran her eye over everything. She didn't have many casual clothes, and she didn't look great in jeans, but she looked worse in sweatpants, so the jeans would have to go in. Would leggings be warm enough? She had some chunky sweaters, and she'd need her walking boots. Grace went to get them out of the wardrobe. On her way she passed the bookshelf. She pulled out her guide to woodland plants and flicked through it. She'd definitely need that.

What else would she need for Cornwall, though? Yaraslava had said the house was near the sea and there were lots of walks. She'd made it sound as if she'd been there, but Grace was pretty sure she must have scoped it out on Google Street View – which was exactly what Grace had done. Then she'd found it on a historic properties website, listed as having six bedrooms, an orangery, an extensive basement and an old stable block. Hawksmoor House had been originally built in the 1800s for the local mine owner, and had been considered very modern.

Grace had tried to zoom in on Google Street View, but it had huge gates and was down a long drive; she could only catch glimpses of it from the surrounding roads. It looked *fantastic*.

Chapter 40

THE MORE SHE thought about it, the more Rosie liked the idea of creating a smokescreen of posts to make it look as if she was still in London. Marmalade watched her stoically as she sat down beside her open suitcase and scrolled through her gallery. Hallie had already sent her a selection of interior shots of the apartment in Cheyne Walk in Chelsea, and there was no point in waiting. Getting things like the weather right, to make sure it looked as if she was in the city, was going to be vital, but she was going to enjoy every minute of deceiving Michael.

'Make him think you're still here, Rosie. I'll be at every showing and will cover for you, but if anyone at the viewings asks for you, it'll be a bloody great red flag. Call those detectives and tell them what we're doing, too. They might even be able to stake the building out.' The thought of Hallie's earnest face made Rosie smile. She had great friends. She didn't know if she could cope with all this if it wasn't for Grace and Hallie. 'You know how you do reels of your everyday stuff, not just the properties. Mix some of those in and everything will look authentic. You can schedule everything, then it won't matter if this place of Sebastian's has no signal. You'll be sorted.'

Rosie had nodded; she knew exactly what Hallie meant. Her reels tended to be her walking into the office on a sunny day, or getting coffee at the weekend, shots of the river, or the rain if she missed the bus. They were the bits that had made her years in Paris so popular: trawling vintage markets; photos of people shopping.

Twisting around to lie across her duvet, Hallie's voice ringing in her head, Rosie clicked on the photos, organising them into folders. They'd been out together looking at a property the month before, and had popped in for coffee to a hotel with the most amazing staircase. Rosie had taken videos and photos that she hadn't got around to posting yet. It was an incredible building: the whole hallway had been constructed in rich ochre and sandy-coloured marble, with black marble pillars. The floor's elaborate zodiac mosaic looked amazing from upstairs, and there was even a bronze dragon on one of the staircase finials whose twin had been on the *Titanic* itself. The *Titanic*'s last stop before it sailed across the Atlantic had been Cobh in Cork, not far from home, so it all dovetailed perfectly for her account.

Rosie added a photo of Marmalade to the folder – lying on her windowsill like a giant draught excluder. Pigeons washing in the water feature in Russell Square. Lots of cups of coffee. Marmalade on her purple armchair. Hallie was right: she should schedule a few and post with a London location, making sure they were vague enough to look real. And Michael loved Marmalade.

Pulling her pillow under her, Rosie found the last of the videos she'd taken in the hotel. She was saving them as an email notification came in from an address she didn't recognise. *Corvus Books*. For a moment Rosie's stomach sank; was this new hell from Michael? Holding her breath, she opened her Gmail and clicked on the message.

Someone from Corvus Books wanted to talk to her about her Instagram posts and her stalking experience – about the stories that had been shared on her account. *Was this for real?* She googled the sender – a Sarah Hodgson, Publisher. Her profile came up immediately on LinkedIn. She read the email again. It sounded as if Sarah was offering her a book deal. *For real?* Rosie sighed. Any other time, she knew she would have been intrigued by this – wildly excited, in fact – but she really didn't have the headspace to think about it at that moment.

Replying quickly, thanking Sarah for her email, Rosie said she'd need time to consider the proposal and she'd get back in touch in due course. She hit *send* just as a WhatsApp message came through from Grace.

> We're all booked!! We're on the 10.03 from Paddington tomorrow. I've got the tickets. I'm packing now so meet you in Leon upstairs in Paddington at 9.15 and we can stock up on snacks? The train gets to Redruth just after 2.30 – there's a taxi booked to meet us. We should get to the house before 4, even allowing for delays. Unfort he didn't book us first class 😟 😂

Grace's excitement was infectious. A bit of Rosie was relieved that she was seeing this as a fun holiday, rather than Rosie running away to the other end of the country to hide, so she could get back a tiny grain of her sanity.

Because that's exactly how it felt to Rosie.

But Grace needed a break, too. Her description of what had happened to Nick was horrific. Rosie was sure Grace would have terrible nightmares; her own were bad enough. Detective Sergeant Nandy's voice echoed in her head: 'The circumstances of Nick's attack do make it look like it was opportunist rather than planned, and that there was a level of anger involved. We think the assailant must have left the property immediately before Grace arrived. They might have heard her calling him, and escaped out onto Hampstead Heath.'

Rosie closed her eyes for a minute, trying to block out the memory. The fact that Nick had been approached from behind still bothered her. He wasn't the sort of guy who you could sneak up on. *But what if Grace had walked in on whoever it was? What would have happened then?*

Rosie didn't want to think about that.

Returning to Instagram, she chose a video of the apartment Hallie was showing in Chelsea, typed up her text and, carefully selecting the location, hit *post*.

 **rosiesparislife**

[image: living room of a period apartment in Cheyne Walk overlooking Chelsea Embankment Gardens, London, a cream brocade sofa faces a glass coffee table. Beyond it is a white marble fireplace with a period mirror above. It's a light airy living room, cosy in winter.]

Hey everyone, I know a lot of you came here originally to see the gorgeous properties I work with, and it's been a while since I've shown you anything new. But today I've been to this beautiful apartment, and I just had to share it. I'm ridiculously excited to be hosting an open viewing here at the end of the week, and I've taken some exclusive shots of the main rooms so you can get a look inside.

But seriously, I'm obsessed – this four-bedroom, three-bathroom apartment is over 100 years old, and it has the most stunning period details. At just over 2,000 square feet, it's been fully restored to the highest standard, with white Carrara marble counters in the kitchen and the most dreamy master bathroom with a huge waterfall shower. The main reception room has sash windows and a white marble fireplace with an original tiled surround, plus space for at least two sofas and a baby grand piano. Bi-fold doors open up the dining area with plenty of room for a table for twelve. And there's a hidden door into the family kitchen, and chef's kitchen. Whether it's the whole family for Sunday lunch,

Christmas lunch or a dinner party, this is an apartment you can *really* entertain in. And talking of secret doors, there's a book-lined study with a hidden entrance into the family kitchen for those midnight snacks. Even if you're working late, we've got you covered.

There's a lot happening in my life, as you know, but anyone who has followed me for a while knows my real passion is beautiful property – and I can't wait to show this one. In case any of you are worried, you have to register to view and I won't be on my own. Apartments like this are built with the owners' personal security in mind. I'll be completely safe.

Property Features:

Four bedrooms
Three bathrooms
Double reception room
Balconies
Lift
Porter
Vaults
Communal gardens
River views

This is the perfect London location, with a guide price of £4,550,000.

Get in touch with the office @Sterling&CoPrime to book, and I'll show you around!

#primeproperty #Chelsea #entertainment #dinner #periodproperty #Edwardian #Londonviews #LondonLiving

Chapter 41

'YOU'RE LATE, WHERE'VE you been?' Ben stuck his head out of the kitchen as Hallie pushed the front door closed behind her.

'I went for a walk.'

He looked at her quizzically. 'It's past six. I got home early, I thought you'd like the company.'

'Sorry, I turned my phone off. I needed some air and some headspace. I popped into the National Theatre on the way back to check what's on next week.' Hallie wasn't about to tell him she'd been pacing up and down the river walk outside, trying to figure out how she was going to ask him about the Sterling & Co Instagram account.

Part of her hoped that when she mentioned it, he'd look incredibly guilty or confess straight away, but Ben had got to where he was today because he was a good salesman. He could be very persuasive.

Hallie glanced around the circular white marble-floored hallway, trying to find her words, but all it did was reinforce what she'd been thinking. You didn't get to live in an apartment like this without cutting a few corners. Would he seriously have compromised her by getting into the Instagram account, though? She thought he loved her. She definitely loved him, but it came down to trust. If she couldn't trust him, they had no future together. It was as simple as that.

And the thought of that was breaking her heart.

'Are you coming in, or planning to stay there all night?'

Hallie slipped off her leather jacket and pulled a hanger from the coat stand to hang it up.

'Coming in, I think. Are you cooking?'

He grinned, a boyish twinkle in his eye. 'I sure am. Monkfish with tomato, ginger and garlic, grilled vegetables, and those baby potatoes you like. Crème brûlée for pud.'

Hallie felt her eyes prick with tears. *He was so perfect. Could this be any more difficult?*

'Come on – wine's chilled.' He vanished inside the kitchen.

Hallie pushed herself off the door. She was just going to have to come out with it.

'Ben, I need to talk to you.' She followed him into the kitchen, her wedge heels squeaking on the floor. She normally kicked her boots off by the door, but the extra height gave her a bit of authority – or felt as if it did, anyway – and she needed every advantage she could get.

Ben handed her a huge glass of white wine. Taking it, Hallie took a sip. It was her favourite. Inside, she cringed. 'I need to talk to you about Sterling's.'

He grinned gleefully at her. 'I heard Yaraslava was picked up by the police today, to "help with enquiries".'

Hallie looked at him, confused. 'I only spoke to her this morning. She didn't mention anything.'

'It was this afternoon. I think she's still there. They aren't buying her alibi.'

Hallie frowned. 'I don't understand. How …? Why would she need an alibi? Yaraslava … Are you sure?'

Ben cleared his throat and went over to the hob, quickly lifting the lid on a pan and checking the contents, releasing a delicious waft of garlic in the process. He picked up his wine and took a slug.

'Oh, I'm very sure. I heard her fingerprints were on the murder weapon.'

Hallie felt her mouth fall open. 'How? And how do you know? What's going on, Ben?' Suddenly she wondered why he was cooking on a Monday evening. What did he have to say to her that might need her to be softened up by one of his amazing dinners?

He leaned on the counter, his face clouding, and took another sip of his wine. 'There's some stuff I need to tell you. I should have told you before, but there never seemed to be a good moment.'

'About Sterling's?'

Here it was. Whatever the news was, she knew it was going to be terrible.

He nodded. 'More precisely, about Yaraslava.'

Hallie cocked an eyebrow. 'I know you can't stand her, but … how do you know she's at the police station? That's mad. Do they think she killed Nick?'

She pulled out one of the white leather stools tucked under the island and sat down heavily. She was going to need this wine. She reached for the bottle to top up her glass.

Ben hadn't answered her, but she could feel him studying her.

'You know I love you, don't you, Hals? Like … properly. No messing. I want—'

Hallie held up her hand. If he was going to propose now, it really wasn't the time.

'Tell me about Yaraslava. I want to hear everything.'

Leaning against the counter, he shuffled and crossed his arms across his chest. It took him a minute to find the words. A minute in which Hallie felt her world begin to spiral.

'You know she used to work for me?'

'Obviously. She hates you, too, you know. She's always going on about Hunt's taking Sterling's business.'

He nodded slowly. 'Part of that is because we had a bit of a thing. Obviously on the quiet. It doesn't do to go around sleeping with your staff.'

Hallie's eyebrows shot up. She knew Yaraslava had left Hunt's because of a row, but she'd never been able to find out what it had been about.

'The thing is … Well, two things. The first is that she's insanely jealous – she has to be in control of everything. That's … Well, I can tell you more about that another time, but the second thing is that she attacked me.' He paused, but Hallie wasn't about to fill the silence. She wanted to hear this. 'She came over after work and … Well, she just went nuts. She'd seen me with this client – I went to school with her, for God's sake, but Yaraslava didn't know that. Alicia had called into the office while I was out and said something to her. Anyway, Yaraslava thought me and Alicia were having a fling.'

Ben took a large sip of his wine and then, remembering the pan behind him, twisted around to turn it down. Turning to Hallie, his eyes locked on hers, his face full of pain. 'Honestly, I thought she was going to kill me.' He cleared his throat, swirling the wine around his glass. 'I know about her getting taken in today because, that night, I had to call the police. She grabbed this wine bottle and belted me with it, broke my jaw. They arrested her and I went off to hospital. When they finally let me out, I came home, but I didn't press charges.'

'That was the row that made her leave Hunt's?'

He nodded. 'My case officer warned me it could happen again. They keep all the records in a case like that, even though I didn't want to take it further.' He raised his eyebrows. 'So when they did a check on the fingerprints on the bit of rock that had been used to bash Nick, hers came up. My guess is they thought she *had* done it again – gone off on one, I mean – and walloped Nick like she did me.'

'Jesus Christ. Do you think she was seeing Nick?'

'I've no idea. I mean, he was a bit young for her, but … Anyway, the point is that I would love you to stop working there, but I can't give you a job at Hunt's because—'

'I know. It would mess things up, working together, living together. Sleeping with the boss isn't a good look …'

'That aside, if I did, I'd be terrified Yaraslava might come after *you*.'

How it ends ...

Chapter 42

THE ONE THING Rosie hadn't taken into account in this whole 'getting to Cornwall undercover' expedition was her lovely suitcase.

She'd woken up for the first day in weeks feeling lighter, a glimmer of excitement flickering at the prospect of an uninterrupted week away, without the fear of what stunt Michael might pull next. She'd made sure Marmalade wasn't hiding anywhere in her flat and watered her plants. After double-locking her front door, she'd carried her suitcase down the many flights of stairs, trying not to bump it off the walls and wake up the two Davids en route.

It was when she got to the passage/hallway and had her hand on the actual front door that she'd realised, if Michael was watching, he'd see the case and know she was going somewhere. She closed her eyes, part of her kicking herself, the other part trying to come up with a plan. Fast.

Just because she was bringing a suitcase with her didn't mean she was going on holiday. She could be going to a conference, *or* she might *not* be going away at all. *Perhaps* the case was full of antique books and old photographs – or something – for staging at the apartment in Cheyne Walk.

Things to make it look welcoming.

Ridiculous but plausible. *Maybe*, with a bit of work.

Rosie had planned to leave early to meet Grace so she could mingle with the morning rush hour and, if Michael was following her, hopefully lose him.

And if he followed her all the way to Paddington? Why would she be going to Paddington? As she leaned on the inside of the front door, Rosie's mind whirred. Why hadn't she thought of this before?

Perhaps she was meeting someone there who was giving her something for staging in the Chelsea apartment. Rosie closed one eye and grimaced as she thought about it. It sounded mad, but it might work. As with anything, it was about doing it with confidence. Make the story sound right and people would believe you.

Rosie sighed. It was a plan of sorts. She'd work out the details on the way. Hauling open the front door, she stepped outside.

Predictably, Paddington Station was heaving with people. It was a huge station, with a double curved glass roof a bit like St Pancras, but lower, and it wasn't nearly as elegant. And, Rosie realised, as she took the escalator up from the Underground and headed briskly through the huge arched main doors, Paddington Station's shape was what led to the chaos.

St Pancras had always been her favourite station in London: she just adored that you could get on a train in Paris, get off in the centre of London, go and see a show, and get the train home the next day. And you arrived into a beautiful building. The red-brick St Pancras Hotel, with its Gothic arches and unbelievable staircase – the one the Spice Girls had used in their video – was at one end, its bedroom windows overlooking the concourse and a massive bronze statue of two lovers meeting. More importantly, St Pancras had a long concourse where travellers could browse designer boutiques or stop to randomly play the piano, all in a straight line.

Paddington, by contrast, had a broad rectangular concourse with a shopping centre and loads of food places and shops at the rear, and the platforms at the front. It meant everyone was constantly criss-crossing backwards and forwards and falling over one another trying to get from the loos to the platform, or to coffee, or to the Underground.

All of this was going through Rosie's head as she navigated to the rear of the station, and the lift leading to the restaurant Grace had suggested meeting in. Her eyes darting, Rosie could feel all her senses on full alert as she searched for faces she might recognise – one face that she might have seen somewhere else.

Heading for the lift doors, Rosie glanced over her shoulder, scanning the crowd. She knew she stood out with this case, even with her navy beanie pulled over her hair and the long stripy scarf in revolting leprechaun colours that Eoin had given her – the least Rosie-like thing she owned – although the scarf probably made her stand out even more. She just hoped she looked enough like someone else to confuse Michael. She'd pulled the beanie on as she'd got off the bus, adding the scarf when she'd changed trains. She had her fingers crossed that it was enough.

Halfway across the concourse, Rosie spotted a tall blond guy in shorts holding a bunch of flowers, and her stomach flipped. He looked very familiar.

Over six feet tall and angular, he was gazing at the departures board, looking sort of uncomfortable. Acne peppered his cheeks, and his bleach-blond hair was cropped around the sides and tousled on the top. Rosie stopped dead and someone coming up behind bumped straight into her.

'I'm so sorry.'

Hauling her case to the end of the bank of chairs at right angles to the shops, she hovered, pretending to look in her bag at the same time as taking a surreptitious look at the stranger.

She felt her phone vibrate with a message. Was that Grace, or …?

But the guy with the flowers wasn't looking at his phone. And then she realised where she'd seen him before. He was a model who had a YouTube channel and Instagram account she followed. She'd seen him in the Place Vendôme once, when she'd been on the way to meet a client at the Ritz Hotel.

Rosie let out a breath.

This was mad. The sooner she got to Cornwall, the better.

 **rosiesparislife**

[image: vintage books piled up on an antique Regency style chaise with a silver cocktail shaker, a black marble case clock with a gold dial and a marble solitaire game. A Victorian round mirror with a heavy gold, bow detail, frame is standing up behind the items.]

I know this photo isn't up to my usual standard, but that's because what I actually have with me today is a secret! One of the things I love most about showing a new home is getting it to look perfect for prospective buyers.

The sellers' taste may not be anything like my clients', so it's important a house looks neutral, and that often involves staging. I've packed up my trusty ice-blue Samsonite with some beautiful things to add a cosy aesthetic to the apartment in Cheyne Walk. It's already stunning, with the most incredible views over Chelsea Embankment Gardens, but tiny touches help a buyer imagine themselves living in the property, and the minute someone can see themselves in situ, I know I'll get an offer.

It's always attention to detail that makes a difference – in everything in life. As you can tell, I'm super-excited about this property! If I had £4.5 million spare, I'd be buying it like a shot. It really is perfect in every way.

Get in touch with the office if you'd like to view it. I always recommend seeing a property at different times of the day, but the evening is best. When we're looking at property, we sometimes forget that it's actually the evening when we want to relax, and that's the time to check out the views, see what the lighting is like, and get a real feel for what it would be like to live there.

And in case you're wondering, yes, Michael is still in the picture. If you're reading this, Michael, I've got a busy week ahead and Sterling & Co have arranged extra security so I won't be on my own for one minute. Look out for the huge guys in the black suits – they'll be looking for you.

#primeproperty #lookslikehome #makeanoffer #chelsea #security #stalker

Chapter 43

ROSIE WAS ON her second cup of coffee when Grace appeared, pulling her suitcase and looking flushed.

'What's with the post about staging at Cheyne Walk?' Before Rosie could answer, Grace continued. 'This place is mad. Where's everyone going?'

Rosie smiled up at her. Grace had her highlighted hair pulled up in a gold clip, and was wearing an awesome bright red duffel coat and hiking boots that looked very new. Rosie had picked a table where she could clearly see the door, and had spotted Grace weaving her way across the mezzanine level a few minutes earlier.

'It feels like everyone is on the move, I know. Sit down, you look exhausted and we haven't started yet.' Rosie indicated the seat in front of her. 'I did the post for Michael. I suddenly realised that if he was watching for me to leave my house, then he'd see the suitcase and might think I was going away.'

'Oh God, you're right.' Grace threw her handbag onto the seat closest to the wall and pulled her wheeled suitcase in under the table beside Rosie's. 'Do you think he's actually watching the house? I never thought about that before, but he definitely seems to know a lot about how you get to work. That's super-creepy, isn't it?'

Rosie didn't need telling. It was one of the worst parts of all of this, and why she'd been living in the dark for the past how-ever-many weeks. Too many – that was for sure.

'You need a coffee. Let me get it.' Rosie stood up. 'For all I know, he could work in one of the buildings across the road. Maybe his office looks right out at my house. Hopefully, if he did see it, he thinks the suitcase is for work now, so I don't have to worry so much about him appearing on the train.'

Grace shivered. 'Jaysus, that would be awful. Could you imagine if he sat down next to us and tried to make conversation for hours?'

Rosie couldn't, and she definitely didn't want to go there.

Grace sat down and leaned over to look at the menu board above the counter. Rosie was about to put her phone away when she saw another email had arrived from Corvus Books. Clicking it open, she saw that Sarah Hodgson was back, offering her money this time. A lot of money. *Rosie hadn't even spoken to her yet.* Rosie closed her email. This could definitely wait. She didn't have space in her head to get to grips with it. Maybe Sarah was real, or maybe she was some friend of Michael's and this was a new level of craziness.

'Cappuccino, oat milk?'

Grace grinned. 'Perfect.'

'I'm sorry, I think those are our seats.' Ahead of Rosie, Grace was looking at whoever was sitting in their reserved seats with raised eyebrows and using her firm voice.

Behind her in the carriage, Rosie couldn't see who Grace was talking to, but she definitely wouldn't want to mess with Grace when she was being firm about anything.

An American voice responded. 'They've cancelled all the seat reservations because the train before this one was cancelled. It's every man for himself.'

Rosie could feel Grace gearing up for a stinging reply, but leaning forward, she tweaked the sleeve of Grace's coat.

'There are two here.'

She indicated the opposite side of the aisle. Two young lads who looked as if they were in their twenties were siting opposite each other, a bag of beer cans on the table between them. The two seats next to them, perhaps predictably, were empty.

Grace turned around and indicated the seat closest to her. 'Are these taken?'

The two lads shook their heads and Grace grinned, hoisting her case up onto the overhead luggage rack with ease.

She reached for Rosie's case and, a moment later, was wriggling the two cases so they sat snugly side by side. Rosie sat down, surprised. Her case weighed a ton, and Grace didn't look as if she could lift something that heavy so easily. But perhaps she worked out and hadn't mentioned it. She was miles taller than Rosie, so that helped, but still.

'Thanks so much, I didn't realise you were superhuman.' Rosie sat down and pulled her handbag onto her knee.

'I have many hidden skills …' Grace reached for her own bag. 'Including the curation of a snacks stash that will make this trip much more bearable.' She pulled a Tesco carrier bag from her huge handbag and opened it to show Rosie several bags of crisps with distinctive red and blue packaging.

Rosie's eyes widened. 'Tayto? Where did you find those in London? I thought I'd have to go home to get some decent crisps. I haven't seen those anywhere.'

Grace laughed and threw a packet at her. 'I'm multi-talented – what can I say?'

Chapter 44

BEN SAT DOWN on the bed beside Hallie, slipping her cup of tea onto the bedside table. He'd used her mug, a giant cream china one with 'Joy' written in a tasteful grey script on the side.

He yawned as he spoke. 'I need to get moving, it'll be lunchtime at this rate before I get in.'

Grinning, she pulled him towards her. 'Don't you think Hunt's can manage without you for a morning?'

He kissed her and pulled away. 'I'm sure the ship won't sink, but—'

'But nothing, Ben Hunt. You're the boss, you can go in when it suits you. Do you have a meeting?'

He smiled and shook his head. He'd put on a freshly ironed white shirt, the heavy cotton woven into stripes, open at the neck. With khaki slacks and the heavy brown leather belt she'd given him for Christmas, he looked delicious. She peeped over the side of the bed. He had a thing about crazy socks; today's were khaki with ducks on them, their orange beaks bright against the green.

Smiling, she reached out to grab his hand. 'The ducks are cute.' She sighed. 'I can't stay now, you know – at Sterling's, I mean. I couldn't work with Yaraslava. It's bad enough her thinking Hunt's are into some sort of corporate espionage, but …' She leaned back. 'Knowing what she did to you, and wondering if she was involved in what happened to Nick, I don't think I could ever want to be in the same room as her again.'

He nodded slowly. 'I should have told you before.' He cleared his throat. 'The thing is, there's more.'

She froze, looking at him hard. She'd wanted to talk about this the night before, but he'd steered her away from the subject, as if he wasn't ready. They'd ended up talking about where to go on holiday. 'More?'

He grimaced. 'The reason she left Hunt's.'

'She broke your jaw.' Hallie could feel her eyebrows rising.

Ben cleared his throat. 'She did, but that wasn't the actual reason she walked out.' He paused. 'I don't have any real proof, so this has to stay between us. Like, seriously.'

Hallie didn't think her eyebrows could go any higher. Leaning on the pillow, she let him speak. It took him a moment to find the words.

'You know how Yaraslava's Russian?'

'Belarusian, but go on.'

'They share national characteristics when it comes to amassing wealth. The point is that Yaraslava has a lot of big money Russian buyers in her little black book. Belarusian or not, they all seem to be connected to shelf companies. There are names attached to them, the only one I remember was a woman called Irina, but essentially they are the sort of businesses that are owned by other shelf companies registered in Switzerland, the Virgin Islands or the Caymans …' He drew in a breath. 'Or all of them. They are the type of companies that are set up to launder money around the world.'

Hallie frowned. 'But we check – and report anything suspicious. The NCA is super-hot on dirty money. It's a massive issue with property – and superyachts, come to that.'

'That's what the row was about – the one when she actually left. Obviously, we weren't seeing each other by then, but she was still working for Hunt's. We had some super-prime properties go through Hunt's, several well over ten million each – well over – and she didn't raise any concerns about the vendors or the purchasers. She didn't even seem to look closely at them.'

'Oh.'

Ben nodded. 'I couldn't risk the company I'd built being used by criminals to clean up their drug money, or wherever it came from. I asked her about it and she walked out.' He sighed. 'It was actually a bit more spectacular than that. This is Yaraslava we're talking about.' He pulled a face as if he had a particularly bad taste in his mouth. 'The deals had all been done by then. It was a penthouse in Greenwich that alerted me. I was looking for something else and I came across the paperwork. It was owned by a company called Landmark. I recognised the names – Landmark and this Irina woman. When I checked back, I realised they'd been involved in a whole load of deals, buying and selling.' He rubbed his face. 'I challenged Yaraslava on it and … Well, you know the rest. She walked out and went to work for Sebastian.'

'You think she's involved with this company, or getting a kickback or something?' Hallie looked at him. The name Irina sounded familiar, but the thought of Yaraslava and Ben together was crowding her mind, making it hard to concentrate.

Ben glanced at her and then at his hands. He had them clasped tightly in his lap, a sign Hallie recognised. She could see that admitting knowing all this was causing him huge stress. He nodded slowly. 'If she's acting for the buyer and the seller, and getting a kickback from one of them, plus the commission, that's an awful lot of money. She's a very wealthy woman.' Ben looked at her. 'Crime is pretty lucrative.'

Hallie shifted against the pillow. 'I can't believe it. Do you think Sebastian knows?'

Ben rolled his eyes. 'I think Sebastian is a bit dazzled by her, to be honest. Most men are. She's like a black widow, she pulls unsuspecting males into her web.'

Hallie couldn't resist a wry grin. 'That's exactly what she's like. She came into the office the other day in a full-length black fur coat. She looked like Cruella de Vil. Have you had any comeback on those properties – the ones she sold?'

'No, thank God. I probably should report them, but honestly, I don't know what sort of people she's dealing with. Well, I can imagine. And obviously they'd know it was me that filed the Suspicious Activity Report. Even if I don't do that and call the National Crime Agency, she'll know it was me.'

'And she's already broken your jaw.'

His eyes widened. 'Indeed.'

'I think you've done the right thing. I mean, she left, so you didn't have to fire her, and what's done is done. Hallie grimaced. 'There's nothing you can do about those sales that have already gone through and, honestly, I couldn't bear it if anything happened to you.' She reached out to rub his hands, still clasped together, putting her own hand protectively over them.

He grinned sheepishly and leaned over to give her a kiss. As he pulled away, Hallie froze. Suddenly all the dots were beginning to join up.

'What?' Sensing a change in her, Ben looked puzzled.

Hallie scrunched up her face, wincing at the realisation that had hit her.

'The woman who is selling Park House is Russian, and I think her name might be Irina. And I have a feeling it's owned by a company called Landmark. Could Yaraslava be doing it again?'

Ben glanced at her, worry etched into his frown lines. 'It sounds like it – and Nick …'

'Maybe Nick realised, and he got caught in the crossfire.'

Chapter 45

'I THINK I NEED to stretch.' Rosie extended her back while trying to stay in her seat and not disturb the lad next to her, who had been nodding since Exeter. They'd shed their coats about an hour into the trip, and Grace had rolled them up and put them on the overhead luggage rack between their cases, but Rosie still felt a bit sticky.

'My brother Fiacra says if you're travelling for over three hours, it turns into an endurance test. I think I believe him now.' Rosie looked across the carriage to the seats they should have been sitting in. The Americans were obviously going the full distance, too, but were on the right side of the train to get the best view of the landscape. Annoying.

'What does he do – your brother? Does he travel a lot?' Grace unscrewed the lid of the water she'd brought and, taking a sip, grimaced. 'Warm.'

The whole carriage was warm – stuffy, too. But Rosie reckoned they were lucky; the passengers from the cancelled train had all joined this one and it was packed. There were people crammed into the spaces between the carriages and, since they'd left Exeter, standing in the aisles. Down beside the loo, Rosie had seen a girl curled up on her rucksack, asleep on the floor. She couldn't imagine anything worse.

Answering Grace, Rosie leaned back in her seat. 'Fiacra's in RTE most of the time. He's a producer. He actually works for an independent company, but RTE buys most of their programmes, so it's like he works for them, really. And my other brother Eoin's in New York, doing something I don't fully understand in financial consultancy. His company basically rescues companies in trouble, or does their best to.'

'Wow, everyone in your family is super-successful. Does your dad run a company or something?'

Rosie shook her head. 'He left us when I was fourteen. He's, as my mam says, "an utter waster". She's a midwife. I think that's where we get the work ethic from – the boys at least. She was always working, or having to vanish if there was an emergency.'

'And you? Don't you think you've got it, too?'

'Me?' Rosie looked surprised. 'I suppose so, but I don't really think selling houses is work. I love it. I'd probably do it for free if someone was happy to cover my rent and bills.' She grinned. 'And Instagram … Well, that's not proper work, is it? Delivering babies in the middle of the night and saving people's lives is work.'

Grace nodded slowly. 'It definitely is.'

'Have you got any brothers and sisters?'

Grace shook her head. 'I'm the one and only. Which is great, but can be a bit stifling sometimes. My mum doesn't work, so when she's not playing golf she wants to know exactly what I'm doing.'

Rosie smiled. 'We had the opposite problem. We had to take care of ourselves, pretty much, but Fiacra's six years older than me, so he's quite responsible. I'm closest with Eoin, there's only a couple of years between us, and then Conor is the baby. I think he was an accident.'

'Sounds fun having siblings, though.'

Rosie nodded. 'Yeah. We sort of needed each other, though. My dad was utterly useless. He supposedly drove a taxi, but when he did live with us, it spent most of its time in our drive. I think he was allergic to actual work.'

'You turned out OK, though. Look how successful you are. You've got a gorgeous flat, everyone loves you,

you're thin and pretty.' Grace put a half joking emphasis on 'thin', but for a second Rosie wasn't sure if she was joking. Then she saw Grace smiling.

'I'm not sure about thin, and I'm not tall like you.' Rosie paused. 'And popularity isn't all it's cracked up to be. It attracts the wrong sort of attention, too.' She glanced anxiously up and down the carriage. She'd searched every face when they'd sat down and, satisfied that there didn't look like anyone who might be Michael within listening distance, had begun to relax a bit. Not that she had any idea what Michael looked like, but from his voice messages she sort of guessed that he was young enough, ordinary, not super-posh and probably professional.

And she couldn't see anyone like that in this carriage, thank God.

Rosie bent down to reach for her own water, trying to hide the tears pricking at her eyes. She had no idea why she was tearful now. Perhaps she was just exhausted; she'd had so little sleep since Saturday, when Grace had come around to tell her about Nick.

Sitting up with her water bottle in her hand, Rosie unscrewed the lid. 'You're doing so well at Sterling's, though, Yaraslava thinks you're amazing.'

As if she didn't want to take the compliment, Grace suddenly looked out of the window. 'I think we're nearly there. Will we wake these two up?'

Both of the lads beside them – when they'd finished talking loudly about a holiday in Ibiza and a friend of theirs who had no friends – had fallen into an alcohol-induced sleep and had been snoring for what felt like about a hundred miles.

Rosie rolled her eyes. 'I'd hate to wake them. But doesn't the train go on for miles after Truro?'

Grace nodded, her eyes full of mischief. 'To Penzance. And I bet it goes back to London then. They might not make their night out after all.'

'Is Redruth like Party Central then?'

'I've no idea. I don't think it's like Manchester or somewhere, that's for sure. I've never been to Cornwall, but I did a load of googling about this place we're going to. The house is magnificent, and there's a village less than a ten-minute walk inland – mainly tourist stuff, but coffee shops and pasty shops …'

'I've never had a Cornish pasty. I follow this guy from Cornwall on Insta and he swears by them.'

'I've heard they are delicious.' Grace grinned. 'The house itself is only a few minutes from the sea. It's really rocky, but there's a bit of a beach. You just have to walk down miles.'

'It sounds very picture postcard'

'It looks it. There's a cafe–restaurant, an art gallery, and a cute shop that has a famous – well, Instagram famous – seagull called Bob.'

Rosie grinned. 'It sounds perfect.' As long as there was no sign of Michael, it would be perfect, but she didn't say that bit.

Chapter 46

YARASLAVA FELT HER phone vibrate in the zip pocket of her fleece as she power-walked along the tarmacked road that wrapped around the edge of Richmond Park. She ignored it.

She needed to think.

There were lots of urgent reasons she should check her texts – too many – but she needed some headspace.

Ahead of her the road was empty, the lush grass borders on either side merging into patches of ferns and then giant oak trees. She didn't usually walk here during the week, and marvelled at the peace: the lack of cyclists in their racing Lycra who seemed to consider that this was their territory at the weekends. She could see a herd of deer wandering across her path. She slowed, letting them meander on their way.

A movement to her right made her start – a flash of red as a fox wove through the tall grass. That's what she needed now: long grass to hide in while safely watching everything unfold.

She hated not knowing what was going on. Since she'd left Belarus, she'd planned every minute of her life. If she was doing a deal, she thought out every single possible outcome and the consequences, always looking ahead so nothing could surprise her.

She didn't do surprises.

Thankfully, when Dimitri had confirmed she was with him on Saturday morning, the police had released her. Her explanation for her fingerprints being on the murder weapon had been logical and convincing enough. They'd turned up the next day to ask her a load more questions, and suggested she go to the station with them. Being questioned in an interview room hadn't been her idea of fun at all. In the end, her lawyer had persuaded them she was a model citizen. You got what you paid for in this life, and he was *very* expensive. But it had started her thinking. Despite what she'd said to Dimitri, London wasn't feeling like the safest place in the world at the moment.

And she knew explaining what was going on to Sebastian would require a whole different level of storytelling. Part of her was still hoping that she wouldn't have to get into any of that, that something would happen to save her. But it didn't change the fact that if there was a trial and they produced the piece of ornamental stone used to batter Nick's brains into the pale oak floor at Park House, Sebastian would recognise it. And he wouldn't be the only one.

Serpentine stone was only found in three places in the world, and one of them was a twenty-square-mile outcrop at the end of the Lizard peninsula in Cornwall. About a three-minute walk from Sebastian's summer house.

And if photos of the crime scene were made available, they'd reveal the distinctive paintings on the walls of the living room by a Cornish artist – an artist Sebastian had introduced her to, who sold his work in the gallery on Lizard Point.

Nick and Grace hadn't made the connection, but she was pretty sure Hallie and Rosie paid attention to their environment, and would see the similarity between the paintings in Park House and the painting on her office wall.

Not that it was her employees who she was worried about.

Yaraslava sighed. Making a house look comfortable was key to getting a sale, and when she'd first viewed it,

Park House had been a rental, the rooms designed to be a neutral blank canvas. That was fine if you had a bit of imagination, but from Hallie's feedback on the Bradfords' viewings, Yaraslava had known they'd need a bit of help seeing themselves as residents in Park House. And she needed them to see themselves living there, so she could seal this deal and get the Grigori brothers sorted.

Mikhail Grigori. The name echoed in her mind as she picked up her pace. The deer ahead of her had moved on and the road stretched out like a runway, long and smooth. One that she could take off from or crash-land on.

But crash-landing wasn't an option.

She'd survived moving to London, living in a hellhole of a single room, buying her clothes in charity shops, doing everything she could to make connections and build her reputation. She felt her heart rate quicken and tried to push the memories from her mind.

It was cold; mist still hung in pockets around the trees, ephemeral and mysterious. Yaraslava had read that these oaks had been here for hundreds of years, imagined that they had breathed in the emotions of all the people who had come here, listening to their dramas as they unfolded around them. She could imagine the stories captured in their gnarly bark, the secrets they'd heard.

She'd survived before and she'd survive again. She just needed to figure out what was going on and outsmart whoever was behind it.

Dimitri had laughed at her when she'd said she thought she could do better than the police. But she had more information than they did. She knew the moves going on behind the scenes. The hard bit was figuring out the 'why' and the 'what next'.

Because she had a pretty good idea of the 'who'.

Mikhail Grigori.

Were the Grigoris finding new ways to pile on the pressure? Did they want to ruin her because she'd tied up their money for too long? Perhaps they were under pressure themselves, for some reason. Now that was a new thought.

Yaraslava felt the breeze pick up, the trees around her rustling their agreement. Perhaps this *was* all about the Grigoris sending her a warning. They couldn't afford for her to get hit by a car or fall off a building, because then they'd never get their money. She was the one who had set up the companies they filtered their cash through; she was vital in the chain.

And they knew her well enough to know that she didn't scare.

But attacking the people around her, the team she'd nurtured and built ... That would affect her.

Not that the Grigoris were her immediate problem. She'd find the cash. Her Swiss account had a very healthy balance, but she didn't want to reveal that to anyone – the Grigoris, Dimitri or anyone else – and moving money quickly sent up red flags across the banking system. That was her last resort.

First, she had to work out how to break it to Sebastian that they needed to come up with a plan to explain the presence of the paintings and the ornament used to kill Nick at Park House. Either one on its own wouldn't be significant, but the two together could raise questions.

And there was only one person who might link those items to Sebastian and, in turn, to Yaraslava. She certainly hadn't even considered the potential fallout when she'd moved the pieces from the property she was currently living in. But Sebastian had his own secrets, and one of them was their relationship.

His wife had long ago tired of going to the house in Cornwall; she was far happier at their villa in Cannes, which was why Hawksmoor was a safe place for Yaraslava.

But his wife's money, family and connections had helped Sebastian get to where he was now, and a divorce that called into question his trustworthiness could be catastrophic for the business. A business they both needed to preserve.

Was she being paranoid? Yaraslava rubbed her face, her cheeks cold in the damp air of the park. Would Sebastian's wife really connect the dots? She'd dropped hints to Sebastian in the past, making snide comments about Yaraslava. So it felt likely. Too likely.

Which brought Yaraslava back around to the 'why'. The Instagram hack, terrorising Rosie, and now Nick's murder: they were all attacks that threatened the business, but also her own position.

Was someone trying to destroy her personally, by framing her?

Chapter 47

HAWKSMOOR WAS A rambling dark grey stone house, with what appeared to be a two-storey glass extension on the seaward side. Looking up at it, Rosie couldn't quite work out which was the main aspect. It had twin gables; the door was a huge wooden affair flanked by pillars, which looked more like it belonged in a church than a domestic property. Not that there was much domestic about this house. It was hotel-like in its grandeur, with thick ivy growing up the three storeys to the slate roof.

It was very impressive.

Getting out of the taxi, Rosie turned and exchanged glances with Grace as she went to the boot and lifted out both their cases, glancing along the car to see if the taxi driver was planning to get out. He'd met them at the station, but it had quickly become evident he didn't seem to know how his windscreen demister worked – or his speedometer, come to that. An hour on the twisting narrow Cornish roads had felt like an actual lifetime.

The driver had opened his door when they pulled up, but seemed to be on the phone now.

'I hope he doesn't expect a tip.' Wheeling her own case, Grace pushed Rosie's towards her.

As they stood looking at the house, the wind picked up and Rosie shivered, pulling her scarf up.

'All OK there?' The driver's voice brought Rosie back to the car. He'd rolled down his window, but didn't wait for them to answer. Instead, he swung the car around the huge gravelled turning circle.

As if someone inside had been watching, the front door opened and a young woman in jeans and a bright stripy sweater skipped down the steps and grabbed their cases. She had her dark hair in a practical ponytail, and looked to Rosie to be about the same age as them.

'Welcome – I'm Anja. Come inside, I've got the fire lit for you.'

The house was perfect inside, the exact opposite of the chill castle-like promise of the exterior. Pale wooden floors reflected smooth walls in shades of white and cream; a huge wide wooden staircase rose on the left of the hallway like a welcome.

'Let me show you around and then I'll take you to your rooms.' Still smiling, Anja dropped their cases by the front door and, guiding them to the right, pushed open huge glazed double doors into a stunning living room. There was a massive stone fireplace at one end; a log shifted and sent a flurry of sparks up the chimney as they walked in. The wall opposite the door was part of the glass extension Rosie had seen from the outside. Sisal carpet turned to more pale floorboards in a sun lounge soaring to a mezzanine level upstairs. Rosie had shown some amazing houses in her career, but she didn't think she'd seen a living room with quite this many sofas before. There were three in the main space, and she could see another three in the sun lounge, plus an enormous old pine table that would seat a small army.

Rosie smiled across to Anja and went into the glazed area. The house was slightly elevated and surrounded by farmland. In the distance, to the left, she could see a lighthouse rising above the cliffs. Below it the land seemed to suddenly end and drop into the sea, a deep grey today. Even from here she could see the white tips of waves breaking and seagulls circling the roofs of what looked like a cluster of buildings on the cliff edge. It was so wild, for a moment Rosie's heart rose. It was like home, and right now she needed fresh air and space.

But would Michael know she was here? She'd done what Eoin had suggested and swapped the SIM in her phone – she hadn't told anyone about her new number yet, so it had been blissfully quiet on their trip down. She hadn't even given it to Grace. Sharing a house, they'd be practically joined at the hip for the next week, so she'd hardly need it.

Rosie had had her head buried in a thriller most of the way – one she'd picked up a few days before, set in Ireland. It had transported her from the cramped table and the nightmare of Michael, back to the lakes and mountains of the west coast.

She had wondered whether reading about women being murdered was a good idea, but she hadn't been able to put it down once she'd started. It was about a kick-arse forensic scientist who rebuilt faces from skulls and who had three little birds tattooed on her arm. And who loved climbing. That made them different enough for Rosie to be able to separate fact and fiction.

'This place is amazing.' Behind Rosie, Grace was talking to Anja.

'I'm so glad you like it. Sebastian has asked me to fill the fridge. Anything else you need, just text me and I'll get it delivered. If you need me to cook or change the beds, please just call. Sebastian said you'd like some peace and quiet, though.'

'Thanks so much, that sounds wonderful.' Rosie came into the main living room. 'I'd love to go for a walk before it gets dark, just down to the sea. Is it far?'

'Less than ten minutes. It gets dark about 6.30, so you've time. There are no street lights, obviously …' Anja said it a little uncertainly.

'Don't worry, I'm from the country. There are no street lights around our house in Cork.'

Anja looked relieved. 'That's good. Some city people have no idea how dark it can get here, especially when there's no moon. It's a bit damp out, but the weather's OK. When it closes in, the cliffs can be quite dangerous.'

Grace slipped off her coat. 'Are you OK going on your own, Rosie? I'd love to get some air and have a look around the garden, if that's OK, Anja? I'll just get settled first.'

Chapter 48

ROSIE PATTED HER pocket to make sure she had her phone with her as she walked down the driveway.

Swinging over the stile beside the gate, she steadied herself on the wet stones, grabbing on to a post designed to stop walkers from slipping. It was quite a drop on the other side; a series of irregular flat stones were placed like stairs down into the field.

Rosie glanced around her. From up here you could see how huge the house was. It seemed like a strange choice for Sebastian to have his holiday home here. Even as she thought about it, she could see mist hanging in pockets across the fields, could hear the waves breaking in the distance.

The light was starting to fade, but as Rosie's eyes began to adjust, she could see clearly. The field was full of sheep clustering around the drystone walls running around the house. As she climbed down the stile, one of the sheep, its coat still thick and shaggy, jumped onto the wall, baaing at her, but she wasn't worried. There were lots of sheep in Ireland, and generally speaking, they weren't the brightest creatures. If she'd been walking across a field full of cows she would have been a lot more cautious, but Rosie strode on.

Even from here she could smell the sea, feel its pull in the bite of the wind, and immediately she could feel some of her worries dissipate. There was something about being close to the ocean, away from the claustrophobic confines of tall buildings, that put things into perspective. Here the elements were your friend, but also, she knew well, your enemy.

Thoughts of friends and enemies nagged at Rosie as she climbed the next stile to the main footpath going down to the sea.

Did Michael know one of her friends? Was that how he knew so much about her? There had to be some way he was finding out the tiny details of her life.

Jumping down onto the footpath, Rosie set off towards the cliffs. The Lizard was the most southerly tip of the UK, and it was beautiful, the fields spanning out on either side of her, peppered with houses, all significantly smaller than Sebastian's. To her left she could see a long white building several storeys high that looked like a hotel, and at the end of it, the tower of the lighthouse.

Rosie was distracted by a whirring sound and, looking up, she started as she spotted a drone hovering above the field to her right. It seemed to be looking at her. Or filming her. Then its lights flashed and it shot off like something out of *Doctor Who*. She stopped walking, watching it fly across to a field closer to the lighthouse and then suddenly drop.

What the actual hell?

Was it Michael? Had he found out she was here, and now he was spying on her with a drone?

Something snapped inside Rosie and, thrusting her hands into her pockets, she strode off in the direction the drone had taken.

What did he think he was doing? How could he have followed her down here? Only a handful of people knew she and Grace were in Cornwall, and she'd only been here what felt like five minutes.

Crossing the narrow lane that swung into a field used as a car park, Rosie scanned the few vehicles parked there. And as if it was taunting her, the drone rose up again from behind a battered VW camper van, this time shooting off in the direction of the sea.

Her blood pumping, Rosie headed swiftly towards the van. Parked at right angles to the sea, the front of the vehicle facing her, it was pale blue and pink, had stickers all over the windows, and was badly in need of a paint job. It looked as if it had been new in about 1965.

As she got closer Rosie realised the rear doors were open, and below them she could just see a pair of legs in jeans and walking boots.

Swinging around the rear door of the van, the words were out of her mouth before she registered who she was talking to.

'What the hell are you doing with that? Are you spying on me?'

The man standing between the open doors physically jumped, almost dropping his control unit. At least six feet tall, he was wearing a battered brown leather flying jacket, the elbow of one sleeve ripped, an orange bandana tied around his neck. His hair, wavy and streaked with blond, was bright against a deep tan. As he recovered from the fright Rosie had given him, she realised he had very large blue eyes and was actually extraordinarily striking-looking.

And she'd seen him before.

A wave of fear hit her at the same time as a wave of adrenaline, the two smashing against each other, making her knees weak. She'd always thought she'd recognise Michael when she met him …

'What the …?' His face shocked, he turned to the drone, navigating it from wherever it had been heading to land on the scrubby grass in front of them. Rosie realised he had a tablet attached to the inside of the open door closest to him, and he had been following the camera shots. The screen was showing a video of their feet.

Relaxing, he turned to her. 'Sorry, I'm not spying on anything, just getting some footage.' He had what Rosie guessed was a local accent, tinged with a harder London edge, and he was looking at her as if she was mad.

Rosie could feel her face flaming. He definitely didn't sound like Michael. 'I'm sorry. I thought … It flashed at me – your drone did.' The words tumbled out. 'I thought it was following me. I thought *you* were following me.'

He looked at her sideways. 'Huh?'

She shook her head, embarrassed, and everything suddenly slotted into place. 'You're not Jago? From Instagram?'

He was already looking at her, his face crinkling in recognition. 'Yes … and you're RosiesParisLife?'

'Rosie. Yes, I'm Rosie. I've been following you since you were in uni in Sweden.'

A grin lit Jago's eyes. 'And I've been following you since I went to Sweden. I needed a fix of decent food, even if it was only photos. That's *so* weird – I feel like I've known you for years. What on earth are you doing here?'

What on earth, indeed …? This was weird. Jago was literally the only person Rosie knew who lived in Cornwall, although she hadn't known exactly where. But it was an Irish thing to meet someone you knew everywhere you went; she shouldn't have been surprised.

'I've had some problems.' Rosie hesitated, but she felt as if she'd known him for years, too – they'd often DM'd. 'You probably saw my posts. I've got this stalker …' She took a deep breath and burst into tears.

'Jesus, come and sit down. I've got a flask of coffee.' Turning, Jago pulled a stool out of the rear of the van and set it down beside him, patting the top. 'Sit.' In one easy movement, he jumped into the van and reappeared with a silver flask in one hand and a pair of pink spotted hand-thrown mugs in the other.

Rosie sat down and rubbed her face with her hands. 'I'm sorry.' *Why did she keep saying that?*

'Don't be, I get it. I shouldn't have hovered over you. I was just … Well, that scarf's a bit mad …' Rosie looked up and realised he was blushing, too. 'I had no idea it was you, but I've seen your posts about the guy following you. It sounds horrible.'

Chapter 49

SEEING THE HOUSEKEEPER off, Grace felt quite pleased that Rosie had taken herself out for a walk. Leaning on the huge front door, she looked around the hallway properly, a tiny bit of her marvelling at the space. Their business at Sterling & Co was incredible houses, but she'd never had the opportunity to actually stay in any of them.

In front of her, the stairs rose to a mezzanine level and a gallery running right around the hallway. Above it was a huge skylight, filling the space with light. At least, it would fill the space with light on a sunny day. On a grey day like that one, the hall was lit by antique lights, giving a warm glow to the panelled walls. Grace could imagine it must be spectacular on a clear night, when you'd be able to see the stars shining down into this space.

Anja had shown Grace where hers and Rosie's bedrooms were – next door to each other, overlooking the fields and what looked like a lighthouse – but while she had a moment on her own, Grace wanted to have a look around the rest of the house.

In her experience, all houses held interesting details about their owner, and this was her opportunity to see if she could learn a bit more about Sebastian Sterling. He was English posh, had obviously been to a private school, but she had been curious since she'd met him about his background. And she was dying to see what the house could tell her.

She glanced up at the skylight. It was getting dusky, but if she had a quick look she'd have time to get out into the garden before dark. And then she was going to make some special soup for dinner. There was gorgeous crusty bread in the kitchen, and a huge basket of organic vegetables that had just been delivered, and the kitchen was a dream.

Skipping up the wide stairs, Grace looked around the mezzanine as she reached the top. Up here the walls were shades of cream as well, the sisal carpet on the stairs changing to a softer deep pile oatmeal at the top. Grace had kicked off her damp boots when they'd come in and could feel her feet sinking into the thick wool pile. At the top of the stairs was a row of three doors; Grace's bedroom door stood open in the middle. On the landing to her left were another four rooms, their views, she guessed, over the village. But to her right, on the seaward side of the house, there was one big set of double doors. It had to be the master bedroom.

Padding around to them, Grace tried the matching crackle-glazed china door knobs, and the doors parted to reveal a magnificent room. Directly in front of her was the very top of the glazed extension: a broad balcony enclosed by floor-to-ceiling windows, which no doubt opened in the summer. Beside the windows, two comfortable taupe sofas faced each other, a walnut coffee table between them. Grace looked around to her right to see an immense four-poster bed with rich cream satin curtains with gold piping that matched the duvet, and about a hundred pillows piled up. Beyond the bed there were more windows, this time overlooking the drive, and Grace could see the twinkle of lights from a house further down the lane.

To her left, another set of double doors stood flanked by two more single doors, all begging to be opened. Silently, Grace padded across the deep carpet to the double doors, swinging them wide to discover the most enormous marble bathroom. A free-standing bathtub, looking as if it must have been craned in, sat in front of the window; a massive walk-in shower was on her right. On her left, double sinks were sunk into the marble counter; above it was a mirror reflecting the whole room. Tucked in opposite corners on the window side, Grace realised there were more doors. Her curiosity growing, she went and opened the one on her left, seeing immediately that it was a vast dressing room, no doubt accessible from the bedroom, too, through the single door she'd seen.

Disappointingly, there weren't any clothes hanging in it. There was a marble vanity unit at one end – French style, with acanthus ormolu legs and a vast mirror above it. Grace pulled out a drawer and took a quick look inside.

There wasn't much there: some Charlotte Tilbury powder and a bottle of distinctive red Chanel nail polish. Grace picked it up and looked at it. It had been opened, but only a tiny bit had been used, as if whoever it belonged to only used it to touch up their nails.

Interesting.

Replacing the nail polish and closing the drawer, Grace returned to the bedroom, closing the dressing room door carefully after her. When she'd seen the size of the windows, she'd deliberately not put the lights on, which meant she could look outside. Beyond the fields she could see a path running down towards the sea. It split into two at a car park; one artery ran into the grassed area where several cars and a camper van were still parked, despite the hour. To the right, the path vanished into undergrowth and then seemed to reappear to wind down along the headland, past a huddle of buildings overlooking the sea. Even from this distance, Grace could see the water was boiling around dark rocky outcrops that rose, spear-like, from the depths.

Turning, she was about to leave the room when she noticed a low table on the other side of the bed, scattered with silver-framed photographs. Crossing to them, Grace picked up the first one: a wedding photo taken outside the front door of Hawksmoor House, unmistakably of Sebastian and a blonde woman in a bouffant wedding dress.

She picked up the next one: a picture of a teenage girl with a horse, and what looked a lot like the dark granite of the house behind her. Grace picked up the wedding photo again, sure it was the same girl. So this wasn't Sebastian's holiday home at all; it seemed to have been his wife's family house.

Grace looked around the room again. The decor was all new, she was sure of it – delicate antique watercolours of birds' eggs picking up the creams and beiges. Someone had spent a lot of money remodelling and refining Hawksmoor.

She thought of the red Chanel nail polish and looked back at the horsey girl in the photograph, puzzled. Perhaps she had changed in the intervening years, but she looked more like a shell-pink nail varnish girl than a Pompier red one.

Grace put down the photos and picked up another one: the same woman, this time with Sebastian sitting beside her on the deck of a yacht. She had her blonde curly hair tied up in a ponytail and looked very outdoorsy. Grace looked closely at the photo – at the woman's hands. She definitely wasn't wearing red nail polish.

Chapter 50

YARASLAVA COULD FEEL a headache coming on. This was all getting out of hand, and that was the one thing she couldn't stand. She needed to be in control. She needed to know exactly what was happening.

She was sitting at her desk in the Sterling & Co office, her door closed to the silence in the main space. The room was dark except for the pool of soft light thrown by the glass deer head above her. She rubbed her forehead.

She could feel things slipping from her grip; everything she'd carefully built was teetering, as if on the edge of a chasm.

Leaning over to wake up her desktop, she opened an incognito window and swiftly accessed Ben Hunt's Gmail folder. When he'd discovered she was reading his messages the first time, he'd gone crazy and changed his password, but not to one that was any more difficult to crack than the original. She shook her head.

She'd been stupid then; she should have been more careful. Ben had already been suspicious about some of the properties she was selling through Hunt's, and he'd started asking her questions that she didn't think were as innocent as they'd sounded. She'd been checking his calendar, trying to work out precisely what a meeting had been about, when he'd walked in behind her and caught her at his desk.

She looked at the time on the screen. He'd be in the gym. She'd called the office earlier to check he was on his way out, and then she'd called the reception at the gym to check if he'd arrived. He was so predictable. Every evening Tuesday to Thursday, and at the weekends.

Yaraslava knew Ben would get a warning that his Gmail was being accessed from a new computer, but he used his work email as the backup. She shook her head; he wasn't nearly as tech-savvy as he thought. She should be able to catch the message and delete it before he saw it.

Not that she cared at this stage.

Yaraslava clicked on the trash can. It was always the best place to start. She just needed to know if he'd been looking at Landmark in any detail recently. If there were any emails about the company and its registration details, they'd probably be in here.

Someone was obviously focused on causing Sterling & Co trouble, and Hunt's was an obvious suspect.

As Yaraslava ran her eyes down the list of senders, she recoiled at one of the names.

Nick Armitage.

This was precisely what she was worried about. Had Ben been asking Nick about Park House and its owners? Yaraslava closed her eyes, her headache increasing in intensity. Nick getting an email from Ben, suggesting that Hunt's had a client interested in Park House, would be completely logical; their client would want to know details about the property. Slipping in a few questions about the seller would be so easy.

She opened the email. It was one line, sent on Friday, the day before Nick's unfortunate clash with that ornament.

Perfect, see you there Sat, won't mention a word to Y 😉 N x

That was it. The whole message. See him where? At Park House? And if she – Yaraslava – was the Y, what wasn't he going to tell her? About a buyer? Or about Ben asking about the house?

Yaraslava had no idea, but she didn't like it one little bit.

She needed to regain control of this situation. And fast.

This had all been caused because Dimitri was too lazy to do the paperwork and set up another company for them to put their business through. Which was ridiculous, when they had all the identity documents they needed for Irina Ivanov and her husband. Neither of them existed in real life, but selling anything was all about creating a narrative. And Yaraslava knew all about telling stories.

There were times when she wondered if that's what her problem with men was – every relationship she'd had was about constructing a story and living in her own fairy tale. She'd always gravitated towards unobtainable relationships that presented a challenge, where she made things happen, where she was the one in control.

She closed her eyes, thinking. Ben had been exactly like all her other relationships. She'd had to work hard to win him, but then she'd lost him. He'd started asking too many questions, and then … Well …

It was as if she needed to keep proving herself.

The email arrived alerting Ben to a new computer accessing his account. Yaraslava deleted it.

Did she need to look around here more, or had she seen enough?

Nick had organised to meet Ben on the day he'd died, and they'd agreed not to mention it to her. What the hell had they been going to discuss?

Chapter 51

BY THE TIME Rosie reached the house, it was dark. Jago had given her a lift in the van, juddering past the footpath where she'd walked across the fields, looping through the village and down the lane the taxi driver had taken. He pulled up outside the gate and looked across at her.

'All OK now?'

Rosie nodded sheepishly. She'd ended up pouring the whole story out to him. It had felt good to tell someone who sort of knew her, but didn't know anyone else involved. And he'd listened, his head on one side, without saying it was her fault or asking what she might have done to attract the attention of a total lunatic. It had been dark by the time she'd finished, and she'd been shivering, despite the fleece blanket he'd pulled out of the van for her to wrap around her shoulders.

It had smelled of lavender and cinnamon and had been incredibly soft.

'I'll be down in my grandma's restaurant tomorrow,' he said. 'I'm baking, but Morwenna will be on the counter, it's not busy at this time of year. Want to try some more of my hevva buns?' He grinned cheekily at her.

Rosie blushed. 'I'd love to. What time do you open?'

'Ten, but I'll be down about 7.30 to get the ovens on. We supply the village shops with bread and pastries, so I'm pretty busy early on.'

'Ten sounds great to me. I'll see if Grace wants to come.'

For a moment she thought she saw a flash of disappointment in his eyes. 'Whatever suits. I'll be there until after lunch.'

'Great.' She swung the door open. She felt as if she should give him a hug. Their chat had been pretty intense.

'Get moving or you'll let all the cold in. I'll see you in the morning, and I'll DM you my phone number in case you need … anything.'

'Thanks, thanks so much.' Rosie jumped out of the van and smiled at him again before swinging the door closed.

She waved as Jago turned the van around, and then walked up the drive to the front door. She hadn't thought to bring a key, but she was sure Grace would be wondering where she was.

The doorbell was a huge iron pull handle that Rosie had only seen before outside churches. She could hear the peal of a bell inside when she pulled it, and a moment later the door opened and Grace peeped out.

'My goodness, where have you been? I was starting to think you'd been kidnapped.'

Rosie couldn't resist a sheepish smile as Grace stepped aside to let her in, closing the front door behind her. Rosie peeled off her scarf and turned to look at Grace, realising at the same time that she could smell something delicious.

'I've been on an adventure. But what have you been doing? What's that smell?'

Grace smiled. 'Anja left us loads of food, all prepared, but there was this gorgeous loaf of bread and loads of veg, so I made some soup. Come on, I've got the kitchen table set and there's wine.'

Rosie groaned inside. When Jago had revealed that he was currently working as a chef in his day job, he'd vanished into the Tardis-like van again and reappeared with the most delicious scones that he called hevva buns. Twice the size of Irish scones, they were full of fruit and cinnamon and frosted with sugar. He'd produced plates and knives and butter and a fold-up table, and they'd had a picnic, listening to the waves and chatting. Perhaps it was the fresh air, and the fact that they were delicious, but Rosie had eaten two and was feeling very happily full. She didn't know if she could manage soup as well.

But Grace looked so pleased with herself, Rosie didn't think she could say no. She slipped off her coat and, kicking off her muddy boots, she dumped her coat and scarf on the end of the stairs.

'Come on, the kitchen is amazing.' Grace beckoned her towards the rear of the house.

'Did you get a look around the garden?'

'I did – it's fabulous and massive.'

Grace led Rosie through to the biggest kitchen she had ever seen: a pale flagstone floor, interrupted by an island the size of Rosie's living room, continuing on to a huge farmhouse table.

Grace had laid out their places, tall glasses beside colourful woven place mats, a bowl of salad and a wooden board with a crusty loaf on it, in the middle of the table.

'Sit down and I'll bring it over.' Rosie quickly went to the island to wash her hands, grabbing a tea towel to dry them, and then sat down, leaving the head of the table to

Grace. She had obviously had fun playing house while Rosie was out; she had even found a cut glass dish for the butter.

'I put plenty of black pepper in, but it might be a tiny bit bitter. I was playing around with the organic vegetables and there might be a bit much kale in it.'

Grace came to the table with two shallow white china bowls.

'I didn't know you cooked, I'm very impressed.' Rosie glanced at her, but Grace was concentrating, getting the bowls just right on the place mats. 'Will I cut the bread?'

'Please. I'd better just nip to the loo. Start without me.'

As Grace vanished, Rosie picked up her spoon and took a tiny sip of the soup. It was quite bitter. It looked fantastic, proper home-made, and despite being dark green, smelled like curried carrot and parsnip. But Rosie really didn't think she could eat it. She looked around frantically and spotted a second sink in the counter.

She glanced at the door Grace had gone out through, and picked up her bowl and nipped over to the sink. As she'd guessed, it was a waste disposal. Looking over her shoulder, she poured the soup away and turned on the tap to wash it down the sink. She couldn't risk turning on the unit, but you couldn't see the soup, which was the important thing. Hurrying back to the table, she picked up the bread knife and cut some slices for them both. Buttering her slice, she ate it quickly.

A moment later, Grace reappeared.

'This is delicious. I was hungrier than I thought – it must be the fresh air.'

Rosie put her spoon down in her bowl and bit into her bread.

'Are you finished already? Would you like some more?'

'It was gorgeous, but I'm stuffed now. Have yours. This place is amazing, isn't it?' Rosie smiled innocently as Grace sat down.

Grace reached for her wine. 'The garden's huge, too. I had a good look around. What did you get up to?'

'I bumped into this cute guy called Jago – I know him from Insta. He did aerospace engineering, but at the moment he's working in a restaurant on the cliff overlooking the sea. I'm meeting him for coffee tomorrow, if you want to come.' Grace had started on her soup and nodded, her mouth full. Rosie picked up her glass. 'He does drone photography. It's mad – we've been following each other for years. His photos are amazing.'

Chapter 52

ROSIE TOLD GRACE that, after all the travelling and fresh air, she needed an early night. It was no word of a lie. Leaving her curtains open, she climbed into the huge bed in her room. She hadn't bothered unpacking; she had opened her case and hauled out her make-up and washbag to put in the bathroom, leaving the case itself open on the floor. She hadn't brought anything with her that needed hanging, and she was genuinely too tired to sort it out now.

Leaning on cotton bed linen so fine it felt like silk, surrounded by pillows, Rosie felt as if she was in a five-star hotel. She picked up her phone to check the signal.

She'd connected to Jago's van's hotspot as they'd chatted about Instagram, and her phone had updated, but blissfully, there were no messages from Michael after she'd switched to her French SIM. She felt almost like she had before all this started – happy and relaxed. Now she could see there was only a glimmer of signal, but she opened Instagram and found Jago's account.

The images took a while to load, but his pictures were amazing: soaring videos of the coastline; the sea crashing on razor-like rocks; seagulls riding the wind. In one, the mist was thick, swirling around an old lifeboat slipway, the doors on the boathouse rusting.

She scrolled down and found a selfie Jago had taken hanging from a cliff face, his blond hair sticking out from under a midnight-blue beanie, his eyes an even darker shade of blue in the photo. As they'd chatted she'd discovered he was a year older than her. She knew he'd studied in Sweden and was a keen climber; some of his best drone shots were of him scaling cliffs. Somewhere along the way he'd wanted a break from tech and had trained as a chef, and so he was home now, cooking in his grandmother's restaurant, helping out while she recovered from a hip replacement.

They'd not stopped talking. She'd been a bit embarrassed, breaking down and telling him about Michael, but she'd been so comfortable chatting to him, she felt as if she must have known him in a previous life or something.

As Rosie scrolled through his feed, she realised she had one full bar of signal on the phone. She'd better check her email, just in case there was news.

Opening her Gmail, Rosie could see a bunch of unread messages. The first was from Eoin, telling her to be careful and keep him updated. She fired off a reply, saying she'd arrived, Cornwall was amazing, and she'd met an Instagram friend already.

Hallie next. Reading the subject line, Rosie frowned. She opened Hallie's message.

Hi Rosie,

Can you call me in the morning? About 10.30? I've tried you but keep getting your voicemail. Something's come up I need to run by you.

Hxx

What was that about? Rosie felt herself tense and prayed it was nothing to do with Michael.

The next message was from Detective Sergeant Nandy.

Rosie, I know you're travelling today, but can you call me as soon as you see this message? Any time day or night, on my mobile. Number below.

Any time day or night. That didn't sound good. Rosie felt her stomach tense again, the familiar sick feeling of anxiety nagging at her. Was it too late to call now? She checked the time. It was after ten, but she did have one bar of reception and it sounded important.

She dialled the number. It rang twice and was picked up.

'DS Nandy.'

'Hi, it's Rosie Kinsella here, I'm sorry. I changed my number this morning and I didn't get a chance to tell you.'

'Are you still in London?' He'd obviously seen the French phone number and sounded confused. 'I tried your office, but Yaraslava said you'd gone on holiday?'

'Not a holiday, exactly. I'm in Cornwall with Grace, but I'm using my old French SIM card. I needed a break, and nobody's got this number.'

'That sounds sensible. Look. I was hoping to be able to meet you to tell you this, but—'

'I'm too far away.' Rosie suddenly started to feel even more sick. 'Has something happened?' She mentally corrected herself; she should have said 'has something *else* happened?'

There was a pause before Nandy replied. 'Do you remember you told us Nick wanted to send your emails to a friend, so he could try and trace them?'

'Yes.' She said it hesitantly. *Where was this going?*

'One of the things we've been considering is that perhaps he'd had a go at tracing them himself. I'm just going to have to put this bluntly, but we wondered if he'd discovered something about Michael that caused him to be attacked – by Michael.'

'I'd sort of wondered that myself.'

At the other end, Nandy cleared his throat. 'The thing is, the friend Nick sent the emails to has been away, hiking. Totally out of mobile coverage. But he's back now.'

Rosie sat up in the bed, her whole back and neck tense. 'And was he able to look at the emails?'

'Not exactly. He picked up a voice message from Nick that was left late on Friday evening, where he said he thought one of the emails had been sent from your office.'

'Nick said that? That one was sent from our office?' Rosie could feel shock spreading through her like a virus, paralysing her mind. 'From *our* office?'

'It seems so. He says Nick said he'd looked at the IP addresses Michael had used – there were several. One was a public library, there was a coffee shop, and the other was a lot closer to home.'

A coffee shop? Had she been right in thinking that's where Michael could have seen her first? Rosie's thinking mind suddenly kicked in. 'You can pick up a Wi-Fi signal from outside a building. It wouldn't mean it was someone actually inside the office, would it?' Rosie paused, the questions tumbling in her mind. 'Did Nick say who he thought had sent it?'

'You're right about picking up the signal. We're looking at the CCTV in the area at the time the email was sent, to see if it was someone hanging about outside, or parked close by. It's possible an ex-employee has the passcode, or it's someone else in the building. But – and this is *absolutely confidential*.' Nandy said it as if he'd have to kill her himself if she repeated it. 'Nick said he was going to talk to someone on Saturday. He was going to ask them about it – those were his words.'

'On Saturday, the day he was killed?'

'Exactly. We need you to be very careful, please, Rosie. This information gives us a solid link between your stalker and Nick's attack. I'm sorry our cyber team has been so slow. We should have had this information by now, but I'm escalating the trace, obviously. We're going to get a full team on your messages. We have guys who look at everything from distinctive word patterns to writing style. We need to move fast.'

'But that means Michael killed Nick, and that maybe someone in the office knows who Michael is … That he's been in my office?' Before Nandy could respond, Rosie said hastily, 'I'm going to have to go.'

Dropping the phone on the duvet, she ran to the bathroom, reaching the toilet just in time to empty her stomach. She retched again and slumped down onto the cool marble tiles. *Someone in their building knew who Michael was, and he'd killed Nick.*

Chapter 53

GRACE WAS ALREADY up and flicking through the local newspaper at the table when Rosie walked into the kitchen. Grace was wearing a fluffy pink jumper and jeans, had tied her blonde hair in a ponytail, and was looking much fresher than Rosie felt. She looked up as Rosie came in, immediately frowning.

'Gosh, you look a bit rough. Didn't you sleep?'

Rosie put her hands to her face. 'No, I was tossing and turning a bit. Probably too quiet. I'm used to constant traffic.'

Grace smiled sympathetically. 'I had a bit of a funny tummy in the night – did you? I was wondering if I'd picked up a bug on the train.'

Rosie had definitely had a funny tummy during the night, but it wasn't a bug. She didn't think Grace could have heard her through the house's thick walls; at least, she hoped not. Instead of answering directly, she said, 'Were you sick?'

Grace shook her head. 'That's what made me think it was some mild bug thing. That carriage must have been thick with germs. After Covid I'm a lot more conscious of public places and handwashing. I had sanitiser with me, but it's amazing how quickly people forget, isn't it?' She shrugged. 'I'm fine now, though. I just had an amazing coffee. There's a machine over there that can probably take you to the moon if you press the right buttons.'

Rosie looked over to the counter running around the rear of the room, to where Grace was pointing. She was right, there was a full-on professional machine, looking as if it was only missing a barista who knew how to use it. The type of machine her landlord Maurizio would love. But she didn't think she was up to figuring it out this morning.

'It's the same make as the one Yaraslava bought for the office.'

The way she said it made Rosie look over at her. 'Is that significant?' What was Rosie missing here.

'I found a bottle of nail polish last night. Chanel Pompier red.' Grace's eyes widened, unable to resist a grin. 'That's the colour Yaraslava wears.'

'You think she's been here?'

Grace nodded. 'I think it's a possibility.' Her face twitched with mischief. 'And she stayed in the master.'

Rosie didn't want to know why Grace had been in their boss's bedroom, but the fact that Yaraslava might have been was certainly intriguing. Not that it was any of her business. She had bigger problems.

Rosie shrugged. 'She's a free agent, I suppose.' She could tell Grace was desperate for a gossip, but she didn't have any spare emotional capacity for Sebastian's relationships.

'I think I'll skip coffee. I'll just have some orange juice and walk down to the cafe to see Jago. The weather looks OK.' Out of the huge windows she could see the sky was overcast again; a soft mizzle was falling, but it could be worse. Rosie guessed the weather here could change fast, like it did at home, with storms rolling in from the sea. 'Do you want to come?'

Obviously not impressed with Rosie's lack of interest in Yaraslava and Sebastian, Grace turned over the page of the newspaper.

'I'm pretty snug here for now. I might walk up to the village a bit later. There's bad weather on the way this afternoon, according to the forecast. I thought I'd light the fire and crash in front of the TV after lunch.' She hesitated. 'Will you be OK on your own?'

Rosie smiled, appreciating her concern. 'I'll be grand, but thank you for asking. Nobody knows we're here and my phone's turned off, and it's staying that way, so nobody can get in touch with me. I've scheduled Instagram posts that make it look like I'm in London, so I think I'll be more OK on my own here than I would be up there.'

'What about Hallie? You said there was security on the Cheyne Walk apartment. Is there really?'

'Those buildings in Chelsea are very secure, and Hallie was going to have a word with Yaraslava about getting someone in to mind her. Everyone has to book to see it, so they'll be able to do background checks. After what happened to Nick, Hallie doesn't want to take any risks.'

Grace let out a sigh. 'I still think it was someone who came into the garden from the heath. Nick could have walked into a robbery or something. The alarm was off when I got there.'

'Nick would have turned that off himself, though, wouldn't he, when he went inside?'

'Oh, yes, I suppose he would. Didn't think of that. It was the back doors being open that made me think someone had come in that way, but maybe Nick opened them. Did the police say anything about fingerprints or anything when you spoke to them?'

Rosie shook her head as she opened the huge walk-in fridge. 'No, they haven't said anything.' Rosie glanced behind her, but Grace was looking at the paper. Thank goodness. She still felt shocked by her conversation with Tristan Nandy. She wasn't ready to talk about it yet. Rosie turned to the fridge. Sebastian had been as good as his word, and it was crammed full with everything from yogurts to chocolate eclairs.

'Does he honestly think we'll eat all this?' Rosie found the orange juice and brought the carton to the table. Grace had laid out a glass and bowl for her, and had put milk in a jug. Several boxes of cereal stood on the table beside a big vase of foliage and spring flowers. 'Were you in the garden again? What time did you get up?'

Grace shrugged. 'Early. Lot on my mind.' She smiled sadly, and Rosie knew she must be thinking about Nick. Finding him would have scarred her for life; she didn't know how Grace was sleeping at all.

'Maybe that's why you were feeling queasy, plus all the travelling. That train trip wasn't exactly comfortable.'

Grace grimaced in agreement. 'I think we should upgrade to first class on the way back – no joke.' She turned her attention to the paper again. 'It seems the big news around here is someone stealing wild birds' eggs. Or many people, by the sounds of things. The police are running something called Operation Easter, which "aims to tackle the thefts". Wouldn't it be great if the only thing the police in London had to worry about was birds' eggs?'

Rosie opened her mouth to explain about the importance of wild birds, and how some were increasingly rare ... but she closed it again. Grace was probably right, and after the night she'd had, she wasn't ready for a debate on preserving wildlife and the ecosystem.

She'd texted Nandy the previous night to say she was OK after the abrupt end to their conversation, and that she wouldn't say a thing to anybody. He'd replied that they'd work as fast as they could.

Now Michael was linked to Nick, it was never going to be fast enough. Suddenly, Rosie didn't even feel like orange juice.

Chapter 54

AS SHE PUSHED open the door to the restaurant, Rosie could see Jago in the kitchen behind the glass counter. 'Restaurant' was a bit of a grand term; it was more of a cafe, with tables clustered around windows on every side, all of which had an incredible view of the sea. And for the moment, it was empty.

The counter was already packed with Jago's hevva buns, croissants and sliced cakes, and the air rich with the delicious scent of baking. It looked as if he'd been busy.

'Good morning, chef,' Rosie called out as she closed the door, an old-fashioned bell jangling above it.

Jago stuck his head out of the kitchen, rubbing his floury hands down the front of a spotless white apron. His grin was broad.

'Bonjour, mademoiselle. Asseyez-vous, s'il vous plaît.'

'Do you speak French?' Rosie knew he'd learned Swedish as part of his course at university, but she hadn't expected French, and his accent was perfect, if a little formal.

He shook his head. 'No, that's it, but I make a mean croissant and the best coffee you'll find on Lizard Point.'

'Is that anything to do with it being the only coffee I'll find on Lizard Point?'

'Maybe.' He cocked an eyebrow. 'What can I get you?'

'A latte would be amazing.'

He came out into the servery and switched on the coffee machine, turning to look over his shoulder. 'Anything from the creepy dude?'

Rosie swung her bag off her shoulder and sat down at the table closest to the door. 'Nope, thank goodness. But he'll realise I'm not looking at my phone pretty soon. I'm mainly going to ignore my email today as well.'

'That sounds like a plan.' The machine whirred and spluttered. 'So how do you know the Lovicks?'

'The who?' Rosie looked at him, puzzled.

'Hawksmoor House – it belongs to the Lovick family. They were mine owners back in the day, employed everyone around here for miles. They still own the rights to a big seam of serpentine stone.' Spinning around, he picked up what looked like a polished black ball-shaped paperweight from behind the counter and spun it around his hand as if it were a baseball.

'What on earth is that?'

'Serpentine. Here – catch.' He pretended to throw it to her. 'Sorry, joke. It's really heavy.' He turned to the machine and, picking up her coffee, brought it, and the paperweight, to the table.

'There's sugar there if you need it.' He put the coffee and the polished stone down, going back to make himself a coffee before rejoining her.

Rosie took the moment to look at the seams in the stone. It was beautiful, gleaming in the overhead lights like black marble with delicate veins of rust and pale green. It looked as if a storm had literally been captured in the rock.

'Is it always polished smooth like this?'

Running his finger over it, Jago nodded. 'Usually. It's carved in all sorts of shapes. Everything from chess pieces to lamps. My gran's got a huge serpentine lighthouse in her back garden. You can only find it in a few places in the world – it's been mined and worked here for generations.'

'It really is lovely. So who are the Lovicks? It's our boss's house – Sebastian Sterling, but maybe he bought it recently. It looks like it's been completely redecorated.'

'Sebastian's your boss?' Jago snapped his fingers. 'Of course ... Sterling & Co. Sorry, I should have realised. I wasn't thinking.'

Rosie sipped her coffee. 'Do you know him?'

Jago shook his head. 'I've only met him a couple of times. His wife is Leonora Lovick, her family owned the house – well, everything around here, really. They invested wisely, and her grandfather's brothers went aboard and built mines all over the place – South Africa and Botswana. They focused on minerals as well as precious stones.' He picked up his coffee. 'I heard it was her money that set him up in business, but I don't think he exactly came from the gutter himself.'

Rosie shook her head. 'Definitely not, he went to a very expensive school somewhere. But interesting that his wife is behind his success. We never see or hear about her.'

Jago rolled his eyes. 'She's not been down here in years. Rumour has it she's got a place in the South of France. Sebastian comes here a lot, though, with "friends", so I'm told. The most recent was a woman with black hair. She looked like a model.'

Rosie glanced at him sideways. She'd bet she could guess who that was. It sounded as if Grace might be right about the nail polish.

Rosie opened her mouth to say something, but the door opened behind her, bringing with it a gust of wind. A young woman came in, her long blonde hair plaited in dreadlocks and shaved at the sides, a silver ring through her nose.

'Blimey, it's getting colder.'

Jago raised his hand in a mock salute. 'This is Morwenna. Morwenna, Rosie. Rosie's a friend of mine from the interweb.'

'Awesome.' Before Morwenna could say more, Rosie heard the insistent call of the foghorn reach them, its haunting tone a higher pitch than the one at home, but a sound she'd recognise anywhere.

'Right on cue,' said Morwenna as she slipped off her coat. 'I think we'll be quiet today, Jago boy, there's a mist coming in.'

He nodded, not looking particularly happy. Realising Rosie was looking at him, he explained, 'This place makes a fortune in the summer, but we keep saying to Gran she should open fewer days in the winter. The problem is, she's—'

'A stubborn old woman.' Morwenna finished the sentence for him. 'But a bloody great one. Did he tell you she was the cox on the lifeboat until she was seventy?'

Rosie shook her head, her eyes widening as Morwenna continued. 'They reckon she's saved someone from every family down here on the Point. She's a force, like the storm itself.'

Jago grinned and looked over at Morwenna as she went behind the counter and pulled on an apron. 'Morwenna's a poet.'

'And he's going to make me famous on Instagram. Have you seen his account?'

Rosie nodded as Jago blushed. 'You'll make yourself famous, Morwenna, you don't need me for that.'

Over his shoulder, Rosie saw Morwenna roll her eyes. 'Right, what do I need to do first? Oh, did you see the *Packet*? There's a front-page article. Those bloody egg-nappers have been out again. It's not emmets, I reckon it's locals.'

She started doing something under the counter involving the clatter of pottery.

Jago turned around in his seat to look at her, his face angry. 'Seriously? I haven't seen the paper yet.' He turned to Rosie. 'We've got loads of rare birds here. This is one of the last places you can see choughs in the UK. There are only about four hundred breeding pairs in the whole country – they nest on the cliffs. We all keep an eye out at nesting time, but there are gangs working around here stealing the eggs for collectors. Absolute scum.'

Rosie was impressed by his passion, just as strong as she'd seen in his climbing posts that put a spotlight on the climate, wildlife and coastal erosion.

'What's an emmet?'

Jago grimaced. 'A tourist. But Morwenna's right – I don't think it *is* tourists.'

Suddenly remembering the time, Rosie looked at her phone. It was almost 10.30. 'I've just got to make a phone call. Where's the best reception around here?'

Morwenna pointed with her thumb behind her. 'Edge of the path. There's a stone bench around the other side. It's a bit blowy, but you can have a proper conversation.'

'I won't be a minute.'

Jago grinned at her. 'That scarf needs to earn its keep.' Then, 'Should I heat you up a hevva bun while you're out?'

Chapter 55

'ROSIE? IS THAT you? Thank God. Are you OK?' Standing in Ben's kitchen, Hallie turned around from the counter and paced towards the window. 'Did you see my email?'

At the other end, Hallie could hear Rosie was outside somewhere, the wind whipping around the phone and snatching away her words.

'Yes, and sorry, the reception is terrible down here. I've had to come to the edge of the cliff to get a tiny pip. But I think I'm OK. I'm here, anyway, and it's gorgeous.'

'Is the house amazing?'

'It's stunning – huge. Way bigger than I expected.'

Hallie could tell Rosie knew she was making small talk. She hadn't emailed to say she needed to discuss their boss's choice of wallpaper.

'Any sign of Michael?' Looking out over the Thames towards the London Eye, Hallie bit her lip.

'No, thank God. I haven't given anyone this number, so I haven't had any texts, but when he sees I'm not picking up my messages he'll probably start emailing. I thought he might last night, but nothing yet.' Rosie sighed. 'What's happening in London? Any news on Nick?'

'Nothing new yet.' Hallie drew in a breath. She could hear the wind whistling around Rosie, seagulls crying in the background. She was just going to have to come out with it, and she needed to hurry up before Rosie froze or lost the signal. 'Look … I don't know how to say this, but I think Yaraslava could be involved in all of this somehow.' Somewhere near Rosie, Hallie caught a burst of conversation. 'Are you OK to talk?'

'I'm down at a cafe near the sea. There are people walking past, but it's so windy I don't think they can hear me. What do you mean, Yaraslava's involved? How?'

'Oh, Rosie, I'm so worried. You know how she's always saying Hunt's are poaching clients and she thinks they hacked the company Instagram?'

'That could have been anyone, honestly. Our followers would be of interest to a lot of scammers.'

'I know, but … Well, I thought the same for a bit …' Hallie could feel the dark hole of anxiety opening in her stomach. 'I honestly thought someone from Hunt's could have got access to my phone.'

When Rosie replied, it sounded as if she'd found somewhere a bit more sheltered to stand. 'How's that possible, though, unless you went out to dinner with one of them and left your phone on the table or something?'

Hallie cleared her throat. 'Well, it wasn't quite that. The thing is, the Ben I'm seeing is Ben Hunt.'

There was silence at the other end while Rosie absorbed this. Dreading her response, Hallie squeezed her free hand tight, her nails digging into her palm.

'Are you serious? He's a real stud.'

Hallie suddenly relaxed; she hadn't expected that. 'Well, I think so, but—'

Rosie interrupted her. 'But, Jaysus, Hals, Yaraslava will kill you.'

Hallie drew in a sharp breath. 'That's why I'm ringing you – that's exactly what I'm worried about. Like, really.' She paused. 'I'm terrified she knows, and she's sent you and Grace off to the opposite end of the country to split us all up.'

There was a pause while Rosie obviously tried to figure out what Hallie was saying. 'I think we might need to workshop that idea, Hals, you could be a bit ahead of yourself there.'

'She was arrested, Rosie, before, for attacking Ben. He didn't press charges. That's how the police knew it was her fingerprints on the rock that killed Nick.' It came out in a rush. Hallie closed her eyes, reliving the moment Ben had told her all over again.

'Hang on, slow down a bit. She attacked Ben Hunt? What …?'

'He was seeing her, secretly, and one day she saw him with a client and thought he was two-timing her. She's incredibly jealous – she attacked him.'

'Was that why she left Hunt's?'

'No, that was another thing. She was doing some sort of dodgy deal and Ben called her out on it. They had this huge row, and Yaraslava marched out and took the business to Sterling's.'

Rosie was quiet for a second, a gust of wind picking up the sound of the sea crashing on rocks. Hallie could tell what she was saying was taking a minute to sink in. Then Rosie said, 'Yaraslava was seeing Ben Hunt? Perhaps she's got a thing about sleeping with her boss.

Grace reckons she's been down here, to Sebastian's house.'

'What makes you say that?'

'Grace said she found some Chanel nail varnish. The same colour Yaraslava wears. And something Jago said. He's a guy I know from Insta who lives down here. He saw this fabulous-looking woman with black hair in the garden.'

'But that could be Sebastian's wife.'

'That's what I thought, but the nail polish Grace found is new, and Jago said Sebastian's wife is from the Lizard. I think he'd recognise her. He said she hates it here. The house belongs to her family, but she hasn't been home for years.' Rosie paused. 'Yaraslava actually *attacked* Ben Hunt? That's a bit extreme.'

'She frightens me, Rosie. Ben said she went nuts and hit him with a bottle of wine, full-on clubbed him with it. I don't think I can work there any more. I don't know what I'm going to do, but I don't think I could look at her across the desk. I didn't want you to get back and find I wasn't there.'

'You need to do what's right for you, Hallie. I'm serious. You could get a job anywhere. You're brilliant at sales, and everyone in London knows it.'

'Thanks, Rosie. I'm just scared.'

'So am I, Hals. If Yaraslava attacked Ben, do you think she could have attacked Nick?'

Chapter 56

GRACE TOOK HER time finishing her breakfast after Rosie left. Sitting in this perfect kitchen was pretty much a dream come true. She was enjoying every minute of this trip, which was surprising even to her, given the stress of the past few weeks.

Picking up her mug to finish the last of her tea, Grace looked around. Sebastian had definitely used an interior designer and spared no expense on the house.

Grace had learned early on in life that knowledge was power, and finding out a bit more about her boss could be very useful currency in the future. With Rosie off on her walk, it was the perfect time to have a bit of a look around the rest of the house and see what more clues she could pick up.

Things were definitely coming to a head with Rosie and the whole Michael thing, and Grace wanted to be sure she had some security if anything unexpected happened. She'd already been sidelined once by Yaraslava, and even if she had had a pay rise and it turned out that she was getting some unexpectedly generous tips, she didn't want to find herself somehow out in the cold.

Putting her mug in the sink, Grace padded out into the hallway, her socks silent on the polished wood. On the right, behind the stairs, there was a door that she'd investigated briefly yesterday – two, in fact. One led to a spiral staircase that accessed the basement; the other opened into a mirrored lift servicing every floor. Grace pressed the button to call it.

Getting in, she selected –1 and the door slid silently shut. In what felt like a split second, the lift carriage came to rest and the doors slid open.

The movement of the doors seemed to cause the lights in a wide hallway to flick on, revealing what felt like a secret subterranean area of the house. Down here, in contrast to upstairs, the floor was tiled in what looked like black marble; the walls were half panelled in deep grey, painted above the panelling in a dove grey. Along the walls, lamps spontaneously lit as she moved out of the lift, motion sensors tracking her.

The hallway down here was cavernous: ornate gold and black French occasional tables were pushed against the walls, huge white marble busts on each one. Grace felt as if they were regarding her critically.

Half slipping on the polished marble, she pushed open the first door leading off the hall. She'd expected it to be access to the pool Sebastian had mentioned, or the cinema, but instead it was a room full of huge gold-framed paintings. She glanced around, recognising what looked like French and Italian Renaissance-style oils, mainly portraits. It was like an art gallery, every square inch of the deep blue walls covered. But why would you keep paintings downstairs in the dark? Grace scanned the walls, the hairs rising on the back of her neck as she suddenly felt as if the eyes of everyone in the paintings were following her. Backing out, she closed the door quickly.

The next room was a gun room: a red leather chesterfield sofa faced a huge black marble fireplace on her right; racks of gleaming antique guns were locked – she hoped – behind glass doors on her left. This room felt just as strange as the previous one. Why did anyone need this many guns? The cabinets were highly polished rosewood, rows of drawers under each one. Grace moved forward, her curiosity piqued, but catching sight of someone in her peripheral vision immediately started her heart racing.

Gasping, her hand going to her chest, she realised there was a mirror above the fireplace, reflecting the room. She closed her eyes, willing her heart to slow down. This part of the house was starting to creep her out, and she wondered for a moment if Anja the housekeeper was supposed to have locked these rooms, but then that would have made Grace even more curious about what was down here. Sebastian obviously didn't think his staff would be wandering about, having a poke around. Grace smirked to herself. People often underestimated her – more fool them.

Pulling open one of the drawers below the gun cabinets, expecting to discover it full of shell cases or something, Grace was surprised to find it was a display drawer, like something from a museum. But rather than anything gun-related, it was full of butterflies, each one pinned against a deep blue velvet background, their wings iridescent in the light from a chandelier that had come on when she'd opened the door.

Grace slid the drawer silently closed and opened another one. It was packed with what looked like birds' eggs in a polished wooden tray, each one labelled in spidery handwriting on a yellowing paper tag. This was definitely a collector's room – one owned by someone with too much money and what felt like a series of slightly bizarre obsessions. Grace pushed the drawer closed.

Out in the hallway, she found the cinema and then, through another door, the indoor pool. The scent of chlorine hit her as soon as she stuck her head inside, lights in recessed alcoves springing on in response to her movement. The pool itself was long and narrow, sunk in more black marble, lights twinkling up through the water. She didn't go in; she could return later with Rosie when they had time to relax. There were things she wanted to do today, and spending half of it lost down here wasn't part of her plan.

But everything she'd seen so far in this house told her a lot about Sebastian Sterling. Grace's mind jumped to Rosie, and the whole Michael situation. He was a bit obsessed as well. Angry and obsessed.

Chapter 57

'NOW, HONEY, TELL me what's bothering you.' Sebastian Sterling leaned on the sofa in Yaraslava's living room and put his head on one side. He was wearing jeans and oxblood loafers, with a perfectly toning checked shirt. His heavy gold watch caught the morning light from the sash window as he lifted the cut glass tumbler she'd just handed him, the smoothie still frothy from her blender.

She should be handing him a whisky. She had a feeling he might need it.

Yaraslava hated it when he called her 'honey'; it actually made her cringe, but she was used to masking her reactions.

Sitting down next to Sebastian, she felt his arm go around her and slip up under her silk T-shirt. His fingers rubbed her back, looking to unhook her bra strap. She wasn't wearing one and, as he realised, his hand moved around her. He was like a dog on heat sometimes, but that gave her power, and she needed all the help she could get at that moment. She twisted, letting him cup her breast and play with her nipple. He put his glass down on the broad arm of the leather sofa and leaned in to nuzzle her neck.

'Tell me. You've been preoccupied for days. I know Nick was a shock, but there's something else, isn't there?'

Yaraslava sighed, taking a sip of her own spinach and ginger smoothie and leaning in to him, arching her back as if his fingers were turning her on.

'You are going to be cross.'

'I doubt I'd be cross with you, my love. Just tell me what it is and we'll fix it.' He was almost purring, continuing to rub her under her clothes.

Yaraslava closed her eyes for a minute, then turned to him and kissed him, his mouth opening to hers. But she pulled away.

'I am in trouble … Nothing I cannot sort out, but I am worried that it is going to impact you.'

'Let me be the judge of that. Come on, tell me.'

Yaraslava twisted so she could see his face properly. He pulled his hand from around her and put it up the front of her T-shirt, moving to her other breast, a flush beginning to rise up his neck. This was it. She just needed to hold his concentration a little bit longer.

She'd learned early on in their relationship that he liked to possess beautiful things. She'd been able to reel him in, but now she needed to keep him on the line.

'It is my brother, Dimitri.' She paused as if she was trying to find the words. 'He has got involved with this woman, Irina Ivanov. She is Russian, from Moscow. She owns a company called Landmark that has bought several properties in London.'

Sebastian's eyes were on her mouth, but he seemed to be listening as he interrupted her. 'Am I joining the dots on "Russian", "London" and "property"?'

Yaraslava nodded. 'Yes, you are. He did not realise. He is in love …' As she said it she cast her eyes down, and Sebastian smoothed a strand of her hair from her face, tucking it behind her ear. She lifted her eyes to meet his. 'One of the properties Landmark has bought is Park House.'

'OK …' He drew it out, his eyes dropping to the revealing deep V-neck of her T-shirt, narrowing as he fought to listen to what she was saying. She could see that he was working through the implications.

'The big problem … one of them … is that Irina owes money to some other Russians. It is better if you do not know who they are. The sale of Park House was supposed to pay them off, but obviously that is not going to happen any time soon and … Well, she is a bit distraught.'

Sebastian pursed his lips, finally focusing fully on what she was saying. 'Were they involved in what happened to Nick?'

Yaraslava shrugged. 'I do not think so. That is not really their style.'

'Too messy?'

She nodded. 'Very. They plan things. They know the cash is wrapped up in the house, so they could easily have hurt Nick to frighten me, but I think they would have done it at the office. The house makes no sense.'

'So how does all this impact me and you?'

Yaraslava closed her eyes again. 'Dimitri wants me to sell Park House as fast as possible, even if I have to buy it myself.'

Sebastian started to tut. 'That's ridiculous.'

Yaraslava took a breath. 'I know. But the thing is, the police think I might have had something to do with Nick's death. My fingerprints are on the stone that he was hit with.'

Sebastian's eyebrows went up again. 'How ...?' He rolled his free hand, careful not to knock the glass. Yaraslava deliberately looked at him from under her lashes, her eyes anxious, her face creased with worry. 'This is where it gets complicated.'

'And it isn't already? Go on.' The hand inside her top slipped to Yaraslava's waist, and he reached for his glass and took a sip of the smoothie she'd given him.

'Park House was leased by the previous owner. She bought it to relocate but then never moved in, so she let it short-term to a tech company. It was a blank canvas – very neutral, but very cold. I knew the Bradfords were interested, but they are not a couple with imagination. We needed to stage it, make it look like home when they viewed it. There was not much time, so I took some of my own paintings and ornaments.'

He nodded, as if he was following but needed more information. She continued. 'The paintings are those Cornish seascapes I have been buying when we go to Hawksmoor. And ...' She took a deep breath. 'The ornament he was hit with was that beautiful piece of serpentine stone, the big one. My fingerprints were all over it.'

'So the police think you were involved somehow?'

Yaraslava looked at him, her eyes full of just the right amount of distress. Her lip trembled. 'They brought me in for questioning, and Dimitri gave me an alibi. But he is getting desperate – or rather, Irina is. He is starting to hint that he may go back to the police and say that he was mixed up about where I was when Nick was attacked.'

Chapter 58

BY THE TIME Rosie finished her call with Hallie and returned to the cafe, a trickle of walkers had arrived, their bright rain gear a riot of colour. On the other side of the counter, Morwenna pointed to the table Rosie had been sitting at before and indicated she'd bring her over another coffee, but Rosie could see Morwenna and Jago needed to focus on their customers.

Behind Rosie, the door opened and a party of four came in, a muddy collie tangling around their legs as it made for a water bowl behind the door. It had obviously been here before.

Rosie moved out of their way. 'Tell Jago I'll message him. You're busy.'

Morwenna held up one finger and, deftly producing a paper bag from under the counter, slipped two more hevva buns into it. She passed them to Rosie with a knowing look. Before Rosie could protest, Morwenna was asking the people who had just come in what they would like.

Rosie shook her head, laughing, and mouthed 'thank you'.

Following the path up the cliff towards the lighthouse and the car park where she'd met Jago the previous day, Rosie paused for a moment, looking out to sea. The cliff sloped away steeply in front of her, thickly carpeted in deep grass that met the path where she was standing, with no barrier or fence to keep people away from the edge. Only half concentrating, she turned over the conversation she'd had with Hallie in her mind.

The police had said that one of Michael's emails had come from the office, and they'd arrested Yaraslava. Her fingerprints turning up on the murder weapon was a pretty conclusive link to Nick's murder. Was Hallie right that Yaraslava had sent Rosie and Grace away for a reason – perhaps not to isolate Hallie in London, but to isolate the two of them all the way down in Cornwall?

Yaraslava had definitely come up with this Cornwall idea with Sebastian. Were they working together?

Rosie shivered, realising as she turned onto the path leading to the car park that the damp mist rolling in off the sea was getting thicker. The wail of the foghorn sounded again. Rosie glanced up, but it was as if the whole lighthouse and the building beside it had vanished into the cloud, or had never been there at all.

Rosie picked up her step and hurried towards the footpath. If she cut across the field again, she'd be back at the house in a few minutes. In the bottom of her coat pocket she could feel the key Anja had left – she'd remembered it this time. There was one for each of them, on matching brass keyrings that looked like knots tied in a piece of rope. Rosie ran her fingers over the knot as she walked. When she reached the stile and the wooden sign for the footpath, she could feel the start of a shower and see the sheep had moved into the lee of the wall again.

The house felt empty when Rosie got back, swinging the heavy door closed behind her, the hallway warm and welcoming, but quiet, as if it was waiting. Grace had said she might walk up to the village. She must still be out; perhaps she was having coffee up there.

Kicking off her muddy boots and unpeeling her coat, Rosie draped her scarf and hat over the banister again and went into the kitchen.

Grace had hauled out a selection of vegetables from the organic box and had left them on the counter:

muddy potatoes, carrots and parsnips. Beside them was a white china plate with a pile of very skinny spring onions on it. They looked as if they'd just been picked and washed. Rosie looked at them, puzzled. They didn't look like the spring onions her grandpa grew, and she didn't remember them being picked this early in the year; she was pretty sure that he only planted them in March.

Rosie didn't know why Grace had suddenly decided to cook for both of them. The fridge was packed full of obviously home-made pies and a lasagne, and Rosie had spotted two big quiches in there, too. But perhaps Grace loved cooking, and it had just never come up as a topic of conversation.

Filling the kettle, Rosie clicked it on and leaned on the counter, looking out of the window. The rain was falling heavily on the glass; the mist was so thick she could barely see the garden. Rosie made her tea and padded out to the hall. She wanted to unpack properly and enjoy the peace of the house before Grace got back.

As she reached the top of the stairs, Rosie heard an alarming rattling sound coming from Grace's room, as if the wind had caught something and was threatening to break it. Hesitating, she knocked with her free hand in case Grace was inside after all. Whatever was rattling stopped for a moment, then started again, more loudly this time. Worried that something might be getting damaged, Rosie knocked more loudly.

'Grace, are you in there?' She waited a moment longer for a response but, not getting one, pushed the door open.

Grace had left a top window open and the wind and rain were whipping the blind and heavy curtains. Water was already starting to pool on the windowsill. Putting her tea down on the bedside table, Rosie ran over to the window and closed it, firmly shutting the weather out. She stood for a moment, looking out at the fields, now shrouded in mist. The weather in Cornwall changed as quickly as it did at home.

Turning to collect her tea, Rosie was picking up her mug when she noticed a book beside Grace's bed: *A Field Guide to Poisonous Wild Plants*. Poisonous plants? Rosie looked at it, puzzled. Why would Grace have a book about poisonous plants?

Rosie could see several bookmarks sticking out of it. Picking it up, she flipped to the first marked page and was greeted by a photograph of a flower that looked a bit like a crocus.

Meadow saffron grows in hay meadows, woodland and is also popular in gardens. Its delicate pink flowers appear in September. The leaves appear in the spring and must be treated with caution as all parts of the plant are poisonous. Colchicine, the alkaloid of meadow saffron, has been used for centuries in the treatment of gout and, more recently, Mediterranean fever, but several cases of poisoning with this plant have occurred when it was mistaken for wild garlic.

Why had Grace marked this page? The photograph was of meadow saffron in flower, its pretty star-like petals shades of purple and lilac.

Mystified, Rosie flicked to another page, immediately recognising the plant marked as one of the bunches of fern-like leaves in the vase on the kitchen table. Hemlock. Not the sort of plant you'd put in a vase. 'Hemlock is highly poisonous to humans and animals.' Rosie flicked to the next marked page. Oleander. She was sure there were branches of this in the vase, too. 'When ingested it tastes quite bitter … Induces stomach upsets.'

Rosie put the book down slowly. What had Grace said about the soup last night? 'It might be a little bitter.' Rosie had thought it was an odd thing to say about soup.

She flicked through the pages to the meadow saffron and read on: 'crocus-like bulbs'. Perhaps the spring onions in the kitchen weren't spring onions at all.

Disturbed, her mind trying to rationalise what she'd read, Rosie put the book down and picked up her tea. She looked around the room, still frowning, still trying to work out why Grace would have brought poisonous plants into the house. It was as if the information was trying to connect with something in her brain, but she was resisting it.

Unlike Rosie, Grace had obviously unpacked properly last night, leaving her case neatly in the corner of the room. Rosie turned to the bedside table, opening the drawer. Perhaps she had other gardening books with her, or something to explain this sudden interest.

Rosie didn't quite know what she was looking for, but something wasn't right. Grace had never once mentioned being interested in plants — or cooking — even when they'd once talked about Rosie's grandpa's vegetable patch.

Finally focusing on the drawer, Rosie realised it didn't have books in it — only an old smartphone. Rosie picked it up and looked at it. She knew Grace's phone was the latest iPhone; she was obsessed with having the latest one, and it had a pale pink pearlised cover that Rosie had commented on.

Was it Grace's? *Why would Grace have two phones?*

Chapter 59

'LET ME GET this straight …' Sitting on Yaraslava's sofa, Sebastian shifted around to face her, his tone serious. 'Your brother is prepared to let you get arrested for murder – why, exactly?'

Yaraslava sighed and glanced out of the tall sash window overlooking the street. The wind had picked up, scattering raindrops against the window like shot. As she formed her answer, she could hear the constant sound of traffic outside and the tick of the mantel clock.

'I do not think – I *hope* – he is not going to withdraw his statement, but he is desperate for me to find a solution to get Park House sold. If these Russians come after Irina, they are not going to be very understanding. He could be next, and then, who knows? If they are angry enough, they will be ringing on my doorbell.'

'Or putting plutonium in your coffee.'

'Something like that. And …' Yaraslava rubbed her hand over her eyes. 'Rosie is being stalked by someone called Michael, and one of the Russians is called Mikhail. It is one of the most popular names in Russia, but still …'

'Rosie's a very attractive girl.' Sebastian paused. 'If they have been watching you, they would have seen her. You can't help but notice her.'

Yaraslava kept her reaction hidden. *What was he talking about – about Rosie? She needed him to focus on her.* She cleared her throat. 'The biggest problem, though …' She glanced at him, her eyes brimming with tears. 'If I go on trial and the press publish photos of the stone, or they get any shots of the house and the paintings, your wife might recognise them, and she will know that I have been to Hawksmoor. If anyone mentions it is serpentine stone, she is going to start wondering how it ended up in Park House.'

Sebastian scowled for a moment. 'She knows about Nick, obviously, but I doubt she'd pay much attention to the trial. With a bit of luck she'll be in Cannes, anyway. I mean, I can make sure she's in Cannes, in the lead-up to it.'

'But trials take ages to come to court. It would be hanging over our heads …' Yaraslava suddenly felt exhausted. Not all of this was fiction. She might be creating a narrative for Sebastian, but part of her felt sick inside. Someone had bashed Nick over the head in Park House, and she was feeling increasingly vulnerable. She was starting to think that things could get a lot worse before they got better.

She closed her eyes. She'd thought she'd never feel this exposed again after leaving home and trying to settle halfway across the world, but unless she found a solution for the sale of Park House soon, God only knew what might happen.

Sebastian shifted next to her. 'Essentially, you need to keep Dimitri sweet so he doesn't consider withdrawing his statement. And if you aren't directly linked to the stone that killed Nick, then there's no reason for my wife to get suspicious. So our priority is keeping you out of court and safe.' He took a sip of his smoothie, as if it helped him think. 'And if you can get these Russians out of the equation, you'll sleep more easily, and by the sounds of things, the lovely Rosie might, too.'

Yaraslava nodded slowly. 'Rosie is incredible. She has turned the whole situation around with her posts about stalking, but I know she is frightened. Terrified, actually. It was wonderful of you to send her to Hawksmoor for the week. I do not think anyone will find her there.'

Sebastian pulled his hand out from under her T-shirt and, wrapping it around her shoulder, pulled her close to him.

'There's a simple solution to all of this. I'll buy Park House for you. I'll put it in your name, so there's no danger of my wife getting at it if we do split. Then you won't have to move around all the time and we can have some privacy.' He paused. 'That'll get your brother's girlfriend off the hook. He'd better not try anything like this again, though.'

Yaraslava looked at Sebastian in surprise, but before she could say anything he continued. 'Are any of this Irina's other properties being handled by us?'

She bit her lip. This was where he went ballistic and everything came tumbling down. It had to happen.

'Get rid of them. Get Hallie to call the other brokers she knows and move all of those properties off our books. If anyone files a Suspicious Activity Report, that's on your brother or this Irina to sort out.'

It wasn't quite that simple, but she needed to deal with one problem at a time.

'You would do that? You would buy Park House?'

Sebastian inclined his head. 'What's the asking price?'

'Ten million.'

'Offer this Irina nine, all cash, seven-day closure. I'm sure that'll help plug the hole in her dam. And then you can move in, my love.'

He kissed her on the lips, but Yaraslava's mind was still reeling. She put her hand on his shoulder. 'Do you really think you might separate?'

Sebastian swirled his smoothie around his glass. 'Let's just say I'm getting a bit fed up of coming home to an empty house when I know you're somewhere in another part of London on your own.'

Yaraslava smiled. 'Thank you. Really, I did not expect you to say or do any of that.' She said it as sincerely as she could, trying to ignore the flare of disquiet in her brain.

Right now, moving Landmark's other properties on to someone else's books would create more issues than it solved. *Out of the frying pan into the fire.*

And moving in with Sebastian was definitely not part of her game plan, either.

Chapter 60

ROSIE PULLED GRACE'S bedroom door closed behind her and padded over to her own room, her mind swirling. Why would Grace need another phone? And a cheap one at that.

But perhaps it wasn't Grace's at all; perhaps a previous guest had left it in the drawer and she didn't even know it was there. Rosie hadn't opened any of the drawers in her own room, but she hadn't put any of her things away either.

Grace had wanted to get out into the garden. Rosie put her tea down beside the bed, pulled her phone out of her jeans, and put it down beside her mug. She pushed back the duvet and climbed in, pulling the cushions up behind her.

Something was wrong here, and Rosie wasn't quite sure she could work it all out. Had Yaraslava sent Grace down here with a second phone so Grace could spy on her and report back?

Rosie could feel herself reaching for logical, safe explanations, but deep inside her mind, an alarm was going off and it was getting louder.

Hallie had said Yaraslava had attacked Ben – that she'd been dating Ben when she worked at Hunt's. Rosie closed her eyes. Everything that had happened over the past few days rolled around her head, making her feel distinctly queasy.

Rosie heard her phone vibrate. The wind must have changed again, and it had picked up a signal. Sebastian had said mobile reception was terrible in the area, but Rosie hadn't quite understood that it was virtually non-existent. She picked up her phone and saw a message in French reminding her about roaming charges.

Ignoring it, Rosie opened her email to check to see if she had enough signal to pick up her messages. She'd told DS Nandy the previous night to double up with an email if he needed her.

As she opened her Gmail folder, Rosie could see that her inbox contained a bunch of new messages. Sarah from Corvus Books again – doubling her offer. Slightly bizarre, but interesting; perhaps Rosie's silence was worrying her. Well, Sarah would have to wait a bit longer.

Rosie ran down the rest of the emails in her inbox and felt herself chill.

Of course, one of them was from Michael. She'd managed almost twenty-four whole hours without hearing from him, but here he was again, like that stone in her shoe, or the knife buried in her back that got closer to her heart every time she moved.

There was nothing from DS Nandy, or anyone else interesting. Her finger hovered over Michael's message. Should she open it? Was that torturing herself a bit more?

At least she was safe here – he didn't know where she was. Her Instagram would have updated this morning with another post about the Cheyne Walk apartment, a view of Chelsea Embankment Gardens from the main reception room.

Rosie almost closed the app, but something pulled her back. She opened the message.

TO: Rosie Kinsella

DATE: 4 April 2025

SUBJECT: Are you OK?

FROM: Outlander

Rosie, I'm so worried about you, are you sick? I'm emailing because you're not seeing my WhatsApp messages –

I wondered if you'd lost your phone or something. Please tell me you're OK.

I really hope the Chelsea apartment viewing goes well next week, it looks incredible, such an iconic building. I know you'll find a buyer who will snap it up, it's amazing, just like you. Perhaps I should buy it and we could sip champagne together in the hot tub to celebrate. It's lashing here today, hope you can put that umbrella to good use.

M xxxx

    Rosie read Michael's email again and began to shake. She was going to throw up.

    Suddenly everything made sense. She knew who Michael was.

Chapter 61

AS GRACE PUSHED open the front door of Hawksmoor House, she could see Rosie had got in ahead of her. She'd abandoned her coat and that disgusting scarf on the end of the stairs. Which Grace found a bit annoying. In a house like this, the least Rosie could do would be to hang up her coat tidily somewhere. It wasn't as if there was a shortage of cupboards.

Grace took off her boots, leaving them neatly beside Rosie's discarded pair.

'Rosie, woo-hoo, I'm back,' she called into the hall, not sure if Rosie would hear her. She could see the kitchen door was open, but if Rosie was right down at the window, or listening to music or something, she definitely wouldn't.

Grace went down the hall and stuck her head through the kitchen doorway. The lights were on at the counter end, but there was nobody in there. Perhaps Rosie was in the living room or upstairs. This house was so vast, she could be lying dead somewhere and you might not know for a week.

Going into the kitchen, checking the water in the kettle, Grace flipped the switch on and reached for a mug from the cupboard above, pausing for a moment to scan the piles of elegant china on the shelves. Most people had a mismatched hotch-potch of mugs, but in Hawksmoor everything was plain white, only the stippling effect in the china creating a sense of difference. It was as if every last detail had been considered and executed perfectly. Grace's mind returned to the room she'd found downstairs, with its very interesting collections.

She leaned on the counter and crossed her arms. She'd had three cups of coffee up at the village and could already feel her mind racing, her heart rate echoing it. This always happened when she had too much caffeine, but it was also when she was at her most creative, ideas flying around her head.

And she'd been doing a lot of thinking while she was out.

It was only a ten-minute walk to the village – at this time of year it was a rather bleak jumble of tourist traps and coffee shops. She could imagine it would be humming in the summer, with all that brightly coloured tourist tat seaside shops seemed to specialise in. She'd settled on a cafe selling delicious Cornish pasties, with long windows overlooking the main junction, choosing a seat in the corner.

As Grace had passed the souvenir shops on the way up to the centre of the village, having a cursory look in their windows, she'd seen ornaments and paperweights, lamp stands and bookends, all made out of a black marbled stone she'd recognised. Which had *really* got her thinking.

One thing Grace had discovered, from almost her first day at school, was that thinking got you a long way in life. Planning ahead, assessing the outcomes, looking at a problem from every angle, had always worked for her.

And creating the narrative, the story around events, was crucial.

The kettle boiled and Grace made herself a cup of strong tea, just how she liked it. Rosie liked her tea weak with sugar; the very sight of it made Grace feel ill.

Picking up her mug, she went into the hall and quickly checked the living room, but there was still no sign of Rosie. Where was she?

Climbing the stairs, Grace was almost at the top when she called out again. 'Hi, Rosie, I'm back. Are you there?'

A moment later she could hear Rosie's voice. 'I'm in here. I'm just having a lie-down, I don't feel brilliant.'

'Oh, can I get you anything? Some soup for lunch, maybe?' Grace hovered on the landing outside Rosie's door.

'No, I'm fine, I think I'm just exhausted. I'm having a rest, I'll be down soon.'

Grace paused. Should she knock and stick her head around the door? She took a sip of her tea, listening hard for any sounds of movement. Nothing.

Smiling to herself, Grace went to her own room and put her hand on the knob, expecting to have to twist it to open the door, but she stopped abruptly. It wasn't fully closed. It was pulled closed all right, but the latch hadn't fully engaged.

Grace was sure she'd shut it properly when she'd left. She knew she had.

Stepping inside, she put her tea down beside the bed and froze. Her book on wild plants wasn't quite as she'd left it, and one of her page markers had slipped out onto the carpet beside the bed. At the same moment, she realised someone had picked up her book, she also realised the small window she'd opened last night had been closed. As a gust of wind blew against the glass, Grace could see the pools of water on the broad white windowsill where the rain had evidently been blown in.

Someone had been in her room and closed the window to stop the weather coming in, but what else had they done?

Chapter 62

LEANING ON HER bedroom door, listening to Grace go into her room, Rosie felt as if all her muscles had locked. She'd read that animals responded to a threat with a fight, flight or freeze response, and right now she was frozen.

When she'd heard Grace coming up the stairs, she'd slipped off her bed to listen at her bedroom door, but with the click of Grace's own door closing, Rosie suddenly realised Grace would see the window was shut, and she'd know Rosie had been in there … unless Rosie pretended it had been Anja, the housekeeper.

She could feel panic rising, threatening to overwhelm her, and now her heart was beating so loudly in her ears, she was sure the whole house could hear it.

But she couldn't just stay stuck here in the corner of her room, praying. She had to get out of the house and get to Jago. She knew he'd help her.

But how could she get out without Grace seeing her? Rosie leaned against the door, trying to catch her breath and think calmly at the same time.

She'd have to act as if nothing had happened – that she didn't suspect anything. Rosie took a shaky breath. This was going to have to be an Oscar-winning performance.

She looked at her phone. The one bar of reception on the display had vanished. If she set up a message to send now, would it go when the phone hit a patch of signal? It was worth a try.

She quickly typed a message to Jago. Lunchtime was almost over now; hopefully he'd be a bit less busy and have a chance to look at his phone. She sent similar messages to Hallie and DS Nandy. She just needed to pray they arrived.

Rosie closed her eyes. She still couldn't believe it, but 'Michael's' last email had absolutely confirmed it. His voice messages had suggested that he was English – she'd been totally convinced he was – but his last email had used two expressions that English people very rarely used. He'd asked her if she'd been 'sick' – in her experience, English people always said 'ill' – and he'd said it was 'lashing' where he was. That was a full-on Irish expression. She'd never, ever, heard an English person use it.

Which meant he wasn't English at all.

And there was only one other Irish person Rosie knew who might have had access to the office, and therefore could have sent the email that Nick had identified.

And that one other Irish person's fingerprints were on the rock that had killed Nick. She'd explained it by saying she'd seen the piece of stone lying in the hall and had picked it up – *but nobody had considered that she might have picked it up for a very different reason.*

Rosie had no idea how Nick could have realised that it had been Grace who had sent the message, but she was sure she was right. Rosie knew you could schedule email – maybe that was how the photos of her house had arrived when Grace had been with her, and miles away from her laptop. She'd scheduled them. And she'd been to Rosie's apartment lots of times – she was always saying how much she loved it, how perfect it was – so she could have taken the photos of the stairs and the hallway at any time.

Had Nick organised to meet Grace at Park House to find out what was going on? Grace might have got suspicious if he'd asked her to meet him at the pub –

they didn't generally hang out outside work – but if he'd pretended he needed help with the viewing, she would have gone without question, especially if he'd persuaded her by saying it could be a co-listing and they'd share the commission. Had he got there early and then confronted her?

Rosie winced. She'd wondered all along about him being struck on his head – she couldn't work out why he would have turned his back on a burglar or someone who was threatening him. But she could see how he might walk away from Grace. He definitely wouldn't have expected her to wallop him over the head with an ornamental rock. But Grace was tall and, as Rosie had seen on the train, she was strong.

Nandy had said he felt this attack was about rage, rather than planning. Had Nick said something about the emails and, cornered, had Grace retaliated by grabbing the nearest object to hand? Had she meant to kill him?

She must have done. There hadn't been just one blow to his head.

The thought made Rosie feel dizzy, just as when she'd listened to Michael's voice on her phone. Rosie had thought he'd sounded like an actor. Now she was sure he was an AI voice generated by Grace's computer.

Perhaps DS Nandy would be able to find something in Grace's internet history to corroborate that – or, better, a saved file.

It didn't matter; right now Rosie was absolutely certain she needed to get out of the house and away from Grace. Grace had failed to scare her to death with Michael's messages, but Rosie was pretty sure she had tried to poison her the night before. Why on earth would she make soup when the fridge was stacked with food?

What Rosie really didn't understand was why Grace was doing all of this. But that wasn't her biggest problem. Getting away to somewhere safe was.

Taking a deep breath, Rosie eased the bedroom door open and ran lightly to the top of the stairs, praying the thick carpet would absorb the sound. She'd got down the first couple of stairs when she heard Grace's door open behind her.

'Feeling better?' Grace's voice had a hard edge to it.

Rosie stopped and turned around with a broad grin. 'Much, thanks. I've got the overpowering urge for chocolate cake. I didn't see any in the fridge, but if I'm quick I'll catch the cafe before it closes. They have "Death by Chocolate". I can't stop thinking about it. Want a bit?'

Jaysus, why had she said that – death by chocolate? Her mouth was running on its own. But at least it would be better than death by deadly nightshade.

Rosie could feel her heart beating as if it was going to explode, her palms sweating on the wooden banister as she hovered at the top of the stairs, waiting for Grace's answer. Then, thinking fast, she said lightly, 'Oh, Anja was here when I came home. She brought some oat milk. She'd forgotten you liked it. She made my bed, too.'

'How did she know that, about the milk?' Rosie could feel Grace looking at her hard. Half in, half out of her door, her head on one side, she was frowning, as if she was confused.

'Maybe Yaraslava messaged her.' Rosie shrugged. 'No idea.' Grace started to come out of her door and Rosie had to stop herself from running down the stairs at full pelt. 'I'll only be ten minutes. Put the kettle on?'

Turning, she scampered down the stairs, pausing at the bottom to grab her coat, desperately trying not to look as if she was hurrying. She didn't turn around, but she was sure she could feel Grace's eyes boring into her back.

Bending to pull on her boots, Rosie straightened and, turning to look up the stairs, waved to Grace. 'Won't be long!'

Hauling open the front door, she pulled it closed behind her and, gripping her phone, ran down the drive, freezing raindrops cutting into her face like knives.

Chapter 63

YARASLAVA HAD DECIDED not to go into the office when Sebastian left. Instead, she'd gone shopping in the new Battersea Power Station centre. She needed to give her mind a break from all the stress of the past few days and focus on something completely different. Wandering around luxury shops – places that seemed to exist only in the pages of glossy magazines when she was growing up, and which had been totally out of her reach when she'd first arrived in London – gave her great pleasure. It calmed her, and even if she didn't buy much, she always came back feeling empowered.

But she'd bought quite a lot this trip. Retail therapy was a real thing.

And she needed to change up her wardrobe a bit.

When she'd first been able to afford clothes with triple-digit price tags it had been a breakthrough, a sign that she was achieving, that she'd made it, and reminding herself of that every now and again was good for her mental health.

Her hands full of the huge stiff paper bags that she'd carried up from the car, Yaraslava was just going to put them down at the bottom of the stairs when she heard a rap behind her at the front door. Freezing, she felt her heart rate increase. She'd literally only just pushed it closed behind her, hadn't even taken her fur coat off yet.

Straightening slowly, she turned and faced the front door. The hallway was narrow, its Victorian floorboards polished to a shine. The door itself was painted a soft sage green and had two stained-glass panels above the brass letterbox. Through the intricate swirling pattern of ivy curling across the glass she could see a dark shape, unmistakably a man, standing at the top of the steep steps leading to the street.

She wasn't expecting anyone.

A hollow feeling was beginning to grow in her stomach, fear nipping at the edges. Had the Grigori brothers sent someone to impress on her the urgency of this sale?

After Sebastian's offer, despite the 'strings' he'd attached, and which she really wasn't particularly happy about, she'd felt a weight had been lifted from her shoulders.

The minute he'd left, she'd called the Bradfords to let them know there was an offer on Park House, just in case they wanted to make one themselves. As she'd expected, they'd decided they'd prefer a house where a murder hadn't recently happened in the living room.

Then she'd texted Sebastian to say that Irina Ivanov at Landmark was delighted with his offer, and had accepted it without hesitation.

The rap of the brass knocker came again, sharper, making Yaraslava jump, the sound like a firework going off. She felt herself start to shake, and closed her eyes. Whatever happened next, if this was the Grigoris' people, now wasn't the time to lose her shit.

She felt her mouth dry as she stepped closer to the door. She was going to have to open it. Being kept waiting this long would only increase their annoyance. She just prayed whoever was on the other side didn't have a weapon. Dying on her own doorstep was even lower on her list of life goals than shacking up with Sebastian, and that was definitely an addendum on the last page.

Stepping forward, bracing herself for the bullet that might come through the doorway the moment she opened it, Yaraslava lifted her hand, eased away the Chubb lock and began to open the door.

'Christ, you took your time, it's freezing out here.'

Sebastian's voice reached her and Yaraslava almost wet herself with relief.

'My God, what are you doing here?' She swung the door wide open.

He grinned at her. 'Twice in one day. Aren't you the lucky one?'

Yaraslava forced a grin. 'Aren't I?' She kept her voice light and stepped aside to let him in.

'Good news, my darling. I called into the office when I left you, and found the Landmark file.' Yaraslava kept her smile fixed in place while her already delicate stomach did a complete flip. Sebastian didn't pick up on her reaction; instead, he beamed at her. 'I've instructed my solicitors and they've initiated the transfer. We don't have to bother with surveyors' reports and all that nonsense. Park House is all yours, my love.'

Yaraslava staggered slightly, before quickly throwing her arms around him and kissing him.

'You had better come in so we can celebrate.'

Chapter 64

IN HAWKSMOOR HOUSE, Grace stood at the top of the stairs for a moment as the sound of Rosie pulling the front door closed echoed through the hallway. She could feel anxiety seeping into every pore.

Had Anja, the housekeeper, really called in this morning when they were both out? Anja had said she would leave them to it and to call if they needed anything, but perhaps Sebastian had asked her to check in on them?

Sebastian, with his strange obsessions and evidently enormous bank balance.

Grace turned and walked slowly back into her room, her skin pricking. If Anja had closed her bedroom window, surely she would have made her bed, as well as Rosie's? Grace had pulled the duvet over and plumped the pillows when she'd got up, but it definitely hadn't been remade.

She went over to the bathroom and, flicking on the light, looked inside. The towel was still hanging slightly askew over the shower door. Anja definitely wouldn't have left it like that. She would have put it on the towel rail or given Grace a fresh one.

Closing the bathroom door, Grace looked from the window to her bedside cabinet, her mouth drying.

Someone had been into her room.

And Rosie had been in an awful rush to leave.

Hurrying to the cabinet, Grace pulled open the drawer to see if her spare phone was where she'd left it. It was, and it didn't look as if it had been moved. So that was something. She pulled it out of the drawer and slipped it under her pillow.

Rosie must have come in and closed the window. And picked up the book on the way out. Had she guessed? Grace closed her eyes. She must have done – or at least, she strongly suspected. Rosie had definitely looked mildly frantic as she'd trotted down the stairs. And Grace didn't think that was due to chocolate cake withdrawal.

Grace could feel her anger building again – the blind fury that only Rosie fecking Kinsella seemed able to induce in her.

This wasn't how it was supposed to end. Rosie was *supposed* to eat the soup and get crippling stomach pains, and Grace would – eventually – after trying the phone several times, but failing to get reception, run for help.

But it would be too late.

The medics would find that Rosie had ingested something poisonous, but Grace would be able to show them the pot of soup they'd both eaten from, so they'd know it hadn't been that. Their bowls and cutlery would have been through the dishwasher at that stage, so the conclusion would be that she must have picked something on her walk. And Grace would remember how much Rosie had said she loved wild garlic, and that sometimes she ate it raw in Paris to ward off a cold, and the rest would be history.

Then Grace would have to post from Rosie's account, to tell her fans what had happened and that she would be taking it over.

I know how devastated you all are by the terrible loss of our friend – one of my best friends – but I won't let her memory die. From now on you'll see me here, bringing you everything you loved about this account.

In time, she'd change the name on Instagram to GracesLondonLife. She had it all worked out.

She had a plan. And she wasn't going to let Rosie Kinsella wreck it, not after she'd come this far. This Cornwall trip had been a gift – completely on their own, with terrible phone reception and no CCTV. Anything could happen to *amazing* Rosie Kinsella down here.

Amazing Rosie, with her perfect life and her fabulous Instagram, her skin and hair that looked incredible even when she was half blown away by the weather. Rosie, who had stepped into Sterling & Co and taken Grace's job; who everyone was always saying was brilliant at selling, and who now would get recognised even more after her stint on national TV. And who, next month, would be spread all over the glossy feature pages of *Delphine*. No doubt they'd take her somewhere *amazing* for the photo shoot, with a team doing her hair and make-up and providing her wardrobe.

And, when they'd been on the train, Rosie had mentioned she'd even had an offer of a book deal about her stalking experience. She was totally conflicted about it, but like the media interest, it came off the back of the success of her Instagram.

Grace could feel her jaw clench as she thought about it, her whole body tense. The absolute last thing she had intended was for Rosie to become famous as a result of all of this. But, of course, this was *amazing* Rosie, who, on top of everything else, was now the poster girl for stalking.

But too much had happened. She'd come too far to lose now.

She'd even managed the Nick situation when he'd challenged her about that email. Grace knew she'd been stupid to send it from the office, but it had been one of those days when only she and Nick were there. Of course, it hadn't taken him long to realise that, once he'd discovered the IP address and the date it had been sent. Everyone else had been off looking at the Caulfield development over by Regent's Park.

Obviously, if they'd included her, Grace wouldn't have been boiling with anger and hit *send* too soon – which was Rosie's fault, too. And then, standing there in Park House, Nick had asked her why she was doing it all, and said how lovely and *amazing* Rosie was, and Grace had seen his face, his puppy dog eyes. On top of everything else, *Nick fancied amazing fecking Rosie*. That had just been too much. Grace had been *very* interested in Nick for ages, had been trying to give him an opening to ask her on a date. She'd been sure he liked her, too, but she'd obviously got that wrong. Really wrong. Overwhelmed by hurt and hatred, that had sent her into a red zone and she'd flipped completely.

Which was exactly how she was feeling now.

But now Grace had an idea about how she was going to finish it, and who she could direct an extra layer of suspicion towards. Someone who had lured them both down here – 'lured' was a good word – and who was already breaking the law.

The headlines in the local paper had dovetailed beautifully with her discovery of that egg collection. Serendipity, indeed.

Hurrying out of her bedroom, Grace ran down the stairs to get her coat. Her plan needed to change, and fast. She'd be virtually invisible in this fog. And the cafe Rosie was going to was right beside the cliff edge.

Chapter 65

THE MIST WAS even thicker down beside the cafe than it had been crossing the field. Swirling like Rosie's fear.

Rosie didn't think she'd ever run so fast, her heart thumping, the cold air making her face sting. She'd focused on the uneven ground, trying desperately not to go over on her ankle. If Grace was looking out of the window, Rosie needed it to look as if she was running because of the rain, not because of the threat behind her.

She had no idea if Grace would try and follow her, but the faster she got to Jago, the better.

The mist had brought rain with it, and by the time she had crossed the field and reached the second stile she was dripping wet, her hair plastered to her head.

The rain blinding her, Rosie sprinted along the pedestrian path, barely able see, running on instinct. There was nobody here now; the car park was empty except for Jago's camper van in the corner. She kept running, trying to measure her steps down the steep path cutting through the vegetation to the cliff top and the cafe, so that she didn't trip and fall. As she emerged from the dense foliage, she could see there were lights on inside behind the counter, but the main seating area was in darkness. It looked very shut.

The whole area was deserted; even the hardy walkers she'd seen earlier had vanished. The wind was starting to howl, and above her Rosie could hear the eerie high-pitched warning wail of the foghorn, the sound almost bouncing off the mist.

Part of her couldn't believe the weather had changed so dramatically, so fast, but she knew that was because she'd been living in cities too long, where you couldn't see the weather coming. At home you could usually see it rolling in; she should have guessed that the morning mist had been the precursor to a storm. The mist was changing to dense fog, brought in on the wind from the sea, and Rosie could see it getting thicker as it enveloped the restaurant.

She ran down the path and around the outdoor tables to the door of the cafe. Her hands on the glass, she could see a dark shape moving inside. She tried the door, but it was locked.

Morwenna must have heard her. She came through to the counter area and, seeing Rosie, came out from behind it to open the door. Morwenna was tall, but she had to reach up to slide down the top bolt before she could unlock it.

'Come in, you'll freeze. There's a red weather warning, you need to get home.'

Breathless, Rosie found she didn't have enough words to explain why she was out. 'I need to find Jago, it's really important.'

'He's worried these egg thieves will try and use the bad weather to get to the nests. We decided to close the cafe, so he's taking a geek along the cliff path, between here and the lighthouse.'

Rosie wasn't entirely sure what she meant by 'geek', but she got the gist.

'Are you OK?' As if Morwenna had suddenly registered the frantic look on Rosie's face, her tone filled with concern.

'Not really. I just need to find Jago.'

'He shouldn't be far, and I'll be here for a bit if you need to come back.'

'Thank you, thank you.' Tempted to go into the cafe, Rosie knew she wouldn't feel safe until she found Jago. If she was right, Grace had already killed once. Who knew what she might do if she'd realised Rosie knew she was Michael?

Rosie's mind didn't have space to form a plan. She just knew she needed to find Jago – she trusted him, and he'd help her.

She turned back to the weather as a gust of wind brought the sting of seawater straight into her face. Pulling her scarf up, she waved to Morwenna and ran around the outside of the restaurant, hesitating as she got to the low wall surrounding it. The fog was getting so thick, she couldn't see any of the nearby buildings, the art gallery or the gift shop. But Jago couldn't be that far away.

Hurrying forward, Rosie ran towards the edge of the cliff. She'd been surprised there was no barrier between the path and the cliffs when she'd been there earlier, but the path was even and wide enough to feel safe.

Calling out, she could hear Jago's name echoing towards her.

Chapter 66

ONE FOOT UP against the mouth of the cave, the other on the narrow grassy plateau outside it, Jago adjusted his harness so he could lean out from the cliff, checking to see if the tiny camera was properly concealed. He should have put one up the year before, when the egg thefts had started, but he hadn't been able to work out *how* to do it without someone seeing him.

There was no question in his mind that the scum who were raiding the nests were local; they could even be members of his climbing group. One thing he was sure of was that word travelled around like wildfire. If anyone saw him messing about with cameras, everyone would be wondering why, and whoever was behind the thefts would get wind of it.

The eggs had to have been taken at night or in bad weather, or the thieves would have been exposed already.

That meant it was someone familiar with the landscape, and who knew to get down here when it was quiet.

A wave splashed up against the cliff and Jago felt its icy lash on his hand. He'd had to take his gloves off to nestle the camera into the crevice, but he was wearing his full waterproof kit with his gaiters to keep the rain and seawater out of the top of his boots.

It was a bit mad doing this in the fog and wind, but he knew this cliff face like he knew his own front garden. He'd been climbing it – usually without any safety equipment, much to his grandmother's ire – since he was old enough to walk.

And he was determined to catch whoever was doing this.

The police were trying, but they couldn't be everywhere, and in this part of the world they were thinly spread on a good day. They might have launched Operation Easter as a campaign in the media, but people would always be more important than birds, and the police had to go where they were needed most.

Concentrating on making the final adjustments to the military-grade waterproof camera, his fingers numb, Jago caught the sound of his name carried on the wind.

He pulled into the cave mouth. He couldn't afford to be seen or they'd never catch the lowlifes involved in the egg trade. He'd told Morwenna he was going for a walk; he didn't even trust her enough to say he was setting up cameras to watch the nests. He heard his name again – a girl's voice. Was Morwenna looking for him? It didn't sound like her – more like …

Rosie clawed at her wet hair, scraping it out of her face. The wind was whipping it into her eyes; her face stung with the freezing rain. Jogging along the path, she screamed Jago's name, trying to peer ahead into the fog. It was moving with the wind, some patches denser than others. Every now and again she could see the white tips of the waves crashing and boiling below her. She had no idea if Jago would hear her, but she had to try. He was here somewhere; she was sure of it.

Rosie suddenly realised she was back at the path leading up to the car park, the sign to the steps looming at her out of the fog. Jago had to be ahead of her further still. His van had been in darkness when she'd rushed past, so she was sure he wasn't there.

Her heart pounding in her chest, Rosie struggled on, the wind buffeting and pushing her. Suddenly her foot hit a loose stone and she went over on her ankle, a shooting pain searing up her leg. The tears came hot and fast, but she couldn't stop now – she couldn't give up. If Grace had realised Rosie knew that she was Michael, she could come after her. Rosie had no idea what Grace might do. She had to find Jago. Morwenna had said he was here.

Taking a deep breath, with the start of a stitch in her side, Rosie hobbled further along the uneven path. She could only see a few feet in front of her. She had read that wreckers had worked this coast for hundreds of years, luring ships onto the rocks with flares mimicking a harbour entrance. She could see how disorientated sailors must have become in weather like this, how welcome a flare on the hillside would have seemed.

She needed a flare now: a glimpse of the reflective stripes on the jacket she'd seen hanging in the van; Jago's smiling face appearing through the fog. How far had he gone along the path?

Rosie yelled his name as loud as she could and stopped for a moment, running her hands over her face, trying to push her hair away again and clear the rain from her eyes. He had to be here … She started to yell again, but …

The shove was hard and brutal, like a battering ram hitting her in the middle of her back. Taken completely by surprise, winded, Rosie staggered forward, trying to keep her balance on the edge of the path, the jagged cliffs plunging down to the sea below her. Fear flooded through her like a wave of electricity, and then she felt a second shove that sent her falling to her knees. She grabbed on to the long wet grass, desperately trying to save herself, but it slipped through her fingers. She plunged forward and slithered down the rock face ...

The scream made Jago jump, whacking his head on a sharp outcrop of rock. Simultaneously, a blur of movement further along the cliff made him react instinctively. Leaping from the entrance of the cave where he'd been hovering, he craned his neck out to listen for his name. Through the swirling fog, he could see something dark had landed on a narrow shelf of rock perilously close to the steep drop to the sea.

Not something – someone.

Feeding the rope through the carabiner on his harness, moving deftly sideways, in seconds Jago was beside the inert body. Using all his strength, wrapping his free arm around the person's waist, he hauled the inert body towards him, registering a mop of blonde hair and a ridiculous scarf at the same moment he realised it was

Rosie, and she was unconscious and bleeding from her head.

Jago could feel his muscles screaming as he pulled Rosie towards him. Gripping her tightly, he used their combined weight to swing her into the mouth of the cave he'd just vacated, scrambling as the loose rock fell away under his boots. Twisting out from behind her, Jago pushed Rosie into the fissure and, rooting under her scarf, checked her pulse, his fingers freezing on her warm skin. Her head lolled to one side, but he could feel her heartbeat.

Jago didn't have time to think what would have happened if he hadn't been here, but the universe had weird ways of working sometimes. Like them meeting the previous day.

Trying to push Rosie further into the cave – more of a deep cleft as wide as his shoulders – Jago crouched beside her. Shielding her with his body at least offered some protection from the weather.

But now he had to work out what to do. If he left her here, unconscious, while he went to get help, she could regain consciousness, panic, and slip down the cliff. If she remained unconscious in these conditions, she'd quickly get hypothermia. Great options. He felt her hand. It was warm compared to his, but she would cool rapidly unless he got help fast.

Pulling out his phone, Jago checked for a signal, knowing it would be weak at best.

It was weak, but it was there.

He dialled 999.

Chapter 67

GRACE STARTED AS her phone flashed with an incoming call from Hallie. She wasn't quite ready to talk to her yet; she needed to prepare herself mentally first. She let it go to her voicemail.

Sitting at the kitchen table, Grace read over the Instagram post she was working on and checked the time. It was hours since Rosie had left the house and the weather had been getting progressively worse. Now a full storm was whistling in from the sea.

She took a breath and hit Hallie's number to ring her back. The phone was answered immediately.

'Hallie? Is that you? Sorry I missed you, the phone signal is so bad here.' She flipped the call to speaker and sat up at the table, her hands in her lap. She needed to concentrate on this call.

At the other end, she could hear Hallie clattering

with something that sounded like the washing-up.

'Yes, I just wanted to see how you two were getting on. Are you OK?'

She sounded a bit guarded, but Grace took a deep breath, adding just a hint of panic to her tone. 'Have you heard from Rosie? She went out to get some chocolate cake hours ago and I haven't heard from her. I'm really worried.'

'Chocolate cake?' Hallie's inflection at the end of the word made it a question.

'She suddenly got this craving. There's a cafe here right by the sea, she said the cake was amazing.'

That word again. *Amazing.*

Rosie Kinsella wasn't so amazing now.

In the kitchen of Hawksmoor House, Grace narrowed her eyes, waiting for a moment.

Hallie filled the gap. 'How far away is it, this cafe? Maybe she got chatting to someone. You know what Rosie's like.'

'But she's been gone hours, and there's a huge storm here. It's lashing rain and the wind is howling. I'm so worried in case she's slipped or something.'

'Slipped where?' Hallie sounded as if she'd moved and was sitting down. Grace could just hear the sigh of a leather sofa.

'I don't know, that's the thing. The cliff path is really exposed. I mean, I don't know why she'd be there and not have come straight back. The cafe must be closed by now. I'm just worried in case …' Grace let her voice catch. 'In case she's met this Michael, or something.'

'But he can't have worked out where she is, can he? I mean, she's been posting about being in London. Do you think he's down there?'

Grace sighed loudly. 'I've no idea, Hallie. The cafe is right on the cliff. What if he followed her and she got a fright and ran, or … I don't know. I don't know what to do, and it's getting dark now.'

'You've tried her phone?'

'Yes, loads of times. The signal is terrible. There's internet in the house, but it's a bit weak, and unless she's got it where she is, WhatsApp won't work. I've tried texting, too, but I haven't heard anything.'

'And you're using her new number? The French one?'

A new number? What was that about? Grace pursed her lips. No wonder Rosie hadn't been getting the WhatsApp messages from Michael – he'd been sending them to her old number. Why hadn't Rosie given it to Grace, the friend who had come all the way from London with her?

'I didn't realise she had a new one.' Grace sounded confused.

'Let me try her. I'll call you right back, but I think it's important you stay there in case she comes back. It would be mad to go out into a storm.'

As Hallie spoke, Grace heard the doorbell. And froze. Who on earth could that be?

'That sounded like the doorbell?' Grace registered Hallie's voice coming out of her phone, but she didn't process what she was saying; her mind was flying in a million different directions.

Surely it was too soon for there to be news? In this weather, Rosie's body shouldn't be found for ages.

'Yes, yes, maybe it's her. Let me go and see.' Grace made herself sound panicked, with a dose of relief for good measure. She needed to sound as if she was rushing.

Picking up the phone, Grace walked quickly to the front door. Through the long window beside it she could see blue lights flashing in the darkness. Several blue lights.

'Oh my God, Hallie, it's the police. Something must have happened. I'll have to call you back.'

Ending the call abruptly, Grace fumbled with her phone and quickly closed the Instagram post she'd been working on.

A knock on the door reverberated around the hall, making her jump. Sticking her phone in her pocket, Grace wiped her hands down her jeans, arranging her face in a worried frown as she went to open the door.

Chapter 68

'ROSIE, ROSIE, CAN you hear me?'
Rosie could hear Jago's voice again, but it was for real this time, not a voice in a confused panicky dream. She reached out for his hand and held on to it as tightly as she could.

'She's back.' Rosie could hear Jago turning away from her, as if he was talking to someone else. She opened her eyes slowly, immediately dazzled by the bright light. She closed them again fast. But she knew he was there. She held on to his hand as if she was never going to let it go.

'What's happening?' Her voice wasn't much more than a croak.

'Let me get you some water.' A moment later she could feel her head raised gently and the cool rim of a glass against her lips. The water was cold, and wonderful. She didn't think water had ever tasted so good. A little dripped down her chin, and she felt whoever had given it to her wipe the drip away.

'Can you hear me, Rosie?' A woman's voice this time. Rosie squinted up, aware of a figure between her and the light. As the figure swam into focus, Rosie realised she was wearing a nurse's uniform.

Rosie tried to say yes, but it came out as a croak again, and nodding hurt. A lot. Her head felt as if it was trussed up, and she began to realise the hand that wasn't holding Jago's was heavy, and aching dully right up to her elbow. She squeezed Jago's hand again with her good hand.

'You're safe now, Rosie. You're in hospital in Truro. You got a nasty whack on the head and concussion, and you've broken your arm, but you're going to be OK.' Rosie felt a wave of relief at the calm authority in the nurse's voice. She was with Jago, and she was safe.

Rosie opened one eye, trying to turn towards him. 'What happened? I was looking for you. I think someone pushed me. I felt a shove, really hard …'

Jago glanced behind him, his hair a mop of unruly curls. He looked as if he'd been through a hurricane.

Suddenly DS Nandy appeared in Rosie's field of vision. 'Hi, Rosie, how are you feeling?'

She looked at him, puzzled, hazy images coming back to her: Morwenna; the fog; falling …

'Like I fell off a cliff.' It was still a croak, but her voice was getting better.

'That's understandable.'

'What happened? How did I get here?'

'Well, you did fall off a cliff, but Batman here caught you.'

Rosie frowned, but it hurt. She opened the other eye and narrowed it against the light. Then everything came back in a rush, and she felt panic coursing through her like electricity: the feeling of someone pushing her hard; slipping and sliding, slithering down; the sharp rock tearing at her skin. Pain in her head and everything going dark.

'Michael … It was Michael.' Rosie tried to sit up, pulling on Jago's hand, her voice husky. 'Not Michael … Michael's Grace. She's got two phones. I think she tried to poison me.' She slowed for a second and the next memory hit her. 'She killed Nick – I'm sure she killed Nick.'

Nandy held up his hand to slow her down. 'Grace has been picked up by the Devon and Cornwall Police. She's been interviewed and detained to give me and DC Owens time to get down here – and for the lads here to examine her devices.'

'There's an old phone in the drawer beside her bed...'

'The forensics boys have got it. And her laptop. And an interesting book on gardening.'

'But how did you know?' Rosie looked at him. 'What time is it?' She didn't know why that was important, but she realised she didn't even know what day it was. How long had she been unconscious?

'Just after midnight.' Nandy sat down on the edge of the bed. 'Do you mind? Sorry, long day.' Rosie smiled at him, tears pricking her eyes. One thing she was sure of was that with these two beside her, she felt very safe.

Nandy crossed his arms. 'I don't know how much you can remember, but you WhatsApped me, and your colleague Hallie. You'd realised Grace had to be Michael, although you didn't go into details as to why, but you said you thought she'd killed Nick.'

He made it sound very practical. 'I got in the car as soon as I got the message and we alerted the local police, but I think your messages took a while to arrive. By that stage they'd had a 999 call from Jago here, and were tied up getting you off the cliff.'

Rosie felt Jago move beside her. 'I managed to get through to the police and ambulance before I lost the signal. They couldn't use the helicopter because of the fog, but one of the guys from the station in Camborne is a climber. When they got the message, he and his mate came to assist the ambulance crew. They winched you up on the body board.' Rosie could remember men's voices and lights, but not much more, as Jago continued. 'You came to when we got you in the ambulance, and you muttered something about Grace before you conked out again. Andy heard you say it and when he asked me, I put two and two together with what you'd told me about Michael.'

Tristan Nandy picked up the story. 'And Andy got put through to me. I was already on the road. Hallie had called me by then as well. She'd got your message, too. The locals called over to Hawksmoor to bring Grace in just after six. We've had a chat this evening, but she's claiming the knock on the head must have made you delusional. Which is interesting, because we didn't tell her anything about your "accident".'

'And Nick? Did you ask her about Nick?' Rosie looked up at Nandy. The shock that Michael was Grace was still sinking in.

'We'll be getting to Nick tomorrow. We're gathering data now, looking at the traffic cameras in the area around Park House to establish what time she arrived.

It is looking very much like Nick suspected her when he discovered that email sent from your office IP address. Our guys are working on the emails now, so we'll know which one it was, and see if we can work out what aroused his suspicions.'

'What happens now?'

Nandy looked at her seriously. 'If you're feeling well enough, we need to take a statement from you. Then we'll see what the cyber team have turned up, and check in with forensics. Turns out our hero here had a night vision camera on the corner of the cafe, trained on the path to the lighthouse. It picked you up passing on the way to the cliff path, and then a figure in a bright red coat passing through the fog moments before you fell. I have a strong feeling, then, we'll be charging Grace Cassidy with both Nick's murder and your attempted murder.'

 **rosiesparislife**

[Image: A stone sign set into the end of a dry stone wall. The words The National Trust are carved into it, with Lizard Point carved below and an arrow pointing to the right.]

I don't know how to tell you all this, but this is Grace, Rosie's best friend and colleague. Something terrible happened last night and there was an awful accident.

I know you thought Rosie was posting from that fabulous apartment in Cheyne Walk in Chelsea, but actually those were all fake posts, and in reality we caught the train down to Cornwall yesterday. We're staying in an amazing house right by the sea, but things haven't quite gone to plan.

As you know, Rosie was being stalked by someone called Michael. After her TV appearance, we thought that by coming down here to Cornwall, Rosie could get some peace from him, and it would give the police a chance to find out who he was.

Rosie's been so distraught. She's been putting on a brave face here for all of you, but in private I've seen how much Michael has truly impacted her. It's been devastating to see her crumbling. The police think he could have been involved in our colleague Nick's murder, which makes my blood run cold. We all loved Nick, especially Rosie. Going into the office without him being there was one of the worst things I have ever had to do.

We don't know what happened yet, but I think Michael pushed her literally to the edge. She was so quiet and not like herself from the minute we got here. I was so frightened when she didn't come home.

I'm posting now to assure you that as her best friend, I'll be keeping RosiesParisLife alive for you and for her, sharing the content you all love of the beautiful homes Rosie and I represent. I'll also be talking to the publisher who approached her, to tell her story about Michael and her stalking experience, as I was there every step of the way and it's vital her story is told.

Rosie was amazing, but now you'll see me here, and together we'll all move forward to amazing things.

Love Grace xxxx

#stalking #suicideprevention #loss #bff #bestfriend

Chapter 69

'WHAT THE ACTUAL ...?' Rosie looked at her phone in disbelief and turned the screen around to Jago.

It was only just eight o'clock, but after Tristan Nandy had left the previous night, Rosie had fallen into the deepest sleep. The drugs must have helped, but she'd realised when she'd woken up, finding Jago sitting in the chair beside her bed, his head on a pillow, that having him next to her had made her feel completely safe.

For the first time in a very long time.

Now the initial euphoria of actually being alive had worn off, Rosie could feel every single muscle aching, but breakfast was on its way, and tea and toast had never been more welcome. She'd spotted her phone on the bedside locker when she'd woken up, and reached for it, discovering that Jago had plugged it in to charge overnight.

And that Grace had posted on her account some time the previous evening.

Making it sound as if Rosie had committed suicide by jumping off a cliff.

Beside her, Jago rubbed his face vigorously with his hands. 'God, I need to brush my teeth. What's that on your phone?'

'Grace is on my phone. Or should I say was. Yesterday.' Rosie read the post again. If it hadn't been there online, she wouldn't have believed it. 'She must have hacked my Insta, but this post is just a bit out of date.'

Jago took her phone and looked at it, his face creased in a frown. 'Maybe it was a draft she posted accidentally. She says, "last night". I mean, she's been in a cell all night with no phone, so it must have been posted before she was arrested. Blimey, look at the number of comments.' His eyes widened as he realised how many likes and comments there were. 'How did she get the password?'

Rosie lay on her pillow, frowning. Had Grace been planning this all along – to take over Rosie's life, to step into her shoes? She felt sick. From the moment she'd read that email supposedly from Michael and realised it had to be from someone Irish, she'd felt the deepest sense of betrayal. Like when you realised someone was cheating on you, times about a hundred. She felt stupid for not realising sooner, and at the same time, intense fear that Grace was two steps ahead of her and really meant to harm her.

She might still be in police custody, but what else had Grace found out about her? What else could she use to hurt Rosie?

And how *had* Grace got her password? That was a very good question. Rosie's mind raced back through their conversations. Then she had it.

'Oh my God … Dashlane.' Rosie turned to look at Jago. He was still reading through the comments on Grace's post. 'She asked me how I saved my passwords and I showed her how to use Dashlane. That's the one password I have that's easy to remember. We talked about the ones she was using, and how having a master password using names or dates or significant numbers made sense. She must have guessed mine, or watched me type it or something.'

His eyes still on the phone, Jago grimaced in response as she continued. 'I know, don't say it. I was an idiot, but I wasn't exactly thinking she was a homicidal lunatic at the time. I thought she was my friend.' Rosie sighed; that was the worst thing in all of this. The betrayal. Grace had known exactly how terrified Rosie was: how she lived with her curtains closed; how deeply affected she was by those photos of her house. But she'd kept going, had kept sending her messages. Rosie felt a deep shudder of revulsion.

'I think you need to put them straight – your followers, I mean. Some of them sound distraught.'

'I'll delete this post first.' At that moment, a grey-haired man appeared at the door of the ward, wheeling a trolley laden with pots of tea and silver cloches covering plates of food. It didn't take him long to get to her.

'Here we are, young lady. I hear you've been in the wars. And I was told to bring breakfast for your hero boyfriend, too. There's a bunch of news reporters downstairs, lad. You'll need shades and a bodyguard if you want to go out the front door.'

Jago's eyebrows shot up. 'You're not serious?'

The orderly's face crinkled as he grinned, his eyes wide. 'This little lady's famous. She was on *Good Morning Britain* – watched it myself. That stalking business is terrible, terrible.'

Jago pointed at the toast. 'Tea and toast – the morning after. That's your shot, Rosie. Do the post now. Keep it simple.'

Rosie sighed. 'I can't believe she's done this. If she's going to try and say she doesn't know what happened, how can she know I fell off the cliff?'

'Perhaps she's just become a victim of her own deviousness. I'm sure your detectives will be very interested in this. Should I screenshot it before you delete it?'

'Please – and can you resize the photo? I've only got one working hand and it's pretty sore.'

Deftly, Jago did as she asked and set up the post. 'Here you go. You just need to say you're OK and you'll post again soon. It doesn't have to be long.'

Three days later ...

Chapter 70

IN BEN'S APARTMENT overlooking the Thames, Rosie leaned into the huge leather sofa and looked across at Hallie. It was almost dark, but Ben and Jago were out on the balcony playing with one of Jago's drones, two figures silhouetted against a bright city skyline. Ben's ridiculously huge cat was sitting just inside the French windows, watching the drone darting around as if it were prey.

'How are you feeling, chicken, really?' Hallie took a sip of white wine, cradling the stem of her glass in her hand.

'Still a bit sore, and this cast is driving me mad, it's so itchy. But I'm definitely on the mend. And honestly, the relief at knowing Michael isn't going to pop up again is just so huge.'

'Have they told you anything about Grace?'

Rosie shook her head. 'Not a lot. I know she's tried to pin everything on Sebastian. He's got some explaining to do about some collections he's got at Hawksmoor House, but they've traced the IP addresses, and he wasn't in the country when half the messages were sent.'

Hallie took a sip of her wine as Rosie continued. 'The good news is that she's been charged with my attempted murder and refused bail.' She tried to keep her voice level. She cleared her throat. 'Grace had that podcast downloaded on her phone – the one by Lily Baldwin about her stalker. I'd thought some of the stuff Michael did and said was very similar.' She drew in a breath, her eyes fixed on her glass. Michael might have stopped terrorising her, but this hadn't gone away. She wasn't sure it ever would. 'DS Nandy said they are building a case against her so they can charge her with Nick's murder, too.'

'He must have organised to meet her at Park House to ask her about everything after he traced that email. He obviously didn't see her as a threat.'

'That's what Nandy thinks. He can't have realised she's absolutely nuts. God knows what made her whack him, but the police said from the beginning that it didn't feel planned, that there was anger involved.'

Hallie grimaced. 'She planned her cover-up, though, that whole story about finding the stone … Poor Nick. He had a real soft spot for you, you know? He wanted to ask you out, but he was waiting for his moment.'

Rosie looked at her, surprised, then felt sadness wash over her again, threatening to suffocate her.

'Seriously? Oh God, that makes me feel even worse.' She leaned forward and, putting her glass on the floor, put her head in her hands as she closed her eyes and focused on her breathing.

She felt Hallie slide along the sofa and start to rub her back. 'I'm so sorry, chicken, I didn't mean …'

Rosie shook her head. 'It's not you.' She took a breath. 'It's Grace. I just need a minute. Talk about something else. Did you ever find out what happened to the Sterling's Instagram account?'

Hallie let out a sharp breath. 'The police reckon it was good old-fashioned hackers. Their cyber people found patterns in the messages, or something, that linked them to hacks of other high-end companies like ours. It seems to be the simplest thing in everything.'

As Rosie took this in, she glanced sideways at Hallie. It was the way she'd said it. 'What? Has something else happened?'

'Well ... a few things. I'm not sure how, but Yaraslava's managed to find a buyer for Park House. But there's something funny going on with that deal. The whole thing feels wrong.'

'Yaraslava would have reported it if she felt anything was off.' Rosie glanced at Hallie, to catch her rolling her eyes. 'Wouldn't she?'

'You'd hope so. I'm starting to think Sebastian might have fewer scruples than Ben does. And he's very fond of Yaraslava.'

Rosie remembered what Grace and Jago had said about the woman who had stayed at Hawksmoor House. 'I think they might have a thing.'

The look on Hallie's face confirmed Rosie's suspicions. 'I think they're made for each other, in all honesty.' She swirled the wine around her glass. 'The police wanted to talk to me about the whole Park House thing. It turns out the number this Irina gave Yaraslava wasn't a real one. It was one of those pay-as-you-go phones.' Hallie paused. 'It was working fine before, and then ... After Nick, apparently Irina stopped answering.'

Rosie looked at Hallie, her curiosity awakened. 'Not many people who own £10 million properties use throwaway phones.'

'Exactly. The police wanted to see if Yaraslava or I could identify this woman. They want a proper statement from her.'

'So who is she? The woman selling Park House, I mean.' Rosie adjusted her arm with the cast on it, resting it on her knee.

'Irina Ivanov – she's definitely Russian. I was telling the detectives I only spoke to her once, when we first took on the sale. I didn't realise it was her at all at the time. She rang in on the main line, but her English was so poor I couldn't work out what she wanted. I put her on to Yaraslava – she told me afterwards what it was about. At least, that's what she said the call was about. Now I'm not so sure.' Hallie hesitated. 'The police are fully investigating Yaraslava and her brother, and right now it isn't looking good for either of them. Yaraslava was arrested today.'

Rosie's eyebrows rose sharply. 'How do you know that?'

Hallie took a sip of her wine. 'I called into the office to have a chat with her. I've handed in my notice.' Rosie felt her eyes widen as Hallie continued. 'While I was there, the police arrived and took her back to the station.' Hallie paused, and looked a little uncomfortable. 'There was some stuff that happened at Hunt's that Ben told them about after Nick – the police, I mean. It involved Yaraslava and this company Landmark that Irina owns. I think she might have got herself into something big.'

It took Rosie a few minutes to take everything in. 'I can't imagine Yaraslava didn't know what she was doing? She's not exactly the type to be conned.' She hesitated. 'It'll be so weird, being at the office without you and Nick. And if Yaraslava goes, too, it'll only be me. How's that going to work?'

'I don't know. The office is never going to be the same without Nick.' The sadness in Hallie's voice echoed the feeling in Rosie's heart. 'Ben's so upset, too, he was good friends with Nick. They were supposed to be meeting on Saturday afternoon to play football. They had to keep it a secret or Yaraslava would have gone nuts.'

Hallie glanced across at Rosie, obviously measuring what she was going to say next. 'I know you won't have to worry about work until you feel ready to come back, but give me a call when you are? Particularly if you decide to leave Sterling's.'

Rosie narrowed her eyes, looking at Hallie; she could feel there was more. 'And …?'

Hallie looked at her innocently. 'How do you know there's an "and"?'

'I can read you – don't keep me in suspense.'

'OK.' Hallie glanced through the glass doors at Ben. 'The thing is, Ben wants me to open another Hunt's office in Mayfair, and … er … we might be getting married.'

Rosie's face cracked into a grin 'Might be? You mean you are.' She laughed. 'That's the best news I've heard in weeks. I need all the details, but I need to see the ring first.' She looked at Hallie expectantly.

Hallie blushed as she showed Rosie a slim gold band encircled with diamonds. It was a bit loose, and she spun it around with her thumb fondly as she looked at it. 'It's a promise ring. We're going to Dubai to get a proper one. But listen … I'd *really* love you to have a think about maybe working with me in Mayfair?'

Rosie was about to answer when the French doors opened to a blast of cold air and Jago and Ben came into the living room, their faces glowing.

'This thing's amazing.' Ben held up Jago's drone. 'We need to get aerial shots of all our properties.' He put the drone down on an occasional table beside a leather armchair, much to the cat's delight. 'What have you two been talking about?'

'Hallie's been telling me about your plans.' Rosie glanced over at Hallie. 'I'd love to work with you, Hals, but I think I'm going to take some time out for a bit. You know that phrase, "You're the hero of your own story"? Well, I need to take my story back from "Michael" and his sidekick. I need to talk some more to a lady called Sarah, and then I think I might have a book to write.'

THE END (almost)

Three weeks later ...

Chapter 71

'I PROMISE I'LL BE back as fast as I can.' Jago slung his rucksack onto his shoulder and put his arms around Rosie to give her a hug as people flowed around them like water. Finding a quiet corner in Heathrow Airport to say goodbye was almost impossible. 'I'm really sorry.'

Rosie gave him a kiss. 'Don't be silly. This is a great opportunity, and they are paying all your expenses. A week in the Pyrenees will be fabulous. Think of the shots you'll be able to take.'

'That's what they want – amazing photos. I wish it wasn't this week, though. It's too soon after everything.'

'I'll be fine. Grace is in custody, she's not going anywhere for a while, and I'm going to be busy working with this editor Sarah has hooked me up with. They want to know the whole story. They can't publish till after the trial, but apparently it takes ages to get a book written and published.' Rosie looked over Jago's shoulder and spotted the time on the departure board. 'You'd better get moving.' She gave him another kiss and he hugged her tight, careful not to squash her cast. 'You won't be away for long – go.'

Waving Jago off, she turned to head to the station and her train home. Heathrow was vast, but as she wove her way through the crowd she felt light and the happiest she had in ages. Only a few weeks before she'd have been terrified walking through this many people – terrified Michael might be following her. And now she was rid of him, and dating Jago.

Rosie smiled as she held her cast against her chest and stepped onto the steep escalator running down towards the underground tunnels linking the Tube and the new Elizabeth Line with Heathrow railway station.

Her mind on Jago, Rosie only barely registered a woman heading up the escalator in the opposite direction, towards the airport. She glanced at Rosie and then quickly looked away. She was blonde, her make-up heavy, shell-pink lipstick set off by a full-length winter white fur coat. She had something light purple in her hand, as if she'd just pulled it out of her Chanel cross-body bag.

It was the bag that caught Rosie's eye – a classic Chanel, but a tiny bit big for her liking. She could almost hear Grace's voice making a comment about whether it was real or a fake. Rosie shook the sound from her head; she didn't need to hear Grace's voice ever again.

When Rosie stepped off at the bottom of the escalator, the woman in the white coat finally registered properly with her, and she did an abrupt double take. Swinging around to look up the moving stairs, she could see the women was just getting off at the top, pulling a sleek black hard-shell cabin bag behind her.

Rosie watched her disappear in the direction of the huge glass wall of the airport.

It was Yaraslava – Rosie was sure of it. Dressed like the Snow Queen from Narnia. And just as duplicitous.

But Rosie was sure she'd had an emergency American passport in her hand; the purple cover was unmistakable. Eoin's girlfriend had had to get one after her bag was stolen when they'd come to see Rosie in Paris.

Why had Yaraslava completely changed her appearance, and what was she doing here? Well, the answer to that was obvious, at least. But Rosie didn't remember her boss mentioning dual citizenship. They'd even talked about it in the office one day – about how useful it could be to have two passports.

Unsure what to do, Rosie pulled her phone from the depths of her coat pocket and searched for DS Nandy's number. It was answered after one ring.

'It's Rosie. I've just seen a woman who looks like Yaraslava in Heathrow. Well, she didn't look like Yaraslava, she had blonde hair.'

She heard Nandy sigh at the other end. 'We had to let her go. We've tracked the company that owned Park House back to an Irina Ivanov, but she's based in Dubai, and has no intention of coming to London or explaining where her money comes from. We're sure it's a laundering operation, but we couldn't make anything stick on Yaraslava. Her brother is a different story. She's told us a lot about him ...'

Just as duplicitous.

'She looked like she was in disguise.'

'I'd guess she'll need a new identity. The Russians she was working with, the Grigori brothers – well, according to Yaraslava – have been bankrolling her brother to buy these properties. We're working on building a case against them.' He paused. 'I can't imagine she'll be popular with them. It seems you can't trust anyone these days.'

Rosie closed her eyes and, for a moment, felt as if she was falling again. You could trust some people. You just had to watch out for the people who weren't quite what they seemed.

Author's Note

I know those of you who follow me on Instagram have been impatient to read this, the full story, but we had to wait till after Grace's trial to publish, and I've discovered that writing a book takes a lot longer than writing an Instagram post!

Huge thanks to Sam Blake for helping me tell this story. Some of you might have guessed that I have read a lot of her books – her name is on the cover because she did the writing here. She says she couldn't have told the story without me, so there's a pair of us in it.

I did try writing this myself – I started writing in first person, but it was way too hard. Michael – or should I say, Grace – had got inside my mind, she was literally watching my every move. When Sam took over, it all flowed.

Hallie went to see Grace in prison and got the information that informed her chapters, but none of us can see how anything I did could have made her want to kill me, or lovely Nick. (Apparently I overuse 'lovely', and Sam's worried that all through this story I needed constant sugar fixes, but that's how it felt.) One thing that is certain, though, is that Grace created a whole narrative inside her own head that involved me, and, let's face it, wasn't entirely rational.

In movies you see that disclaimer: all names have been changed. But not all names have been changed in this story. Suzy Lamplugh is a real person who was working as an estate agent when she disappeared in 1986, and who has never been found. Sam's mum met Suzy's mum, the late Diana Lamplugh, in the early 1990s, and Sam can clearly remember the news reports about her vanishing. My story will be published forty years after she went missing, hence the dedication. This story is very different from hers, but her influence is still strong. Suzy was declared dead in 1993 – the year that, in Ireland, Annie McCarrick went missing and hit the headlines. There were too many in between, and there have been too many women who have disappeared, since.

Stalking is something that can happen for all sorts of reasons, none of which are about the person being stalked, but *all* of which are about the person who is doing the stalking. The other name that hasn't been changed in this book is Lily Baldwin's. Her podcast is incredible, and you can listen to it on your podcast platform – she really was stalked for thirteen years. I kept thinking that Michael's behaviour was a lot like her stalker's, and in the early days, when Michael was leaving me voice messages, I discovered that Grace had been listening to it, too.

It's only through the work of organisations like the Suzy Lamplugh Trust, that was set up by her mum and dad after Suzy disappeared, and podcasts like Lily Baldwin's, that many people get an idea of the reality of stalking and how often it occurs. The Ask for Angela campaign has recently been in the news – it's vital that all staff in bars and restaurants understand what that means. It keeps people safe – women and men.

You can find more information about the Suzy Lamplugh Trust and get their advice at www.suzylamplugh.org. They offer bystander training and operate the National Stalking Helpline in the UK.

Rainn provide a helpline and resources for survivors of stalking and cyberstalking at rainn.org.

The Cyber Helpline gives support to victims of cybercrime: www.thecyberhelpline.com.

If anything like this is happening to you, please reach out for help. It's not your fault.

Huge thanks to Sarah Hodgson at Corvus Books for wanting to publish this story, and her brilliant editing. After an epic night out at home in Cork (thank you, Catherine Kirwan and the River Lee Hotel), when there were far too many cocktails drunk, one of Sam's friends, another crime writer who you might have heard of, Catherine Ryan Howard, offered to do the graphics for my Instagram posts. She's truly multi-talented – thank you! This book has been a team effort – thank you to literary agent Nicky Lovick for lending her Cornish name, and to one of Sam's closest friends, Andrea Hayes, for being me in the posts printed here. (Some of you might have recognised her; she's a well-known face on Irish TV. My mum was so excited when I told her – it's almost made up for me not telling her about Michael when it all started.) And Sam's friends from Dublin, Mave Hooper and John Agar were fantastic (they'll tell you what their input was, if you know them) – thank you.

Laura, Felice and Dave, the PR, marketing and sales team at Corvus, are fab too. Steve O'Gorman is Sam's incredible copy editor – she says that he always spots something (a lot) that she's missed. In Ireland, Gill Hess looks after PR for Sam fantastically, and her wonderful agent, Simon Trewin, is very lovely (I did it again) as well as being a bit of a superstar in the literary world. I need to say a massive thanks to Jago, too, for supporting me while I relived this experience, but you're right, we might not have met if it all hadn't happened like this. It's a cliché, but every cloud really does have a silver lining.

Huge thanks to *you*, too, for reading. Without you, the reader, there would be no book – as Sam says, your support, reviews and feedback are invaluable. And the same goes for the wonderful booksellers and bloggers who support authors. We love you, thank you.

R & SB xx

SAM BLAKE

Think you know thrillers? Think again...

Join the
READERS' CLUB

Get exclusive writing and an insight into bestselling author Sam Blake's books delivered straight to your inbox.

Members are the first to hear all the latest book news, find out when new books are published and have the chance to win books and other prizes in regular competitions.

Plus you'll get a FREE THRILLER by Sam Blake as soon as you join.

Scan the QR code
to join or visit:
www.samblakebooks.com